HARD LATITUDES

Hard Latitudes

A Mike Travis Mystery

Baron Birtcher

OPEN ROAD

INTEGRATED MEDIA
NEW YORK

ISBN: 978-1-5040-8203-7

This edition published in 2023 by Open Road Integrated Media, Inc.
180 Maiden Lane
New York, NY 10038
www.openroadmedia.com

For Christina
Aloha pau ole

HARD LATITUDES

"Feel the bile rising from your guilty past
With your nerves in tatters
As the cockleshell shatters
And the hammers batter down your door
You'd better run . . ."

—Roger Waters/Pink Floyd
Run Like Hell

Echoes

(Eleven Years Later)

Fuck it.

"Okay," I said, finally. "I'll do it."

We'd had this conversation dozens of times. One hundred, more like.

"You'll tell me everything?"

I had relived it often enough inside my head, inside my dreams, like irresolute images projected onto a filthy window pane, never there, but never really gone. Razor wire insinuated itself around my heart and pulled tight.

"The best that I can remember," I said.

Time sometimes has a way of blunting sharp edges, altering both shadow and light until it dulls to a soft-focus surrogate for reality. This was different. Time had turned this to chiaroscuro.

I had tried. And that simple fact made it all the worse, for in trying I had failed. Perhaps that wasn't the whole truth; what was that anyway? But it felt like the truth, or something as near to it as I could ever know.

"When?"

My eyes cut sideways, out the narrow slit of window, and fixed on the gray sky. Clouds had been gathering since late last night, and the wind had begun to push them across the horizon with increasing speed. There would be rain, and soon.

There are things we tell ourselves we need to know, and the

longer the desire goes unsatisfied, the more rapidly it metastasizes into a psychic tumor of obsession. These are the things that deprive us of sleep, eventually invade our dreams and swell to unbearable proportions until the seeking becomes an end in itself. The great irony is that once learned, the object of that fixation vanishes and becomes instead a black hole where no comfort is derived from the achievement of the aim we had sought, had expected, or even deserved—the knowledge no less a poison than the obsession had been.

"When?"

"Now," I said.

I was ready to tell it. As ready as I ever would be.

PART ONE

A Momentary Lapse of Reason

Macau, 1994

CHAPTER ONE

The gunshots could have gone unnoticed, could have been lost inside the clamor and confusion of the late afternoon rush. But they hadn't.

A listless breeze blew across the Pearl River Delta, rolling in from the South China Sea, sluggish and humid as spring gave way to the oppressive heat of summer. Tourists strolled along the busy Rua da Praia Grande, clutching bags marked with the names of high-end shops, while workers pressed their way home through the bustling crowds. The air smelled of the waterfront, of the smoke from distant rubbish fires, spices from open food carts, and the ubiquitous musky odor of sweat.

Tai Man Duk stopped walking when he neared the entrance of the Lisboa Hotel. He watched another group of gamblers arrive for the evening, most of them fresh off the hydrofoil ferry from Hong Kong. For a moment he imagined himself as one of them, well dressed and elegant, smelling of fine soap and aftershave, no concerns for anything, least of all money. He eyed the slender and beautiful women, whose hairdos alone cost more than a month's worth of the rice and dried fish that he and his sister could scrape together.

But all of that would change in time, he thought, now that he had become a "49" in the White Orchid Tong, a soldier on his way up through the ranks, a young soldier determined to be noticed by the *lung tau*—the Dragon Head—of the White Orchid. If he could only have the chance to demonstrate his worth, to let them see that he was no ordinary soldier, but a man of bold action. This was what had brought Tai Man Duk to Macau in the first place. Not yet nineteen, here was his chance to prove himself, pick a few tourist pockets, deliver some cash or maybe even a foreign passport and a fresh set of credit cards to Joey Soong, the underboss who ran Duk's crew. Nevertheless, it was a delicate balance. Duk had been conditioned not only by his culture, but reminded by Joey Soong himself, about the ancient adage: *The nail that sticks up gets hammered down.* Even so, those reminders only served to roil the flame in Duk's youthful belly.

Joey Soong was a man on the rise, a man who had earned the *lung tau's* ear, and a growing measure of his confidence. It was Joey who'd arranged for Duk's illegal transit to Macau, even though it was far outside Soong's turf. Duk's success tonight would bring him great respect, and be a slap in the face of the Green Snakes who acted as though they ran the whole of Macau. But within the next four or five years, Britain and Portugal had both agreed to transfer sovereignty of the entire territory back to China, and everything would be ripe for the taking. Even the Green Snakes had to know that.

If Joey Soong and his crew succeeded, it was said that he would be moved up inside the Tong, be given a territory outside of China: Chicago, Honolulu, maybe, or even San Francisco. Duk wanted nothing more than to ingratiate himself to such a rising star.

A rude shove from behind him shook Duk from his daydream, and put his mind back on business. He wanted to fill his pockets as quickly as possible, catch the eight o'clock ferry back to Kowloon and safely return to his apartment before his sister returned home from her work. She was only thirteen and, ever since the accident that had killed their parents, was prone to horrible bouts of panic if Duk wasn't there when she finished her job cleaning and stacking fruit for the produce vendor at the open market on Shek Lung Street.

The sun was beginning to slip behind the jagged hills in the near distance, the last of its orange light glinting from glass and steel, and throwing long shadows across a street coming alive with the hum of neon. A pearl of sweat ran down his back, and he dried his palms on the front of his pants.

Duk scanned the sidewalk for a mark, selected a tall European man walking alone, the bulge of his wallet clearly visible in his back pocket. Duk threaded his way through the crowd, steadily working closer until he was an arm's reach behind. He would do as he'd been trained and wait until they both became part of a tight pack of pedestrians waiting for the light to change, impatiently anticipating their turn to cross the busy street. It was then, in that crush of distracted and perspiring humanity that he would best be able to make his move unnoticed.

As usual, the street—designed two centuries earlier for horse and carriage, handcart and rickshaw was clogged to a near standstill. Cars, buses and trucks congested the lane and revved their throttles, filling the clammy air with noxious gray clouds of exhaust. The only vehicles able to move were the mopeds, *tuk-tuks* and motorbikes that threaded between the bumpers of unmoving traffic.

Duk felt the press of the growing crowd behind him and used it to maneuver himself closer to his mark, closer to the curb where he could make his escape.

The light changed.

At first, no one noticed the two Japanese motorcycles that

glided down the adjacent Rua Salado, weaving through traffic as pedestrians stepped off into the crosswalk. Duk kept the European in his peripheral vision and pretended to watch the dapper Chinese man just then crossing the Rua from the opposite direction.

Duk reached for the mark's wallet at exactly the same moment that an eruption of semiautomatic gunfire scattered the crowd and the scene dissolved into chaos. He watched dumbly as a hail of bullets tore into the Chinese man, standing him up like a marionette, jerking him about spastically and dropping him onto the dirty street. The thin leather briefcase he carried flew from his hands, skittered along the asphalt and bounced off the curb just a few yards away. Without hesitation, and with the training of the thief he was seeking so desperately to be, Duk moved against the wave of fleeing bystanders and snatched the man's fallen attaché from the gutter.

He shot a glance in each direction, and watched as a cloud of pungent smoke poured from the pipes of the escaping motorcycles. Duk retreated into the refuge and anonymity of the frightened mob as the high-pitched whine of the engines died away. There was a peculiar moment of displaced silence, suddenly broken by the searing scream of a young woman as her eyes landed on the shredded body of the Chinese man whose briefcase Duk now clutched tightly to his chest. He walked as quickly and calmly as he could manage, in the direction of the ferry terminal, and the crowd began to panic in earnest.

Sirens wailed impotently in the distance as Duk chanced one last look behind him, into the street. The Chinese man lay at the center of a widening pool of blood as cars began to move slowly past. Duk's breath was shallow, the skin of his face hot with the rush of adrenaline, heart pounding with excitement, altogether unaware that he had been observed.

＊ ＊ ＊

Joey Soong closed his cell phone, allowed the faint smile to pass from his face before he returned to the study where the Dragon Head and the other two men waited for him to finish his call.

He bowed in the traditional way when he reentered the room.

"It is done, *lung tau*," he said to the older man.

Three sticks of incense burned on an elegant altar at the far side of the study and filled the air with the sharp, earthy scent of sandalwood. Joey watched the thin trails of smoke intertwine as he waited for a response.

"The case has been recovered?"

Joey hesitated a moment before he answered. To succeed in killing the Green Snake *sheung fa,* but fail to deliver the cash the man had been transporting could prove to be extremely awkward. He chose his words carefully. I have been told it was retrieved by one of my crew."

The Dragon Head gazed out the window that overlooked Hong Kong harbor. The lights of the tall buildings on the island side were beginning to glow as the sky faded from silver to black. He clasped his hands behind his back, and turned away from the night.

"You have an enviable future, Mr. Soong," the *lung tau* said.

Joey bowed graciously-once more. "I will try to be worthy of it."

The older man nodded. "Yes," he said. "This you must always do."

May Ling felt a stab of ice inside her chest when she reached the top of the stairs. The air in the narrow hallway of the apartment building was heavy, ripe with the odors of cooked vegetables, mildew and rodent urine. The dim light from the solitary window at the far end of the hall cast her doorway in deep shadow. Another stab of panic as she found the doorknob unyielding. Duk had always left it open for her once he got home. He knew well the depth of the fear she harbored at the prospect of being left alone. Her hands began to tremble as she reached into her backpack for the key she kept there, just in case.

May Ling opened the door slowly, craned her head into the tiny gap between door and frame, and peered into the unlighted room.

"Duk?" Her voice was barely a whisper.

Her pulse quickened as she withdrew the key from the lock and stepped inside.

Something smelled wrong, sour like rotting meat, so strong in the small apartment that it overwhelmed even the odor outside in the hall. Her mouth went dry as her hand fluttered blindly along the wall, searching in vain for the light switch. A tear slid down her cheek as she prayed for Duk to be home, prayed that he would not leave her in this place, on her own, after the night had come. How many times had she begged him?

Her frantic fingers found the switch, temporarily blinding herself with sudden light.

"Hello, May Ling."

The voice rumbled like thunder inside the tiny apartment, startling her so badly that she wet herself as she dropped her backpack to the floor.

She heard two men laughing as she swiped at her tears with the back of her hands.

"This one leaks from both ends," the big one said. He was standing close, his breath stale and overpowering, the skin around his eyes pitted deeply by the scars of childhood disease. He slammed the door behind her.

The smaller of the men had seated himself on the tattered couch that was situated beneath the room's only window. His arms were outstretched along the seat back, fingers drumming an aimless rhythm on the faded upholstery, legs crossed casually at the ankles. He bore the arrogant air of a man accustomed to authority. "Where is your brother, May Ling?"

She licked her lips and attempted to speak, but words would not come.

The big one laughed again and came around from behind her. He made a rude show of looking her over, evaluating her young body. He reached out as if to run his hands along her cheeks.

She shrank back as he frowned at her, his eyes small and vacant. She caught the stench of his breath again as he made a move to grab her arm.

May Ling backed away from him until she had nowhere left to move, and found herself pinned against the wall.

"Please," she said. "Stay away from me."

He stared down at her, his face a rough, blank canvas, a void.

A rustling sound outside in the narrow hall stopped him, the sound of a key slipping into a lock. He threw a glance at the smaller man, who put a finger to his lips and whispered, "Shhh."

A moment later Tai Man Duk opened the door, out of breath, his forehead varnished with perspiration. He had been running, trying to get to the apartment before May Ling.

Confusion flickered across his face when he saw Joey Soong sitting on his couch, but a fist seized his heart as the big, pockmarked "49" who Soong had long employed as his enforcer, came out from the shadows with his sister gripped firmly in his hands. May Ling lunged toward her brother, but Joey caught her arm, tore her from the grip of his enforcer, and pushed her roughly to the floor.

Joey's eyes never left the item Duk held in his hand.

"You have the briefcase," Joey said. "Very good. Bring it to me."

Duk felt his knees go weak, and the room began to spin. He struggled for control of himself, and brought the case to Joey. May Ling flinched at the loud snaps of the shiny brass locks as Joey Soong thumbed them open. He lifted the top and gazed into it for long seconds before turning his eyes back to Duk.

"What is this?"

Duk felt the hot rush of blood throbbing at his temples. "I don't know what you mean," he said.

"Where is the rest?"

"The rest?"

Joey shook his head calmly, but his eyes betrayed his rage. He glanced down at May Ling still sprawled on the floor at his feet, face wet with tears, blank and uncomprehending. Joey gave her a vicious slap with the back of his hand, then returned his attention to Duk. A thin rope of blood and spittle dripped from her mouth as she turned to watch her brother.

"Where. Is. The. Rest?"

"I lost it."

Soong's face went hard. How was the Dragon Head supposed to believe that all that cash had simply been lost by an underling, and not merely pocketed by Soong himself? How could Joey possibly set this straight without looking like a fool? Or worse yet, an embezzler? Here he was, so close to becoming the head of his own branch of the White Orchid, so close to the Golden Mountain, and this fucking toad makes him look like a liar and a common thief.

"How did you *lose* it?" Joey's voice was preternaturally calm.

Duk glanced at Joey's enforcer, then at May. Ling. Blood ran freely across her plum-colored lips and stained the white collar of her blouse. Duk's eyes pleaded for her forgiveness.

"At the tables."

All he had wanted was to make some extra money for the two of them. He was supposed to have won. It was such a good plan. He would put the profits in his pocket, the original sum back in the case, and no one would have been the wiser. If he had won, he would have been a hero to both Soong and his sister.

"You gambled with White Orchid money?"

"I didn't know this belonged to the White Orchid," he said. "The man on the street . . . I'd never seen him before. I thought—"

"The man on the street was a Green Snake," Soong interrupted.

"I didn't know," Duk rasped.

"The men on the motorcycles. *They* were White Orchid. You understand?"

Duk's words all ran together now, tumbling out in a last-ditch effort to be heard, to be understood, to be forgiven.

"I didn't know it was White Orchid money. On my mother and father, I didn't know. I thought I'd just gotten lucky, picked it up from a dead man in the street. I went to the Lisboa to win even more. I wanted to come to you with a fortune. I was going to give it all to you, I swear.

Joey Soong examined the briefcase one last time before slamming it shut, snapping the latches. There was only one way he could think of that might, just might, appease the Dragon Head, and more importantly, help him requite an untenable loss of face.

"Stupid boy."

He grabbed May Ling and pulled her to her feet.

Her eyes flew wide, and the look on her face felt like shards of glass in Duk's heart.

"Please, no . . ." he whispered, tears filling his own eyes.

Soong shoved May Ling toward the big man, where she

stumbled at his feet. Duk made a futile move for him, but the pockmarked man spun, landed a fist deep into his solar plexus and delivered two, three brutal kicks to his ribs and kidneys once he was down.

May Ling screamed and the enforcer clapped a callused hand over her mouth.

"Stupid, stupid boy. Do you have any idea what I have to do now?"

Joey shook his head in mock sorrow as Duk writhed and clutched his middle, felt the sharp grinding pain of his broken ribs as he rolled onto his side and retched. A moment later, Joey knelt down, pulled the belt from Duk's pants, and used it to tie his hands behind his back.

"You know, of course, that the White Orchid must be repaid," Soong said.

"No, please," Duk breathed.

His sister cried out as the big man's thick fingers squeezed tender flesh to the bone, pressing her into the couch cushions as he viciously tore at her clothing.

"This is how it begins," Soong said.

Duk attempted to avert his gaze, but Soong took Duk's head into his hands, held it in place through the agonizing minutes, the animal sounds and his sister's unanswered pleas for mercy.

"It will not go well for her, stupid boy. She will come to wish she had as easy a road as you."

With one hand, Joey grabbed a fistful of Duk's hair and yanked back savagely, immobilizing him as he reached into his own back pocket with the other. The unmistakable *twing* of metal on metal as his sister wept in pain and humiliation only six feet away, the last sounds Duk was to hear, the last images he would carry with him before Joey Soong's straight razor slid silently through muscle, tendon and vein.

May Ling was barely conscious when they finally carried her from the apartment, wrapped only in the soiled sheet they had ripped from her bed. Her brother's body lay where they left him, motionless, his head twisted at an ugly angle, at the apex of a vermilion fan of blood opening slowly across the floor.

PART TWO

One Slip

Kona, Hawaii 2004

CHAPTER TWO

I was sitting at Snyder's bar, doing what I could to avoid the crush of tourists that the cruise ship had disgorged onto Kona's sundrenched streets. I was drinking an Asahi on ice, waiting for Dave, and enjoying the last hour of normalcy I was to have for a long while, a fact I didn't know at the time.

The place was relatively quiet for a Friday afternoon, still a little early for the local *pau hana* clientele, and the tourists hadn't yet discovered the place that day. Snyder wiped a damp rag across the hardwood bar, then tossed it in a plastic bucket on the floor. He leaned against the wall not far from where I sat, crossed his heavily muscled arms and squinted into the afternoon light.

Rumor had it that Snyder was a retired pot grower from Humboldt County. It was said that he held his assets in the name of some offshore trust in an effort to distance himself from legal trouble either past or present, real or imagined. The islands are awash with wild stories and hearsay. The coconut wireless worked seven days a week, but I did my best to ignore it. I didn't care to know a thing about Snyder's past, or anybody else's; it had nothing to do with me anymore.

"Charter this weekend, Mike?" Snyder asked.

I shook my head. "Just finished a three-day. Nothing more for a while."

I had begun chartering my seventy-two-foot sailing yacht, the *Kehau,* for private scuba and luxury cruises around the island, like I had back in the days when I lived in California. It was my constant reminder of how far I'd come since my time with Los Angeles Homicide, and I liked it that way.

He nodded.

"Long weekend for you then."

I followed his gaze out past the batwing saloon doors into the hot afternoon.

"Looks that way."

Snyder turned, and tapped a draft for a dishwater blonde in a tank top and board shorts a couple of seats down from me. I'd seen her in here before. Heavy breasts rested on the top of the bar as she leaned in to watch him, studiously avoiding eye contact with me.

"So, you hear about Yosemite?" Snyder asked.

Yosemite is Dave's nickname. His voice, stature and long drooping mustache make his resemblance to the cartoon character Yosemite Sam almost uncanny. Dave was a friend of mine from Avalon, a small resort town on the island of Santa Catalina off the Southern California coast where I used to run my charter operation. He and another buddy, Rex Blackwood, crewed for me on the trans-Pacific escape I'd made from there following an overly publicized murder case I'd worked. I had returned to Hawaii, my mother's ancestral home, to put twenty years with the LAPD behind me and restart my retirement. Rex had subsequently bought Dave's deep-sea fishing business and returned to Avalon; Dave stayed in Kona, and was now a captain for Jake's Diving Locker, and everybody called him "Yosemite."

I took a swig of Asahi, wiped the foam from my lip with the back of my wrist.

"What'd he do now?"

Snyder smiled and shook his head.

"Got himself ejected from that public hearing a couple nights ago."

"The navy deal? The one about the whales?"

"Yeah," he said. "It was in the paper."

I remembered the yellowing stack of newspapers I'd retrieved from Snyder's backroom office. Since I live aboard my boat, Snyder lets me use the place as a permanent address. Whenever I went out on a charter, I temporarily lost touch with the comings-and-goings in our little town. But this navy thing was heavy on everybody's mind. At least, anyone who gave a damn about the ocean.

"They're still going ahead with it?"

"Looks like it," Snyder said. "These hearings were just a show, man. Didn't matter what the hell anybody around here had to say about it."

The navy was about to conduct tests of a sophisticated sonar system that used ultralow frequency sound waves to track submarines. It was experimental technology, and they wanted to test it in the waters off Kona. No problem, unless you were in the water when they fired it up. The sound waves had proven to be extremely harmful, even deadly, to mammals. Turned their insides into tapioca pudding. There were documented cases of entire pods of dolphins beaching themselves during panicked attempts to escape the subsurface blast of noise. Humans weren't allowed within a mile of the test area. Now the navy wanted to run system trials off the Kona coast, aim the sonar at the whales that came to give birth every year, test it on something they deemed less valuable than a submarine. Unbelievable.

"Unbelievable," I said.

Snyder pursed his lips and nodded like that said it all.

We both turned toward the shaft of sunlight that followed a pair of tourists through the swinging saloon doors. Sunburned noses and loud print shirts they'd never wear at home, huarache sandals on stockinged feet. They padded past the tables toward the bar.

"Piña colada, please," the first one said.

The second one nodded agreement.

"Make it two."

Snyder shook his head. "No piña coladas."

The tourist looked puzzled. "Then how about a Lava Flow?"

"No blender," Snyder said.

"I see," the taller one said after a beat. "Mai Tai?"

Snyder cut me a sideways glance, and the blonde at the bar stifled a smile.

"What else," was all he said.

I was on my third Asahi, and Yosemite still hadn't shown. Warm tropical air mingled with cigarette smoke—you could still smoke indoors back then—and jukebox music. Snyder was busy at the stick when my cell phone rang. Something told me I shouldn't answer, but I did. Like I always do.

I got up off my stool and took the call outside, catching Snyder's eye, letting him know I'd be back.

The slender trunks of palms formed graceful shadows across Palani Road as the sun moved toward the horizon. A blue sliver of Kailua Bay shone between the shops along Alii Drive and I caught a familiar scent of plumeria and sea salt as I flipped open the phone.

I was right, I shouldn't have answered it. It was my brother, Valden.

"Mike?" All my cop instincts prickled. Those habits never go away. Just like the Beretta automatic I still carried. And the other arms I had stashed aboard *Kehau,* beside my bed and in the galley drawer.

"Where are you?" I asked.

"LA," he said. Satellite static wrinkled across space for a long moment. "I think I might be in trouble."

I fought the urge to tell him to call back when he was sure.

My brother and I rarely, if ever, saw eye-to-eye. It is a problem that goes back many years, and has its roots in mistrust and a mutual lack of respect. But there was something unusual in his voice.

"Don't you have private security for shit like this?"

"No, Mike. This isn't business." He hesitated again.

I waited him out.

"It's a . . . uh . . . personal matter."

"Don't jerk me around, Valden," I said.

"I don't want to talk about it on your cell," he whispered. I didn't blame him. It was easier than people thought to eavesdrop on cell phone calls. Ask the NSA.

"Then what'd you call me for?"

There was another long silence before he answered.

"It may turn out to be nothing," he said. "But I wanted to know you'd be there if I needed you."

Not like Valden to ask for anything from me unless he felt he had run out of choices.

"Get a pen, write down this number," he said. "Call me in an hour."

"Valden—"

"On a land line, Mike," he interrupted. "Please."

I took down the number he gave me, and told him I'd call him back. He sounded relieved, even thanked me. I shut the phone and slipped it back into my shirt pocket, unconsciously ran my fingers across the scar on my shoulder. Even after all this time, it was still tender, raw. Like my mood had just become.

When I went back inside, I heard Snyder talking in whispers to the big-breasted blonde. I couldn't hear it all, but enough to get the drift.

". . . Kamahale-Van de Groot . . . wealthy family . . . used to be a cop . . . lives on his sailboat . . ." Giving her the rundown on me. The whole thing, including the name I had been born with, but hadn't used in a long, long time. She was nodding.

When he noticed me, Snyder stood up straight, threw a guilty look in my direction.

"We were just talking about you," he said.

"I know," I said as I took my seat. "You must've learned how to whisper in a sawmill."

The girl turned to get a better look at me, clear blue eyes giving me a cool once-over.

"Van de Groot?" she said. "I thought your name was Travis."

"It is." I cut my eyes at Snyder, but he turned away and feigned concentration as he repositioned the small Plexiglas box that sat atop his cash register, the one that contained the crude carving of a jackrabbit that he refused to discuss or explain.

"Van de Groot?" she said again. "Like the company?"

"Yes. Like the company."

"My God, it's like the Kennedys or something."

"Let's hope not."

"Seriously."

"Snyder," I said, "you started this. Make it stop."

Sun-bleached eyebrows frowned. Little furrows in a tan, unlined face. Seconds ticked by while Snyder continued to pretend to ignore us.

"You gonna tell me the story?" she asked.

I smiled. Persistent little thing.

"No."

I poured the last of the beer over the ice in my glass. Snyder took the empty as she eyeballed me. I watched the foam reach for the rim and melt back.

"Will you tell me if I buy you a drink?" She showed me a crooked grin, and she looked better that way.

"For a beer, I'll give you the short version."

She moved down the bar and slid onto the chair next to mine. Snyder brought us both fresh drinks.

I told her some of it. How I had dropped my hyphenated last name in order to avoid being treated as The Rich Man's Son. Michael Travis Kamahale-Van de Groot is a cumbersome mouthful, and carried more baggage than I wanted in this life. I told her about my twenty years with LAPD, fourteen years of it spent as a detective. But that's where I left it. Nothing about the case in Catalina, or about the cases of Ruby Orlandella or Ashley Logan. Those things belonged to me.

"So now you're just a *hapa haole* boat bum," she said with a smile.

I felt the heft of the lightweight Beretta tucked in the small pouch I'd had sewn into the pocket of my shorts. I had a permit to carry, and I did. Some guys, they get shot and don't ever want to touch a gun again. Me? I'd have the thing surgically attached if I thought it wouldn't interfere with foreplay.

"I suppose so," I said.

She saw something in my expression and started to speak.

I cut her off.

"Thanks for the beer," I said, and offered my hand. She took it and squeezed gently. "Let's just keep this between us, okay? Kona's a small town."

I slipped a few bills from my wallet and tossed them on the

bar for Snyder. As he rang them into the register, I said good-bye to the blonde.

I never did get her name.

CHAPTER THREE

Twilight is my favorite time of day to walk the Kona waterfront. The flickering lights of the village begin to cycle on, piercing the encroaching darkness, the heat of the day leeching from the concrete and up through the soles of your sandals while cool wind drifts in off the water.

As I crossed the street from Snyder's, I glanced out into the bay where the *Kehau* pulled at her moorings, bow and stern lights glowing. At the foot of the pier, sun-browned children played and swam in the rippling tide that was just beginning to reflect the setting sun. My mind flashed back to the orange glow of flames against the ruined storefronts of South Central LA, the weight of the riot gear I had worn, the heat of my own breath inside the helmet. All of us had been called back into uniform for that, detective or no.

I pushed through the doors of the King Kamehameha Hotel and into a wall of air-conditioning that carried that familiar hotel smell. Carpet cleaner, Windex and a hint of mildew. A few guests wandered the lobby, window shopped in the wide promenade as I headed toward a bank of pay phones that still hung along the far wall.

I turned my back to the reception area, pulled the number

from my pocket and placed the call. An hour and ten minutes since I'd spoken to him last. An operator at the other end put me through to Valden's room. When he picked up, he sounded even more agitated than before.

"Mike," he said. "I've got a problem. A big problem."

"Take it easy, Valden. Take a breath."

He made a sound that was half sigh, half laugh, and all desperation. "I'm not sure where to start."

"The beginning," I said, feeling like a cop again. "What are you doing in LA?"

"Business. A couple of meetings and a political fund-raiser."

"How long've you been there?" I was trying to calm him down, get him to think straight. If he got any more worked up, he'd have to breathe into a bag.

"Two days," he said. "I got here Wednesday night. The political thing is Sunday afternoon."

"Uh huh."

"Day after tomorrow."

"I get it," I said. "Then where to after that?"

"Home," he said. "Back to New York."

I looked over my shoulder and out through the glass doors of the lobby. A man in pressed white slacks and Hawaiian shirt was lighting the tiki torches that lined the entry. I smelled the fuel and flame and thought again about those long nights all those years ago, the meltdown in Los Angeles. Same planet, different world.

"So what's going on, Valden?"

I could hear the rattle of ice in a cocktail tumbler.

"I've been, ah . . . been *caught*, Mike."

I had to process that for a second. But not much longer. "LeeAnn?"

"No."

If it wasn't his wife, the alternatives were worse. "Blackmail?"

"Yes, blackmail," he said, something resembling shame coloring his words. Though he'd had plenty of opportunity, shame wasn't an emotion with which my brother was overly familiar.

The hairs on my neck stood on end. See, he and I shared an unpleasant secret—a thirty-year-old confidence involving the death of a friend named Stacy Thorne. We never speak of it. Never. I'd spent more than half my life trying to erase it from my memory, trying to forget his culpability, and my own, however tacit it may have been. Now my mind crawled with the possibility that it may have been uncovered. And if it had, there was no part of his life—or mine—that would ever remain as it had been.

"Go on," I said. "And choose your words carefully. Are you hearing what I'm telling you?"

A lingering moment of silence hung between us. When he finally spoke, his voice was thin. "Something came up here at the hotel."

"Please tell me it's a woman."

"You could say that."

The fist that had been crushing my heart let go, and I felt I could breathe again.

Valden and his women. His wayward pecker had caused more trouble for Van de Groot Capital than any ten litigation firms in the country put together. God only knew of how many indiscretions Valden's wife, LeeAnn, had been spared knowledge. She was a fine woman and a good mother. The better part of me knew he deserved to be caught, deserved what would follow. But LeeAnn didn't. Neither did my niece and nephew.

The only thing that kept me on the line now was that I knew something my brother didn't: blackmail can be a very slippery slope. If someone caught him at whatever this bit of misconduct was, worse could easily follow. And nobody needed that. Nobody.

"What's the play?" I asked.

"They've got me on video, Mike."

"How the hell—"

"Hotel security cameras caught me in the elevator."

My pulse began to slow, and I thought about how the security system would likely lay out.

"And probably the hall outside your room," I said. "Got you going in, coming out. Time coded. Probably have you inside as well."

Valden sighed again. "They couldn't have—"

"You talk to the local cops?"

"What, are you kidding? The note said if I don't pay up by Sunday, they're going to post the video on the goddamned Internet. The cops are the last place I'd go."

These guys were slick. They knew who Valden was, knew he had ready access to large amounts of cash, knew he couldn't stall for time on that account.

"How'd they get to you?"

"Shipped me a DVD with the demand, payment instructions, and a sample video clip."

"Let me guess," I said. "They'll send one to your home if you don't pay."

"That's what the demand said. Plus, copies to all our corporate clients and every major TV station in the country."

"And a posting on the Internet," I repeated.

"I *know*," he interrupted. "I need your help, Mike. Can you do it? Can you help me?"

When our father died, everything between my brother and me had changed. The years hadn't been kind to our relationship.

But he was the only family I had left; Valden, LeeAnn and their kids. I thought about whether I could help him anymore even if I wanted to, about whom I still knew in Los Angeles, how much time it might take.

"I'm not a cop anymore, Valden. I'm just a PI." A goddamned reluctant PI, at that.

I'd been conscripted by the local police captain a few months earlier, pressed into service on those occasions there was work that needed doing off the books. My license allowed me certain extrajudicial freedoms not afforded to law enforcement. In pursuit of a bail jump, I could cross state lines. I could kick down doors without a warrant, could detain a suspect indefinitely and generally deprive him of his legal rights and treat him like property. I had not yet been put in a position to question the morality of that situation. The captain was a decent man, and so far my efforts had only resulted in taking some genuine degenerates off the board.

"I don't care. I'll send the jet."

"Forget the jet," I said. "I'll catch the red-eye. You can pick me up at the airport in the morning."

Relief slithered down the phone line.

"Thank you, Mike—"

I broke in. There wasn't time, and I didn't really want to hear it.

"Just be there. Hawaiian Airlines. It arrives about six in the morning. Look it up."

I walked back to Snyder's. Yosemite still hadn't shown, so I left a message for him, asked him to keep an eye on the *Kehau* while I was gone. I knew he'd probably use it as an excuse to spend the weekend aboard with his live-in girlfriend.

I debated phoning Lani, who was working the bar down at

Lola's. But I drove down to see her instead. She wasn't going to be happy.

The place was all whirring blenders and Buffett music, cruise-ship tourists three deep at the bar. Lani was making change from the register, blowing a stray lock of dark hair out of her eyes. It was a good five minutes before she came up for air. When she saw me, her face brightened in a way that hollowed me out.

"What brings you down—" She stopped herself short when she saw the look on my face.

"I just got a call from my brother," I said.

A question flashed across her brown eyes, and I saw the wind come out of her sails.

"You're canceling on me again," she said. The last time had been a last-minute charter. This was different, but I knew it wouldn't make any difference to her.

"I'm sorry, Lani," I said. "I have to go to the mainland."

"When?"

"Tonight."

Even in the noise of the place, a silence hung between us. I came around the bar to kiss her good-bye, and she offered me a cheek, her body rigid.

"Why?" she asked.

"I can't really go into it now, Lani."

She turned to take an order before I could say anything else.

Lately, it had been nothing but false starts and bad timing, a lingering sense of almost. But I will always think of her the way I'd seen her that time at the beach by the old airport. It had been a birthday party for somebody we both knew, long tables full of food and coolers jammed with ice and beer. I'd met Lani some time before, when she worked at the Harbor House, but that night at Shaloma Marks's birthday, she came in off the beach and almost made me forget who I was. She was dark, with long, thick black hair down to her waist, the trim body of a dancer. A light dusting of sand speckled her ankles and the tops of her feet, and she smelled of the sea and the sun. That night, it was like no one else was there. We talked and drank until the party had long since been packed away, and the moon rose over the rim of the volcano.

Lani told me she'd been married before, but it hadn't lasted long. Three years. He was a part-time fisherman, part-time truck driver, and a full-time crackhead. The marriage lasted just long enough to ruin her credit and scrape away the last patina of her innocence. But she came out of it with a quiet strength, one void of any hint of self-pity. She called herself a romantic realist, though I didn't think I completely believed her.

Now, it was like she'd discovered one more splinter in the little bit of hope she still allowed herself. And deep inside that shadow was a piece of something I wasn't sure I'd put there.

I watched as Lani spoke to the other bartender, crooked a thumb in my direction and came out from behind the bar. She strode past me, walked outside and waited at the quiet end of the lanai. I followed her out, took up a place beside her.

Wind ruffled the deep green leaves of a banana tree as we stood in silence, Lani's face half in shadow in the last of the afternoon light.

"You're nothing but contradictions, Mike," she said softly.

My expression asked the question.

"You're rich, but you don't spend money. You have friends who are more loyal than any I've ever seen, but everyone else is scared to death of you. You say you came here looking for peace, but you had blood on your hands before you'd even been here two weeks. You're tender with me, Mike, but violence hangs on you like a dirty sheet."

"What am I supposed to do with that, Lani?"

Her eyes skipped past me again, stared into the distance as she answered. "I don't know. I love you, Mike, but sometimes you scare me, too."

"I'd never do anything to hurt you."

"That's not what I mean," she said, looked into my face, and what I saw there cut me to the bone. "I know I'm what you want, but maybe not what you need. You have everything you say you want right here in front of you, but you won't reach out and take it."

I felt like a stranger in my own skin, caught in the lie my life was becoming, the empty place between what I actually was and what I had thought I wanted to be. She saw it on my face, and I saw myself in hers. It wasn't the depth of what I felt for her, or even the magnetic poles of my desires that were breaking her heart, but my hesitation. Happiness was the emotion I had never learned to trust.

"I won't bother asking when you'll be back," Lani said.

She showed me the most sorrowful smile I had ever seen, brushed the tips of her fingers across my cheek, and she was gone.

CHAPTER FOUR

A shrill and discordant voice awakened me from a sound sleep. The flight deck announcement of our initial descent into Los Angeles International Airport. I yawned, stretched my legs and slid open the window blind.

The rising sun glanced off the thick blanket of smog that spread across the horizon and tinted it a mottled brown. Below, an unbroken line of headlights snaked off to the north along the freeway, taillights flashing red in the opposite direction. I blinked my eyes and tried to focus on my watch. Six twenty on a Saturday morning. Jesus.

I often said that I hated this city, but that was only a half-truth. At some level it still lived inside my brain, and exposed my inner feelings unexpectedly, like an old lover sharing a smile with me from across the room.

I straightened my seat back as directed, and tried to avoid further conversation with the guy sitting next to me by thumbing through the in-flight magazine. It didn't work.

"Coming home?" he asked. A business type returning from a trip he'd won in a sales contest. I'd already heard about it before we took off from Keahole airport.

"No." I stared at an article about Herman Melville.

"Hmmm," he said. "Connecting, then?"

I shook my head.

"No."

He gave me the salesman smile.

"Not much of a talker, huh?"

I looked out the window as the wheels skidded against the tarmac. The sky looked like tarnished pewter.

"No," I said. "Not much."

Valden was waiting outside the security area, standing on his toes to see over the crowd. He was wearing a silk club tie, Allen Edmonds loafers and a gray Louis Roth suit, tailored to diminish his growing paunch.

I was the third person off the plane.

"First Class," he said. "Joining the establishment?" It fell flat, didn't work with the dark semicircles beneath his eyes.

Valden and I come from different ends of the gene pool. At six two, two hundred ten, I like to get a little leg and elbow room when I can. My brother, on the other hand, packs about the same weight on a five-foot nine-inch frame, and has lost a little more hair every time I see him. Strangers never guessed we were brothers.

"Sure, Valden. Lifestyles of the One Percent," I countered. He looked like he had enough trouble to deal with.

"Just kidding, Mike. Got any luggage?" He was eyeballing the two carry-ons I held.

"This is it," I said, and let him take my bag. I kept the brief-case. "Let's go somewhere and talk, maybe get some breakfast."

"You know this town better than I do," he said. "Just tell my driver where to go."

We walked quickly through the terminal, pushing our way past weekend travelers, and out to the curb where Valden's limo idled in the white zone. Gray clouds of condensation puffed from the tailpipe and blew away on the brisk November wind. The limo was a brown Lincoln Town Car with a modest stretch. A uniformed driver got out and opened the trunk.

My brother introduced us.

"This is Jimmy," he said. "My driver."

We shook hands.

Valden handed my bag to Jimmy and ducked into the back-seat. The driver tucked them away and reached for my briefcase.

"I'll keep it in back with me," I told him.

"Fine, sir," he nodded smartly and closed the trunk. "And where are we headed this morning?"

I gave him an address off Figueroa, an old cop hangout that was open all day. I got in the car and Jimmy shut the door behind me.

Valden pressed the button that raised the privacy screen as we pulled away from the curb. The rich smell of leather and the thick wool carpeting beneath my feet felt like money. That's how it was supposed to feel in Valden's world. That's how you wined and dined your way into sponsoring some of the largest IPOs in the last decade.

It's also how you became a target.

My brother looked haggard and worn, hardly a trace of the usual slickness and condescension. I was sure other people could see it as clearly as I could. When he spoke, it was almost manic, a sleep-deprived energy that burned like a three-day coke jag.

"Let me start from the beginning—"

I held up my hand.

"Not here," I said. "Wait until we get where we're going."

"The walls have ears?"

I glanced at the thin privacy panel that separated us from the driver.

"That's right, Valden," I said. "Eyes, too."

He looked confused.

"What? You mean Jimmy?"

I put on my sunglasses and looked out into the early morning glare, then turned back to my brother.

"You start by suspecting everybody," I said. "Sometimes the problem's right under your nose."

"But—"

"Let me tell you a story, Valden."

"Okay."

"See, there was this border guard at a backwater crossing along the border of Slovenia. Every day he sees this young kid pedaling a nice, shiny new bike across the border with a sandbag hanging over the middle of the handlebars. After a couple days of watching the kid, the guard stops him, makes him dump out the bag. Surprised as hell, he finds it's only sand. He lets the kid go, but makes sure to keep an eye on him.

"He watches the kid for a few more days. Same thing happens. Every day, the kid comes through with a bag of sand over the handlebars. So the guard stops him again, makes the kid dump out the bag. Again, it's only sand. It drives the guard nuts.

"Finally, one day he stops the kid and makes a deal with him. 'I know you're smuggling something valuable through here,' he tells the kid. 'But I don't know what it is. Tell me what you're bringing across, and I promise never to stop you again.' The kid sizes him up, smiles and says, 'Bicycles.'"

Valden blinked, responded only with a blank look.

"Write down the names of everyone who knows you're in town. Everyone who knew you were coming."

"Now?"

I looked hard into his tired eyes.

"Might as well," I said. "Because we aren't going to do any more talking inside this car."

He started to say something more, but I stopped him.

"The list, please," I said.

He stared for a long time, past the tinted windows at the long blocks of tall buildings that lined Century Boulevard. When he finally turned back to me, his expression betrayed his loneliness.

"Okay."

The place was called the One-Oh-Seven. A cop reference to the ten-seven radio code that meant *Out of Service*. I watched the guys at a table by the window throw us the stink eye as the limo glided to a stop at the curb.

The kitchen was always open, always busy, and nondescript in every, sense. Even at this hour on a Saturday there were cops coming off shift preparing to go home, some grabbing breakfast before going on duty. Most were in uniform, though a handful wore plain clothes. In the back was a small room that they used for private parties, poker, and after-hours drinking. Every club needs a clubhouse.

Jimmy appeared at the curb on Valden's side and opened the door for him. My brother looked past him and gave the sixties-era river-rock facade a grim once-over. I knew what he was thinking.

As I slid across the seat, Valden made for the entrance. But when I got out of the car, Jimmy the driver latched on to my elbow.

"I don't know who you think you are, but I resent what you said to Mr. Van de Groot in there."

He was close enough that I could smell his breath: Dentyne and cigarettes. I jacked my arm away and faced him squarely.

"Come again?" I said.

I had startled him, but he tentatively held his ground.

"I'm a loyal employee," he said, his jaw stiff. "I'm a good man and a good driver. I would never do anything to hurt Mr. Van de Groot."

I took off my sunglasses and let him see my eyes.

"Good to know," I said.

Jimmy nodded, his honor defended.

I took a step toward the restaurant, then halted. I turned back to the driver.

"You proved my point, though, didn't you Jimmy?"

Traffic blew past him on Figueroa, ruffling his hair. He cocked his head.

"How would you know what I said to my brother back there?" I said, and followed Valden into the One-Oh-Seven.

My brother waited just inside, drumming his fingers on a glass counter case that displayed an assortment of breath mints and antacid tablets, waiting for the hostess I knew would never appear. I steered him to the back of the place, pointed to an empty seat in a booth against the wall.

"I'll be right back," I said.

I pushed through the swinging doors that led to the kitchen and found a waitress I still knew from back when. She hugged me, grabbed three plates of eggs, toast and bacon, and told me she'd be back in a minute. Through grease-dimmed diamonds of glass set into the kitchen doors, I watched Valden pick imaginary lint from the sleeves of his suit coat. Tables full of cops, in uniform and out, took turns glaring at him.

When the waitress came back, I was holding the keys I'd lifted from the hook hidden beneath the counter. The keys to the private room in back. I held them up where she could see them, flashed a question with my eyes.

She kissed me on the cheek and whispered in my ear.

"We miss you around here, honey."

The back room was smaller than I remembered, windowless, and smelled of tobacco smoke, stale beer and testosterone. The handles of two taps stood up behind a truncated wooden bar top, rows of clouded glassware on the counter behind. There was seating for maybe forty people on mismatched furniture set upon a faded checkerboard of green-and-white linoleum. Framed photos of cops, yellowed by age, covered two walls; a pair of dartboards and an oversized TV occupied the others. Dust motes floated on beams of dull incandescent light that glowed inside ceiling fixtures that hadn't been cleaned since I was a rookie.

Valden's eyes darted around the place; his lips made a nervous smacking sound.

I took a table in the back corner, the one that faced the door, and pulled my laptop from the briefcase, set it on a scratched and dented table. Valden handed me the DVD he had told me about on the phone and paced the floor as I watched it. Every now and then I'd catch him looking over at me, gauging my reaction.

It started with about twenty seconds of video footage of my brother and an unidentified young woman standing in an elevator. Her face was turned to the side, but had the look of someone who'd ridden that car before. At the right side of the frame, the doors eased closed, and floor numbers began to click by on the digital readout. They wasted no time. By the time the indicator read *three*, Valden had pressed the woman into the corner of the car and begun running his hands over her breasts and buttocks. By the fifth floor, he had buried his face into the crook of her neck and was working the hem of her dress high enough to see thigh-length stockings and a garter. She had one shapely calf wrapped around the back of his thigh.

The video abruptly went black, images on the screen replaced with a written demand that $3 million dollars be wired to a numbered account that was sure to reside in the Cook or Cayman Islands. It went on to say that further contact would be made on Sunday, when Valden would be provided the number of that account. If the funds had not cleared the wire by noon local time on Monday, then every US news network, business magazine, and major client of Van de Groot Capital would be sent a copy of the unedited video, and given the name of a web address where the full version would be posted for anyone in the world to access.

The words disappeared from the screen as suddenly as they had appeared, where my brother and his new friend were back in action.

Valden stopped pacing, took a seat in the corner as I watched the last of the footage: an image of him and the elevator woman entering a room on the thirty-fifth floor, the time code clearly marked 23:49:17. Nearly midnight. This was followed by a jump cut to 01:22:44, which showed the woman leaving Valden's room, adjusting a shoulder strap and blowing a final kiss into the room. The number on the door was as clearly visible as was Valden's face when he leaned out and kissed her one last time.

The screen went dark, then flashed an address: that of my brother's New York home, followed by the names of his wife and children.

My stomach was an icy pit, and I heard the rush of blood in my ears.

I turned to face my brother.

"The thing with blackmailers is," I said, "you've got to pull them out by the roots or they keep coming back. You understand that?"

Valden nodded, staring a hole in the linoleum.

"No mention of how they're going to contact you on Sunday," I said. "Any thoughts?"

By the look on my brother's face, I knew the other shoe was about to drop.

"That political fund-raiser I mentioned to you on the phone?" he began. "It's on Sunday."

"Who is it for?"

"Congressman Kelleher."

"Bill Kelleher?" I knew his name from the news. Everybody with a television and an IQ over fourteen knew who he was by now. He held some serious views about immigration and foreign trade, and wasn't shy about sharing them, establishing his bona fides early and often as a viable contender in the next round of presidential elections.

"Where?" I asked.

"Phillip Lennox's estate." Another name familiar to the world.

I didn't say it then, but I knew the blackmailers meant to reach out to Valden at that function. It was the smart thing for them to do. It would demonstrate to my brother they were deadly serious, that they could get to him anywhere they chose, and would underscore my brother's abject dread of public humiliation. They knew it would put the fear of God into him, and at precisely the right time, mere hours before the $3 million was to be transferred.

"There's no guarantee I can help you," I said. "I'm not a cop. I'm barely a PI, and there's no fucking time on the clock. You get that, right?"

"I'm out of options, Mike."

"You know there's a simple way out."

He looked at me out of the corner of his eye.

"And what would—No."

"Tell her, Valden. Confess this thing to LeeAnn, take your licks and be done with it. Salvage your family and your name. And the company name."

"That's not going to happen."

My eyes roamed back to the laptop where the names of his wife and family still glowed in stark block letters.

"You're willing to risk bringing a shitstorm down on yourself, your family and the company our grandfather built out of nothing."

He held my gaze for the first time since I'd arrived, with eyes that were glazed and shot through with fatigue and uncertainty. I hoped he was weighing the potential cost of his hubris.

I punched the eject button, slipped the disk from my computer, and packed them both into my briefcase next to the empty place where my Beretta should have been. Thanks to bin Laden—that vile and despicable fuck-stick—traveling with firearms wasn't as simple as it had once been, even if you were former law enforcement and had all your paperwork in order. I felt naked and ill-equipped for making my way around a city where you could get a slug planted in your brainpan just for mistiming a lane change.

Muffled racket from the kitchen thrummed against the walls of the tiny room, and somehow charged the emptiness we found ourselves in. I looked once again at my brother. He was rubbing his forehead with one hand, flexing a fist with the other. I wondered whether he had the stones for what was coming.

CHAPTER FIVE

"I was having drinks in the hotel bar with the congressman. The girl was there with a friend, sitting at a table not far from ours. One thing led to another."

"It was just the two of you?" I asked. "You and the congressman?"

Valden's feet were twitching as he crossed and recrossed his legs. His eyes were all over the room, sliding across the gallery of cops' faces that stared out from the walls.

I stood and went behind the bar. I unlocked the cabinet with a key from the ring that had let us in, and pulled out a bottle of Chivas. I poured three fingers in a glass for my brother and brought it to him.

"You need to try and calm down," I said.

The glass trembled as he brought it to his lips. Valden closed his eyes as he took a long swallow, gave me a curt nod and looked back to the floor.

"Congressman Kelleher . . ." I prompted him.

"Yes," he said again. "It was just the two of us."

"How many other people in the bar?"

He glanced up at the ceiling, blinked several times.

"I don't know," he said. "Twenty, thirty?"

"Anybody you know? Anybody seem to know you? Or the congressman?"

"It was pretty quiet. We were in the back, at a table in the corner. And no. Nobody seemed to give us a second glance. It's LA."

"What about Kelleher?"

My brother picked up the Chivas again, looked into it for the answer.

"He crapped out early."

"But you didn't."

Valden slammed the tumbler down hard. Scotch spilled over the rim and onto the table. His outburst didn't impress me.

"Don't be a hypocrite, Mike." His laugh was dry, brittle.

I crossed over to the bar again, grabbed a roll of paper towels, came back and tossed them on the table. They landed in the tawny pool that had begun to drip onto the floor tiles.

"She a pro, Valden?"

"What the hell difference does that make?" he said, pushing the Scotch-soaked napkins away.

"Talk to me, goddamn it," I said. "It's important. Was she a pro?"

It was an old story. Men such as my brother tend to screw down, marry up, and think they get to make the rules.

He brought the Chivas to his lips, tipped away the last of it as he absorbed the images on the aging portraits along the wall. He stared at them for a long minute before he shook his head.

"It's all so simple for you guys, isn't it?"

I didn't answer, dragged a chair across the floor and took a seat across from him.

Valden poured himself another three fingers and threw it back in one smooth motion. I watched the whiskey smolder at the back of his throat and saw the liquid glaze wash across his eyes.

"Everything's all spelled out for you," he said. "Your uniforms, your chain of command, your rules." He turned and looked me in the face. "The real world doesn't work like that. You have no idea what real life is like."

I smiled sadly at what my brother had become. I let the irony hang there in that tired room, surrounded by the portraits of cops who had been killed for nothing other than doing their jobs.

"I'm not your judge, Valden." That inclination, if it had ever existed at all, had been hacked away, piece by piece, over years of prevarication and mistrust. You had to have a stake in something to be a judge of it. All we shared now was a name and a secret. I had agreed to help him solely out of a sense of obligation to our family.

"I need to know, Valden. I need to know where to look." I asked again: "Was she a pro?"

The tumbler bounced noisily as his open hand came smashing down on the table. He stood suddenly, sent his chair crashing into the scarred wainscot.

"Fuck you, Mike," he said.

Valden dropped me at the Alamo lot near LAX. There were people I wanted to meet with, and I needed to get around on my own. My brother offered me the use of his car and driver, but a limo was not my speed, nor was being spied on by a curious chauffeur. I told him I'd get in touch after I'd had a chance to talk to some friends of mine, and had a little time to think things through. I knew he'd spend the rest of the morning pacing his suite, maybe pick up where he'd left off with the Chivas.

I watched the limo's brake lights flash as it bullied its way into the flow of traffic, feeling something approaching pity crop up inside me. My brother had spent his life in the pursuit of the premise of success. He desired the trappings, the illusion and the rush. But that was all it had become. Wealth and status had become ends in and of themselves, solipsistic victories in an endless war that raged inside his head. And like any addict, he danced closer to the flame of self-destruction every day of his life. The greatest irony of all was that the willful use of the power he craved was the very source of the slow ruin he was courting so blithely.

I know now that hindsight looks through a misshapen glass, affords a view that is not as accurate as we would wish to believe. Most often, it only shows us what might have been, what we wish had been, but was not. Perhaps I was as much in need of absolution as he was.

The initia call I made was to Vonda Franklin, an old friend from the crime lab, and the only person I knew with the expertise to help me with the first part of the problem.

I called her office, but she wasn't in. I found her home number, still filed away in the old-school address book I keep in my briefcase, and woke her up. After a predictable outpouring of bitching and moaning, she gave me the address of a coffee shop not far from where she lived, and told me to meet her in an hour.

The place smelled of old coffee, burned toast and disillusionment. Two young women, newly minted junkies, amateur whores, or both, shared a newspaper at the counter, where a dull-eyed waitress sucked a breath mint and leaned idly against the pass-through. In back, a tired Hispanic cook wiped kitchen grease off his cheek with the back of his hand.

I took a seat in the back, at a table that faced the door, and waited.

Vonda showed up fifteen minutes late, which had given me time to write some things down. I think best when I think on paper.

She pulled up a chair and glanced around the place. "Not how I remember it," she said, shaking her head. "I swear to God, this neighborhood's going straight into the shitter right before my eyes."

I leaned over and kissed her cheek.

"Not exactly paradise, eh, Mike?"

"Never was," I said.

She pulled some reading glasses from her purse and put them on the table beside her. "So, how's my favorite white man?"

I smiled. It was an old routine.

"You look tired," she said. Vonda reached over, placed a soft brown hand on top of mine and patted me. "And a little wound up?"

"This thing has a short timeline."

"Then let's get to it," she said, tossing a glance over her shoulder toward the kitchen.

The waitress came around from behind the counter, boredom and indolence defining everything about her. Vonda ordered coffee and whole wheat toast. I asked for hot water and a bag of tea. The waitress rolled her eyes and turned away in a draft of stale nicotine.

I slid my notepad into the light where I could read it.

"I see you still make your little doodley notes," she said.

I tilted it toward her, showed her the jumble of words, the lines and twisted angles, the geometric shapes and odd patterns that reflected the inner pattern of my thoughts. Vonda always had found them amusing.

The waitress came back and tossed our order onto the table.

I told Vonda about the blackmail scheme, the DVD, and the

threat to post the video to the Internet. I didn't tell her we were talking about my brother.

"Clever," she said, spreading strawberry jam on a slice of toast. "You've got the disk?"

"Yes."

"Got it with you?"

I nodded.

"Let me see it," she said.

I dipped into my briefcase and came out with it.

She slid it carefully from the sleeve, touching only the outer edges and examined it in the light. A rainbow of refracted light swirled across the silver surface and caught the attention of the women at the counter, who turned to watch for a moment before rapidly losing interest.

"That's one thing, at least," she said.

"What is?"

"It's not commercially reproduced. At least this one wasn't."

"Which means?"

She took the glasses from her nose and looked at me, amber eyes direct and clear.

"It was burned onto a type of disk that's made for consumer use. If it had been mass produced, I'd be able to tell."

"Then there aren't many copies floating around," I said.

"Probably not. This was likely done on a low-volume burner. Like something you'd use at home."

"Or to back up a security system," I said.

"Given what you told me about the hotel, could be a good guess."

"You said something about low volume. How do you know?"

"You'd have to go to a different kind of disk, a whole different process to mass-produce them."

She slipped the disk into its sleeve and handed it back to me.

"Any way to identify who made the copy?"

"Not exactly," she said. "But you can tell which *machine* did the copy."

I pushed my cup away, leaned forward on my elbows. I looked past Vonda's shoulder and winked at the two eavesdropping hookers. They turned away.

"How?"

Vonda smiled.

"Little known fact, Travis: every digital burner has a machine-specific alphanumeric code that marks everything it does. A small concession to the software industry to protect against piracy."

"A signature," I said.

"Better," she nodded. "More like a fingerprint. Completely unique."

"We'd need something to match it to," I said.

"That's true," she said. "Or you could run the numeric code by all the hardware manufacturers and try to trace the machine; who made it, who sold it, who bought it."

"It's Saturday," I said. "I need the information before noon tomorrow."

"Then you're going to have to identify the *people* who burned that disk."

We both went silent when the waitress brought the check.

"One more thing, Vonda," I said. "What about posting it on the Internet?"

"Short version?"

"Please."

She told me about IP addresses, about data packets and protocols, domain names and dedicated servers, but my mind was drifting elsewhere, even as I made notes in my little book.

I watched a young mother in a Nirvana T-shirt briefly struggle with the glass door while she balanced a baby on her hip, a row of silver studs marking the outline of her ear. Her eyes were washed out and gray, like she had spent the better part of her life in tears.

I thought of the *Kehau*, floating in a bay halfway across the Pacific; and of Lani, sitting alone with her first cup of coffee, where the sun was only now showing itself from behind the thin layer of cloud cover that cloaked the early morning shoulders of Hualalai.

"You still with me?"

"Yeah," I said.

"Thing is, Travis," Vonda went on, "to have their scheme work, they'd have to have a domain name ready to go. You know, a way to drive folks to the site once it was up and running. Something like Blackmailers.com *or* DouchebagsandThieves.net, you get the idea. Whatever the domain name is has to be registered to somebody."

"They already have one. How long would it take to track the name of the owner?"

"If it was done legit, not long at all. But if they're smart, it'd be hidden deep inside a series of shells, like a set of Russian nesting dolls."

"How long?"

"A long time, but I'm just LA police." She shrugged. "The Feds, though? That'd be something else altogether."

I put down my pen on top of the notepad and pushed them away. My eyes drifted out the window past the parking lot and onto the flow of traffic in the street beyond.

"I haven't been much help," Vonda said.

"You've helped plenty."

Tiny lines fanned from the corners of her eyes as she

showed me a sad smile. "You look like you have a hundred people inside your head."

I squinted as a stray glint of sunlight glanced off the windshield of a passing car and into my eyes. I turned to face her.

I had been engaged for the greater part of my adult life in an attempt to negotiate an ocean that had no definition, no shape, no markers or boundaries, no plumb line to gauge its depth. I had bartered away the quiescence of discovery in exchange for an aptitude for navigation.

"I'm considering marriage for the first time in my life," I said. "Lani and me."

She was silent for several seconds as the smile reached her eyes.

"That's a beautiful thing, Mike."

"I don't know why I told you that," I admitted. "I don't really want to talk about it."

"You're happy?"

"When I'm with her, I'm home."

Vonda reached across the table and touched my fingers with the tips of hers.

"You ever miss LA? You used to like this town once."

"I used to love it."

She averted her eyes and a heavy silence hung between us for long seconds.

I thanked her then, slid a ten under the napkin dispenser and we slipped out of the booth.

Fifteen minutes later, I watched Vonda's car ease out of the lot, her arm hanging casually out the driver's side window. She tossed me a little wave, gave two taps on the horn, and melted into the city.

CHAPTER SIX

I walked to clear my head.

My mind was vibrating with pent-up energy, my blood-stream like electric currents running in every direction, seeking ground. So I walked, it didn't matter where, to find traction for my scattered thoughts.

The sun was shining brighter now, beating back the last of the thin gray sheet overhead, but the onshore wind was picking up, growing colder as it blew in from the west, from the coastline where it gathered strength and a bone-dampening chill from the Pacific not far away.

I found myself several blocks from where I had parked to meet with Vonda. Across the street, a wide-shouldered man wearing a Seattle Seahawks jersey and a black apron swept the sidewalk outside a bar whose OPEN light he had just switched on. The banner over the doorway advertised five-dollar pitchers for the game that afternoon. As for me, it was already the fourth quarter. I was third and long on the opponent's fifteen, down by six and no time on the clock by the time my brother had brought me into a game I hadn't even known was on the schedule.

I had two plays left: a balls-out run up the middle or a Hail Mary for the end zone. I flipped my phone open and placed a call that would set the Hail Mary in motion, and if that didn't work, it was straight up the gut. That's it. That's all there was.

Rex Blackwood had been on his third tour as a Navy Seal when he had his skull caved in by the Vietcong during a firefight that took place in a village that had long since been reclaimed by an overgrowth of philodendrons and elephant grass, five hours' hump through dense jungle from the nearest LZ. He awakened in a military hospital in Saigon days later, where he endured seemingly endless hours of physical and psychological testing by US government spooks before being whisked back to Virginia and assigned to an NSA operational team tasked with missions so black that they had their own gravitational pull. He bore a tattoo that hinted at the nature of his activities, and suffered only periodic nocturnal visitations of phantoms, but when they came, they would linger beside him for days.

We had become friends after my retirement from LA Homicide, and I had moved my yacht to Catalina Island, where Rex also had sought refuge as a boat captain. He had crewed with me on my trans-Pacific escape on the *Kehau* from California to Hawaii, stayed in the islands long enough to see me take the better part of a poorly aimed shotgun blast to my shoulder—a shot that was meant for my skull—at the hands of a meth-dealing junkie who later died of wounds sustained by return fire from my Beretta. Rex returned to Catalina shortly after I was released from the hospital, but not before another body had dropped. It had been an eventful trip.

The phone rang three times before he picked up.

"Go," was all he said.

"It's Travis. I could use a little help."

"I'll call you from a landline at the hotel. Fifteen minutes. Use it to find a pay phone." The line went dead.

I crossed the street and stepped into the bar with the five-dollar pitchers. The place was empty, but for the guy in the Seahawks jersey who was now wiping down the counter. Classic rock blared from dusty speakers while muted television sets displayed a trio of former pro athletes in designer suits having an animated discussion about the relative merits of the replay rule.

"You got a pay phone in here?" I asked.

"Get with the program, man, it's 2004," he said without looking up from his work.

"That was a yes or no question."

He stopped wiping and eyeballed me for a second before answering.

"I think we still got one that hasn't been torn off the wall yet."

"What's your business number?"

"Why?"

"Your phone number. What is it?"

I knew he was weighing how much trouble I was worth as he studied me again. He gave me the number.

"Anything else?"

"Beer."

"What kind?"

"Cold. And I'm going to need change for a dollar."

I glanced at my watch, had seven minutes to wait before I would hear back from Rex Blackwood. I leaned on the bar, one foot on the rail, and looked out the window toward the foothills. I pictured Rex motoring his way across Avalon bay in his skiff, heading toward the pier where he would tie off and jog the short distance to the hotel lobby. Though he never told me outright, I had cause to believe that Rex had been a part of the remote-viewing operation that the NSA has persistently denied ever existed. I had further cause to believe that the spooks had never completely let him go.

"Pay phone's in the back?" I asked, hooking a thumb in the direction of the bathroom sign painted on the wall with an arrow pointed down a narrow hallway.

"Yeah," he said, his back to me as he drew my beer. He turned slowly, his face slack, and I could read him like a highway sign. His pupils were dilated and his throbbing pulse clearly visible in the vein that stood out on his neck, a heart rate fueled by adrenaline. He was measuring the distance between himself and the aluminum bat or cut-down twelve-gauge tucked away beneath the bar.

"Relax, pard," I said. "A phone call, and I'm gone."

He knew what I knew. It's not like the movies. Real-life violence is rarely presaged by bellicose behavior, verbal threats and wild gesticulation.

"There's not going to be a problem, here, right?" he asked.

Instead, mayhem is most often visited upon you from unexpected quarters; a couple eating a quiet dinner in the corner whose conversation slowly escalates until it ends with a fork being jammed into the other's eye socket. Or random rifle shots fired from behind the concrete balustrade of an overpass or from the rolled-down window of a passing car.

"It'll be like I was never even here."

I made my way across the room, down the hall, and found what I was looking for. I jotted down the number off the pay phone, writing it on the palm of my hand with a ballpoint, and returned to a seat on a stool in front of my beer.

Exactly fifteen minutes from the time I had first reached out to Rex, my cell phone rang. I answered with the number the bartender had given me and hung up. Less than thirty seconds later, the bar phone rang. The bartender answered, and passed the receiver to me without another word. Rex read me a thirteen-digit number and killed the connection. It was an old code arrangement: the first two numbers were to be disregarded, as was the last.

It was a lot of cloak and dagger for one fucking call, but it was the only way that could defeat the wiretapping capacity of the NSA on the fly. We would keep it as brief as possible. Not even the super geeks at the puzzle palace would be able to arrange a trap on our conversation in so little time.

I scooped four quarters off the bar and hustled back toward the pay phone again. I punched in the number Rex had given me and he picked up immediately. I gave him a brief rundown on the blackmail situation without mentioning any names, Rex's and mine included.

"So," he said. "You need a name."

"Yes. Like, five minutes ago."

The line was briefly silent, but I thought I could hear him breathing.

"You know there's no guarantee that the server is in the same location as the guy who owns the domain, right?"

"I'm banking on this being a very closely held operation. All things considered, it's a small amount of money they're asking for. It doesn't have the smell of organized crime with a capital 'O.'"

"I think I have a guy."

"I'm out of time."

"Call me in four hours at this number. Use a different phone."

"Copy that," I said, but the line was already dead.

The bartender stood behind the bar when I came back out, failing in his attempt to appear as though he wasn't tracking my every move. One of his hands aimlessly worked a rag along the countertop, and the other out of my view below. My beer glass had disappeared.

He tensed as I reached into my back pocket.

I slowly withdrew my wallet, dropped a five in front of him and rapped my knuckles on the wood.

"Like I told you," I said. "As though I was never here."

CHAPTER SEVEN

Outside on the sidewalk, silver sun glare stung my eyes. I slipped on my RayBans against the dull throb of the late morning as it burned through the haze. Brisk gusts of cool wind cut through the thin fabric of my jacket and chilled me to the bone.

I stood there a moment, my hands jammed into my pockets, and thought about home. It was nearing nine A.M. in Kona, and I knew Tino had long since arrived at my plantation, slamming across the red dirt road in his old Ford pickup, looking out past the dense green fields of coffee, southwest toward Tahiti, the trade winds drifting down off the volcano at his back.

I felt jet-lagged and empty, attempting to repress my growing anger toward my brother for dragging me back to this goddamned place. I think I had known it since my first year on patrol: When you're out there, you're constantly wading in the current of other people's lives, but only when the tide is going out. Nobody calls a cop when they're having a good time. It was a daily diet of bullshit you encountered on the street—and the real danger wasn't as much about corruption as corrosion.

I shook myself out of it and slipped the cell phone from my pocket, punched in a number I knew I'd never forget. It rang twice.

"Homicide," the voice answered. In the background were familiar sounds, the daily chaos of ringing telephones and office machines.

"Detective Yamaguchi, please," I said.

A measurable hesitation, then: "One moment."

There was no music on hold, only the sounds of passing traffic and the ambient noise of the city as I waited. I looked into the stainless steel sky, then off to the east where the tips of the mountains disappeared into the inversion layer. I was about to hang up and try again when my call was finally transferred.

"Detective Johnston."

"Jeff Johnston?" I asked.

"How may I help you," he said. His tone was all business.

"This is Mike Travis."

"Sorry, Mike, they didn't tell me it was you."

"They didn't ask," I said. "Where's Hans?"

Johnston was silent for a second too long; time enough to tell me that something was wrong. I heard the sound of his desk chair shuffling, could almost see him hunch over as he spoke to me in a voice so low it was nearly a whisper.

"Listen, Mike . . . uh . . . Hans is on admin leave."

That's not the kind of leave you take voluntarily.

"What the hell for?"

Another hesitation.

"You'd better ask him yourself," Johnston said. "He's been off for four or five days now."

"He at home?"

"Far as I know," he said. "But listen, don't tell him you heard it from me, all right."

"Yeah, sure. Thanks for the help."

"Sorry, Mike," he offered. "I know you guys were tight."

Partners. More than that, even. Brothers. And unlike my blood brother, Hans wasn't a man to tread uneven lines, certainly not in any way I could imagine that would bring Internal Affairs down on him. I hung up with a sour feeling in my stomach.

I had to talk with Hans, and the phone wasn't going to get the job done.

Hans Yamaguchi lived with his wife, Mie, in a late-forties vintage bungalow near Old Town in Pasadena. The streets were lined with shade trees; a bucolic appearance more like a small Midwestern town than you'd expect to find in greater Los Angeles. It was the kind of place where neighbors still spoke to one another and children played ball on freshly mowed front lawns.

When I pulled to the curb, I saw their cars parked bumper to bumper in the narrow drive beside the house. Hans's was dusted with a layer of grime and looked like it hadn't been moved in several days. A weather vane in the likeness of a gamecock twisted slowly on a rooftop cupola.

I rang the bell and waited on the porch, listening to the mockingbirds and neighborhood sounds. Across the street an elderly couple busied themselves with yard work.

Mie came to the door wearing a simple housedress, a pink cardigan sweater draped loosely around her shoulders and buttoned at the throat. She was surprised to see me. She had cut her hair since I'd seen her last, and was still as petite as I remembered. She threw her arms around me, pressed her face against my chest, and took my hand in both of hers. She pulled me outside, softly closing the door behind us.

"I am so happy you are here," she said. Her voice carried the cadence and inflection of her native Tokyo, but was uncharacteristically laced with emotion.

"How's he doing?"

"Not very well, I think. He does not go out. Only stays home working on the house. He pretends to find things that need to be fixed."

She looked past me, losing focus for a moment.

"He does not tell me anything. Only that what the people say about him is not true."

I placed my hands gently on her shoulders, but looked squarely into her almond eyes. She felt fragile and childlike.

"You know what kind of man Hans is," I said. "You know you don't have anything to worry about."

She drew a paper tissue from the pocket of her dress, dabbed at her eyes and pulled me through the doorway and toward the back of the house.

Hans was in the backyard, hunched over a two-by-four that rested on a pair of sawhorses, working it with a belt sander. He looked up as I approached, but I couldn't read his expression behind the safety goggles he wore. He stopped what he was doing, stood straight and unyielding, and stared at me for long seconds.

"What the hell are you doing here?"

When he took off the goggles, I saw the luggage he carried underneath his eyes. He hadn't shaved in a couple of days. A fine layer of sawdust powdered his clothes.

"Nice fence," I said.

"It's a gazebo."

"Nice gazebo, then."

He dropped the sander to the ground and hooked the goggles over the corner of the sawhorse. His eyes bored into mine as he brushed wood shavings from his shirt.

"You look like you're running on the rims, Hans."

"You don't have a phone?"

"It was a last-minute thing," I said.

Hans nodded.

"Yeah," he said. "So you know."

"Less than you'd think," I said. "You all right?"

The muscles in his square jaw flexed and he stared inward.

"Sure," he said finally. There was a tone of resignation in his voice that I'd never heard before.

"Listen, Hans—"

"Assholes," he interrupted, speaking more to himself than to me.

"I'm guessing you're referring to Internal Affairs?"

"Who else?" Hans squinted and looked out over his backyard fence, shook his head. "But that's not the best of it."

"I'm not following you."

"Wanna know who's working my case?" He pulled a pack of gum from his shirt pocket, offered me a stick. He didn't wait for my reply. "Dan fucking Kemp."

Kemp had been assigned as Hans's partner after I retired. But not for long. Kemp's father had political connections that had gotten him moved up to Homicide. But after fewer than six months in the unit, Kemp's own ineptitude had gotten him booted right back out.

"I thought he'd been sent over to Fraud," I said.

Hans snorted and peeled the wrapper off the gum.

"Daddy got him a transfer to the rat squad instead."

"Thought you had to be a sergeant for that," I said.

"Promotion came with the transfer."

"Kemp doesn't fuck up," I said. "He fucks *upward*."

"Yeah, well he's loving this shit."

"Be grateful you don't have a real cop on your ass," I said. "He's not splitting atoms on his day off."

Hans smiled, but his eyes had the lifeless appearance of a taxidermic animal. A twin-engine plane droned overhead. Hans let it pass before he spoke again.

"Still drink tea?" he asked.

He reached out and finally shook my hand.

An hour later he'd told me the whole thing.

About a month earlier, Hans and his new partner, Roger Gaines, had been contacted by a detective from Austin, Texas. The Texas cops had arrested a suspect on an aggravated assault charge down there. When they ran the suspect's prints, the guy came up as a suspect in a murder in Los Angeles. It was a case that belonged to Hans and Gaines.

After a boatload of haggling between the district attorneys for both jurisdictions, the cowboys agreed to allow him to be extradited to California to face the charge that carried more weight. So Hans's lieutenant flew him and Roger Gaines down there to pick up the guy and bring him back to LA.

"The Austin detective—shithead's name is Moss, by the way—picks us up at the airport," Hans said. "We landed about six or so in the evening."

"So you can pick up the suspect the next morning," I said.

"Exactly. You know the drill."

I nodded.

"So Moss says since it's early, why don't we get a couple of drinks down on Sixth Street, show us the town. I say fine, it's been a long day. But I should have known better, Mike." He shook his head. "I didn't like the look of the guy from the start. A walking stool sample."

Hans took a deep breath, exhaled a long sigh.

I waited while he regrouped.

"But I go along anyway," he said. "I don't know why."

"Where was your partner?"

"Gaines wants to get dropped at the hotel, get us checked in, call the wife, blah, blah, blah."

"So, you and Moss go on alone?"

"Yeah," Hans said. "But we meet up with this other guy that Moss introduces to me as another Austin cop. I forget that clown's name. Anyway, the three of us hit a handful of bars, have a beer or two along the way, listen to some blues and move on."

I pictured the hot, smoke-filled clubs, could almost hear the Texas blues of Kenny Wayne Shepherd, Buddy Guy and Stevie Ray Vaughan. I pictured young waitresses with legs all the way to the floor, bearing trays full of sweating longneck bottles of Shiner Bock and weaving between the tables.

I tilted my eyes upward, squinting into what remained of the high overcast. Shadows were beginning to show themselves on the ground between my feet and brought me back to LA.

"A couple hours later," Hans went on, "we ended up in this dump a few blocks off the main drag, a T and A club I wouldn't let my dog walk into. After a couple minutes, Moss and the other cop get up from the table and disappear. I'm just sitting there nursing a ten-dollar beer, knowing I have to get up in the morning and haul our dirtbag back to LA, right?

"Moss and the other jack-off are taking a long fucking time, but I don't really think about it. I got other things on my mind. But when he and his buddy finally come back, they're in this big rush to take off. Moss waves at the bartender, and we all leave. I don't even think about the tab. Never even crosses my mind."

I waited, but Hans seemed to be finished.

"That's it?"

Hans took a sip of his coffee, squinted against the emergent light of midday.

"Yeah," he said. "That's it. Except about three weeks later, I get called into the lieutenant's office and there's Kemp and this other IAD ass-hat sitting in his guest chairs. They got a call from Austin PD saying that Moss has been indicted down there. He'd evidently been on the pad for I don't know how long. The other Texas cop we met up with was wired. They'd been watching Moss for a couple months. And the strip joint we went to is a front for some southern-fried wiseguy that Moss had been in bed with."

"What does that have to do with you?" I asked.

"Well, according to Kemp, the fucking mobster is connected to organized crime all over the southwest."

"Including Los Angeles," I guessed.

"Yeah. Including LA. So they're investigating me for conspiracy and a bunch of other crap. At a minimum, even when they clear me, it's a rip for Conduct Unbecoming."

The job was everything to Hans. There had been a time when I felt the same way. He wore the betrayal on his face and in his eyes.

"It's all bullshit, Hans," I said. "If Kemp had to eat the truth to survive, he'd weigh about a pound and a half."

Hans stroked his chin and looked past me, lost again in some private thought. He looked older than when I had arrived, like he was going gray from the inside out.

"They can still bounce me, Mike," he said finally.

"What does Loo say?"

Lafayette Delano had been in charge of Homicide since I'd first come to the squad. I knew how highly the lieutenant thought of Hans.

"Loo's not there anymore, Mike," he said. "He's a captain now. West Bureau."

That was Hollywood, West Los Angeles, the Wilshire district. A good promotion.

"New boss doesn't know me from Adam," he finished.

Hans had more time in than me. Nearly twenty-five years for him now. I had clocked out after twenty. I knew it was killing him that the department was putting him on the outside.

"Kemp's Teflon. He'll do me on his own time just for the hell of it."

"And what'll he come up with? He couldn't find a turd in a sandwich bag."

"I'm not sure it matters," he said. "I don't know if I even want to stick around after this."

"I've done things I wouldn't admit to a cockroach," I said. "Don't let that douche bag run you out."

Hans shook his head.

"It's not just Kemp," he said. "He's just the icing on the cake."

"So what are you saying? You're going to quit?"

He stared into his coffee cup, then up at me.

"I don't know," he said. "Maybe."

"And do what?"

I followed his gaze as he glanced in through the kitchen window, at Mie standing at the sink. She couldn't see him watching her through the glare. He turned back to me.

"I'm not sure yet," he said. "But even when they clear me . . . I don't know. Hell with it."

I sat there in silence longer than I'd meant to. Hans was studying my expression.

"You came here for my help, didn't you, Mike?"

I debated saying no. Hans had enough to deal with as it was. He didn't need to get involved with my brother's bullshit. But he was right: I did need someone to watch my back. And there was no point in lying to him. Nobody knew me better than he did.

"Forget it. They're watching you, Hans."

He shrugged.

"It's like I told you," he said. "I don't believe I give a shit anymore."

I shot my eyes toward the kitchen.

"What about Mie?"

He thought about that for a minute.

"She'll back my play."

I'd known them both a long time, knew he was telling me straight.

"They let you keep your shield?"

"Just my knockoff," Hans said.

You learn young. When you're a cop, there's no greater sin, no greater humiliation, than losing your badge or your gun. Like most cops I knew, Hans had a replica of his department-issue badge—about seven-eights scale, and virtually impossible for a layman to distinguish from the real deal. More often than not, we'd carry the knockoffs when we were on the street, and leave the authentic ones in a safe place at home.

"Close enough," I said. "One more thing."

Hans eyeballed me in silence.

"I need a piece."

One of the perks of being a detective with the kind of record Hans had was his access to confiscated weapons. On their way to the crusher, certain guns can be "requisitioned from source for training purposes."

Without a word Hans disappeared into his bedroom. When he came back out, he handed me a mean little Stoeger Cougar with a fifteen-round magazine stacked with nine-mil rounds, wrapped in a cotton dust rag. It would nest nicely in the Mitch Rosen pocket-carry holster I had brought from home. I felt better already.

"You better get a shower and a shave. We don't have a lot of time," I said.

"This gonna be any fun?"

I told him it would be the investigative equivalent of a two-day search for a pair of reading glasses that were perched on the top of your head.

Hans smiled. And for the first time since I'd arrived, it looked like the real thing.

CHAPTER EIGHT

The fact that the city of Los Angeles represents the center point of the universe for the conceptualization, design and creation of the deluge of filmed fantasy that our world has come to know as entertainment should be sufficient warning in itself as to the proficiency she possesses as a liar.

Most modern-day Angelinos have no idea that even her name was in contention from the very day of founding in September of 1781, when Spanish maps were marked with *El Pueblo de la Reina de los Ángeles* (The Town of the Queen of Angels), while Catholic diocesans christened her *El Pueblo de Nuestra Señora la Reina de los Ángeles de Porciúncula* (The Town of Our Lady the Queen of Angels of the Little Portionú). Either way, the city was to become the stage for some of the country's most savage, corrupt and atavistic acts—acts that small-time politicians, petty functionaries and misanthropic predators would play out against ordinary citizens.

From a time two hundred years before title was ever transferred to the United States as a part of the treaty that ended the Mexican-American War, Los Angeles has worn the blood of every race, creed and ethnicity from the conquistadores to the Rodney King riots on her sidewalks, streets and alleys. At one point in 1848 with the arrival of the California gold rush, the city had come to be known as "the toughest and most lawless city west of Santa Fe," a place where the absence of any type of legal system created a vacuum into which every mode of outlaw, thug and swindler freely roamed the streets and profited from all the loan-sharking, prostitution and gambling that had been kicked out of San Francisco.

In 1871, gunfire erupted in the burgeoning Chinatown that had developed upon the completion of construction on the transcontinental railroad. Two rival Chinese factions, at war over the abduction of a woman, accidentally shot and killed a white man. In response, a mob of more than five hundred Anglos and Latinos descended on Chinatown and lynched nineteen men and boys, only two of whom may have even been *suspected* of involvement in the shooting.

By the 1920s it had become common practice for the mayor, councilmen, attorneys and other city officials to accept contributions and bribes from bootleggers, madams and organized crime. The mayor's brother was selling jobs at the LAPD and the vice squad acted as the citywide collectors and enforcers for both the mayor and the mob.

Bloody battles over water rights raged for decades from the 1930s and beyond; in 1943, clashes between World War II navy seamen and Latino zoot-suiters escalated into running street battles and brutal beatings in which boys as young as twelve and thirteen were dragged from movie theaters and bludgeoned with tire irons and steel pipe; oil was discovered and spurred yet another land rush and vehicle for scandal, corruption and violence.

The decade of the forties was ushered in by the rise of Mickey Cohen, an associate of Bugsy Siegel, who moved west from Chicago and transported an outbreak of heroin addiction, white slavery and extortion with him like a disease for which there was no cure, but had to be put down like a rabid animal.

Jump-cut to the Watts riots of 1965, in which thirty-four people were killed, more than one thousand injured and there was $40 million in property damage; and to 1992, the year in which a jury acquitted white LA cops of beating a black motorist. The Rodney King riots lasted four days during which more than fifty people died, and property damage, this time, was measured in the billions. That's billions with a 'b.' I was there for that one, and sometimes I still think I can smell the smoke on my skin.

So, when you see those pristine images of sun-soaked beaches and palm-lined boulevards, the blue Pacific coastline and Rodeo Drive, don't believe for a minute that it's all fun, fun, fun 'til your daddy takes the T-bird away. Don't believe it for a fucking second. The city of Los Angeles is a liar. She is a liar and she'll break your heart. She can't help it. It's in her DNA.

The Mandalay Plaza was one of the new breed of luxury hotels that had sprouted up in the city. In the short time it had been open, it had become one of the hottest of playgrounds for the rich and famous, known for both its elegance and privacy. The Bengal Room Bar was especially well-known as a watering hole for rock stars, movie people and other glitterati, but one unwritten rule was expected to be honored: what went on in the B-Room stayed in the B-Room. Like Vegas without the poker machines. If you wanted to make a deal, and you were young and beautiful, you did it at the Bengal Room. Let the old guard keep the Polo Lounge; if it was happening in LA, it was happening here. All you had to do is keep it cool. Now that rule had been broken, and it had brought me nearly twenty-five hundred miles from my yacht, my charters, and my life.

I retrieved my briefcase and carry-on from the trunk of the

rental car and took my ticket from the valet. I tipped him a couple of bucks and headed for the lobby. Hans followed me close behind.

The hotel was a gallery of nouveau-Asia tropicane, all lustrous teak, wenge and low lights. A cluster of slender palms arched up into a five-story atrium, and the sound of cascading water resonated off of hand-troweled plaster walls that had been hung with antique botanical etchings of exotic birds and flowers. A crisply uniformed staff stood at the ready behind a hardwood reception desk that looked like it had been hewn from a single slab of African mahogany; each one wore an expression that was the trademark blend of ennui and obsequiousness that typified world-class luxury, rarely encountered outside of Bangkok or Singapore or the Raj Palace of Jaipur.

Ten minutes later, I had retrieved the keys to the suite Valden had arranged for me and preregistered in the name of his subsidiary companies. I let us in. Hans and I passed through the spacious living room and stood before a seamless glass curtain wall that opened onto an expansive view of the Hollywood foot-hills. The decor appeared as though it had been shipped intact from a royal mansion in Rangoon, original artwork and all, but smelled of new carpet and expensive soap.

"Jesus," Hans said.

It was a three-room suite, with a living room and full-service wet bar that occupied the space between two master bedrooms. Hans and I took seats in matching sofas that faced each other across an ornately carved teak table. A ceiling fan made lazy circles above our heads, and stirred the air with blades crafted from bamboo and white sailcloth and reminded me of the *Kehau*.

I grabbed a couple of bottles of mineral water from the bar, placed one in front of Hans and cracked the top off one for myself. On the drive from Hans's place to the hotel, I'd filled him in on Valden's situation, but I wanted to watch the DVD again, this time with two sets of eyes. I popped the locks on my briefcase and extracted my computer and the disk.

Hans drifted away in the short time it took for me to ready the laptop. I tried to read his expression as he wandered the room, taking in the artwork that hung on the walls. His eyes locked onto a painting of Asian fishermen hauling nets from a jade sea, and his thoughts seemed half a world away.

"Video's loaded," I said.

Hans heaved an involuntary sigh and headed back to where I sat.

We ran the video twice, neither of us speaking a word, only watching as the floor numbers passed by on the LCD screen that was mounted on the wall of the elevator we'd just come up on. More silence as we watched my brother dry-hump his way into a $3 million dollar blackmail scheme.

A palpable hush as we parsed through our own thoughts. Finally, I stood and crossed the room, pulled open the draperies and absorbed the heat that radiated off the glass.

"Who's the girl?" Hans asked.

"Valden says she picked him up in the Bengal Room downstairs. He'd been drinking with Congressman Kelleher."

"The trade embargo guy?"

"He's here on a fund-raising mission, getting a head start on a run for president. Valden's an early supporter."

"I thought your brother was a big-time Democrat."

"My brother, as you know, has a negotiable relationship with the truth. He treats his politics the same way."

People found it easier to believe that my brother and I hated one another than to recognize that Valden was often as puzzled and embarrassed by my conduct as I was of his. I made no apologies for him, nor he for me. Ours was a bond of blood, but not of free will, not unlike many other families of brothers.

Valden masked his insecurities with promiscuity and profligate displays of wealth, which in itself did not make him a bad human being. He embraced both the accolades and the ideology that accompanied his sincere belief in the principle of noblesse oblige; he was a limousine liberal equally comfortable with a six-figure contribution to Habitat for Humanity as he was to the campaign coffers of let-them-eat-cake political tools who would sooner chew broken glass than set foot inside the neighborhoods of their own constituents.

Hans stepped back toward the coffee table and picked up his bottled water. The thing nearly vanished inside his meaty fist. He took a swig and sat back down in front of the computer.

"You think she's a working girl?"

"Probably," I said.

"You know there's got to be footage from inside the room."

"Probably," I said again.

Hans gestured toward the laptop.

"Have you got a printer for that thing?"

"Not with me," I said. "We'll have to use one in the hotel's business center."

"Let's cue up the best still shot of the girl's face, print it, and show it around. See if anybody knows her."

"The best angle we've got is the one from the elevator, but the definition's for shit."

"Yeah," Hans said. "But it might be good enough for a bartender to ID her. Something tells me they've seen her around here before."

I thought it would likely prove to be a waste of time. If the girl had been a part of the scam from the outset, the blackmailers would have obscured her face on the video before they'd ever delivered a copy to Valden. Which would mean that this black-mail scheme was a crime of opportunity. But I also knew from experience that assholes that pull stunts like this weren't always the brightest bulbs in the box.

Either way, I had a plan, and bird-dogging the girl's picture would be a good lead for Hans to handle while I did my part.

I saved the frozen image of the girl in a separate file, and burned it onto a blank disk.

Hans shook his head. The smile on his face was devoid of humor.

"Something else bothers me," he said. "Why Sunday?"

"The fund-raiser?"

"Yeah," he said. "Why bother to make contact on Sunday when everything Valden needs to know in order to make the payment is already right there on the video?"

"Except for an offshore account number."

Hans shrugged. "Why not just e-mail it to him?"

I told him what I knew about tracing IP addresses.

He fidgeted with the plastic cap he had twisted from the bottle, and stared past me out the window. "Still . . . that takes more than a couple of days. They could be long gone by that time."

"You're thinking it could all turn to shit if Sunday goes wrong."

"I'm sure they figure it's worth the risk."

I turned and gazed down at the cars on the street below. Mercedeses, Porsches and limousines doing the slow crawl along the avenue.

"They're trying to show Valden they can get to him any time, any place. Increases the odds he'll pay up."

"And how's that strategy working so far?"

"Like a charm," I said. "It's the last place in the world my brother wants to have anything go wrong. These are his people."

I could see Hans's mind at work, like the old days when we'd been partners, returning to a familiar rhythm.

"How big a security staff you think they have in this place?" Hans asked.

I pulled the valet parking stub from my shirt pocket, handed it to Hans. He looked it over and gave it back.

"Notice anything?" I said.

"Just a ParKing, Inc. logo."

I nodded.

"So it's a good bet if they farm out the parking, they contract the security for the lot right along with it."

"That leaves only the inside of the building," he said.

"Right. And with, what, a hundred rooms plus or minus—"

"All in a single tower . . ."

We both did some mental calculations.

"I'd bet there aren't any more than three guys per shift," Hans said.

"Maybe fewer," I finished. "You sure you're down for this?"

A dark luminescence filled his eyes, weighing the possible consequences one more time. Hans moved toward the door.

"You coming or what?" he said.

I popped the disk I'd just burned from my computer and handed it to Hans.

Hans badged the hotel manager with his knock-off and introduced me as his partner. Two lies to get this thing kicked off in the proper spirit.

I stepped into the manager's private office while Hans went to get the photo printed in the business center, and talk to the bartender.

The manager introduced himself as Fernan Desilets. We shook hands and I watched his eyes land on the crosshatched grip of the Stoeger protruding from the holster at my hip.

"How can I help you, Detective Travis?" He took a seat in a tufted blue leather chair that occupied the space behind a neat and orderly desk, and motioned me to a place across from him. His salt-and-pepper hair was neatly coiffed, nails well manicured, his suit finely tailored and expensive. He spoke with an accent that hinted at the Canadian plains.

"Just a couple of things, Mr. Desilets," I said. "I need a list of your employees and the work schedules for your front desk, IT, and security personnel for the entire month. Two weeks back, and two weeks forward."

Something flashed inside his eyes momentarily, then was gone.

"Is there some trouble I should know about?"

"You'll be the first to know," I told him. Another lie. "It's important that, for the time being, we keep any details under wraps. I just need what I asked for, please."

He studied my face for a long moment, then plucked the phone handset out of its cradle and spoke to his assistant. We sat in ungainly silence as we waited. I stood and crossed the room, studied a scale model of the hotel that was displayed inside an acrylic case in the corner near a window that looked out over the pool. Hanging on the wall behind the model was what I really wanted to see: a framed rendering of the first floor, beside it a matching blueprint of the same area, where the lobby, the Bengal Room, and the executive offices were all located. I made a special note of the location of the security office.

Before he had time to ask what I was doing, I turned my attention back to him.

"Is your head of security on duty today?"

He shook his head as he plucked a pen from the matching set on his desktop and made-believe he was studying some paperwork.

"I'm sorry," he said at last, not sounding it. "He's off on weekends."

The manager's assistant knocked gently on the office door before entering. She showed me a thin smile, handed Desilets a small sheaf of papers and left without a word.

He passed me the stack of paperwork and started to say something to me just as the phone on his desk began to ring. He picked up the receiver and made a gesture that I should stay. I pretended to take it as a wave of dismissal, nodded politely and walked out the door, making sure to pull it shut behind me. It was the quick exit I'd hoped for, one that allowed him no time for any further questions of me.

I thanked the manager's assistant on my way out, calling her by the name embossed on the nameplate at the corner of her desk.

"Would you please call security and tell them I'm on my way?" I asked.

She showed me an obsequious smile and I heard her make the call as I headed down the hall and through the door that led back into the lobby.

I took a seat in an overstuffed divan and used a couple of minutes to leaf through the security staff schedule until I found the one for the night of my brother's indiscretion. I shot a final glance toward Desilets's office, then folded the pages of the schedule lengthwise and slipped them into the breast pocket of the blazer I was wearing.

CHAPTER NINE

In any clandestine operation, compartmentalization is the key.

The best way to avoid being jammed up in an undercover operation is to make certain that you never tell anyone anything they don't have an absolute need to know. Keep your story loose and flexible if you can. If you're forced to evade the truth, keep the prevarications within limits that at least have an appearance of authenticity if they're investigated by the people you deceive. And, most importantly, always keep track of your lies.

I shot a quick look behind me to be sure Desilets hadn't come looking for me after departing his office the way that I had.

The door to the security office was locked when I tested the handle. I knocked twice with the flat of my hand and waited, using the time to shift the holster from my hip and clip it to a more obvious position on my belt. I bloused my blazer to give cursory cover to the bulge and knocked again, harder this time. A few seconds later the door was opened by a rangy, long-faced kid who barely looked old enough to buy a legal drink.

Like Hans, I still keep a duplicate of the gold shield I used to carry, back when I was in Homicide. I unbuttoned my coat, pulled the black leather case that housed the badge, and flipped it open just long enough to see his eyes skim past it and come to rest on the pistol clipped at my waistline. I was sure hotel security personnel didn't carry weapons, and the fact that I carried one conferred a certain authority I intended to fully exploit.

"Police," I said. "Step aside."

Take charge right away, preempt any questions—step one in selling the successful evasion.

I saw the kid's Adam's apple work up and down behind the loose-fitting collar of his shirt as he pulled at the knot on his striped necktie. A red sport coat draped from a hook affixed to the back of the door.

"What—"

"I'm here to ask you some questions regarding procedure," I interrupted. "I've already spoken with Mr. Desilets." Which were the only things I'd said to the kid that were true, so far. It was not something I was proud of, and I intended to be twenty-five hundred miles and half an ocean away by the time anybody thought to question my actions.

I watched his expression carefully, saw it register something that resembled acceptance.

"Have a seat," I said.

He did.

The room hummed with the sound and a smell that was peculiar to electronic equipment, and was suffused with a dim blue glow from the video monitors that had been mounted on the wall and arranged in two long rows above the main work-station. Two smaller desks sat unoccupied in the middle of the room, beyond them several shelving units containing rows of clear-plastic CD cases.

"How long have you worked here?" I asked.

"Since the grand opening."

"Get the marbles out of your mouth, son. How long would

that be in actual time? I lost my invitation to the grand opening."

My tone had exactly the effect I was looking for.

"Uh, maybe a little over a year."

His voice was dry, deeper than I had expected. Nervous fingers explored his tie and shirt buttons again.

"First off," I pointed at the CD boxes, "tell me about those things. What are they for?"

"Those are the daily video downloads."

"You don't save them to a hard drive?"

"No, sir."

I rebuttoned my blazer and leaned against the wall, appearing to ready myself for the long interview I had no intention of conducting.

"Give me your daily routine. From the beginning."

"Well, uh, we've got three shifts a day, two guys per shift."

I nodded. "Uh huh."

"One guy walks the building, the other stays in here and keeps an eye on the monitors and phones. We rotate every two hours."

"How many video cameras do you have?"

"Well, I can't say right offhand."

He looked at my expression and made another try.

"We've got one in each elevator, so that's three right there. We've got one that points down each hallway, so that's another two per floor; two more behind the reception desk; one in every emergency stairwell."

"What about the bar?"

He seemed surprised by the suggestion.

"The Bengal Room? What, are you kidding?"

"Not even behind the bar?"

"No, sir."

That was the answer I wanted to hear. Good news for Valden. And a lot of other people, including the congressman, no doubt.

"The lobby?" I asked.

"Yeah, sorry," he said. "We got two wide-angle cams in the lobby and one more outside at the valet stand."

"How about the parking lot?"

"No, the valet company handles that."

As I had thought.

The security office was windowless and close, not a shred of natural light. Less than a foot away, on the other side of the wall, strolled, sauntered and staggered some of the wealthiest and most celebrated people in the world; so close you could touch them, yet these guys watched them, like everybody else, on television screens.

"Where is your server?"

His face was blank. "Our what?"

"Internet server. Show it to me."

"We don't have a server."

I pinned him with my best cop stare. "This would be a very bad time to bullshit me. You follow?"

He nodded.

"If you lie to me, your future at the Mandalay Plaza ends now. You'll be lucky to work night security at Taco Bell."

"Yes, sir."

"Show me the Internet server."

"I told you." His Adam's apple bobbed behind the knot of his tie. "We don't have one."

"How do your guests get online then?"

"It's an outside commercial system."

"How do you send your e-mail?"

"We can't. We're not even allowed to bring cell phones in here. The only e-mail access we have is in the business center."

"Is there a server that runs the business center?"

"Same one the guests use. It's external."

"And the hotel's website? The reservations system?"

"Contracted out. It has nothing to do with the hotel."

"Who's your IT guy?"

"We don't have one."

"What's his name."

"We don't *have* one."

"You like tacos?"

"I'm not lying."

"Let's go back to the security video," I said. "You keep all the footage you shoot?"

He shook his head. "You already asked me that."

"Answer me again."

"It's all converted to digital disk at the end of each shift."

"Every day?"

"Yeah," he said. "Each camera's input is downloaded to a video disk, labeled, and stored right over there." He hooked a thumb toward the racks I'd seen when I first came in. "One disk per shift."

"Show me the machine you copy the disks with," I said.

He started to speak, then thought better of it. He crossed to the far corner of the room, to a stack of electronics arranged on a tall steel shelf unit, pointed to a nondescript device on top.

"How many of these do you have?"

"Just that one," he said. "What do—?"

"What do you do with the disks?"

"At the end of every month we take them out of the cases, stack them on a set of spindles that holds the whole month's activity."

"Then what?"

He shrugged and passed his eyes across the monitors.

"I don't know," he said. "That's beyond my pay grade. The disks don't take up much room, you know? They probably vault them for a while and toss them. Whatever the insurance company wants, right?"

The Mandalay's lawyers probably loved the system, too. I strolled over to the shelves and read the dates on the spines of each cover, making a show of exaggerated indifference. I slid out the one from Valden's big night with his new friend. Proved one thing: whoever had copied the disk had been smart enough to replace it afterward, keeping the hotel's security sequence intact. I did the same, though I removed the disk, and replaced the empty box with the date on the spine.

"I need to take a sample," I told him.

"Uh, I don't—"

"I'll be sure to have it back to you when we're through," I lied yet again.

I pulled the papers I'd folded into my breast pocket and flapped them around. They were the schedules Desilets had given me. I left them folded, so I knew that the kid couldn't see what they were, but the hotel's letterhead was visible enough to convince him I had something official in my possession.

"I've got permission from management right here."

A look of relief crossed his face and he leaned back in his chair.

I slipped the disk into my side pocket, felt the Stoeger's reassuring shape as I smoothed the pocket flap down. I had what I had come for. Now all I wanted was to get the hell out.

I asked a couple more innocuous questions and thanked him for his time. I made it sound official, told him not to mention our discussion to anyone, and that I'd be in touch if I came up with any more questions. As I reached for the door handle, I read the name on the brass plate pinned to the uniform jacket that hung on the door. I recalled seeing the name on the list. Springer, Steven.

I turned to face him one last time.

"Remember now, Steven," I said. I put my index finger to my lips. "Not a word. I may need to speak with some of your coworkers and I don't want them knowing what we discussed. You read me?"

"Yes, sir."

"That's good. You truly do not want me to have to come back."

Hans was in the Bengal Room when I came out of the security office. I could tell by his expression that he had made at least some headway with the bartender, and I was more than a little surprised that the guy would have told Hans anything at all, given the unwritten code of the B-Room. I caught Hans's eye, and angled my head toward the front door, giving him a subtle hurry-up gesture. He folded the printed photo into his pocket and met me in the lobby.

We found a private place to sit before either of us said a word.

"Did you get a name?" I asked.

"He doesn't know."

"But she's a pro?"

"More of a free-lancer, on the troll for a sugar daddy."

"She's come to the right place."

"There may be another small problem with Valden's girl-friend," Hans said, as his eyes scanned the room.

"What's the problem?"

He hesitated, taking longer than necessary to fish his sunglasses out of his pocket and wipe the lenses with a handkerchief.

"She's seventeen."

"This just keeps getting better," I said. "Like bobbing for apples in an outhouse."

"Might explain your brother's heightened sense of, ah, urgency on this thing."

"And nobody's got her name?"

"Bartender swears he has no idea. Said he'd seen her in there a handful of times. He says he boots her out when she comes in while he's on shift, but can't vouch for what anyone else does. For what it's worth, he says she doesn't look seventeen."

"Then how does he know she's seventeen?"

"One of the other customers said his daughter knew her once. From school. She had come by their house a time or two."

"And the customer? What's his name? Where do we find him?"

"He didn't remember. Said he wasn't a regular. Just happened to be there when the girl was in the room."

"So nobody knows who the hell she is?"

"Are you asking me whether I know how to conduct a proper interview?"

I let it slide.

"You talk to the concierge yet?" I asked.

"You think he's pimping for her?"

I shrugged.

Hans took my ticket to the valet stand while I stepped over to the concierge desk. The concierge eyed me as he finished a phone call. His expression was cautious, and sent alarm bells ringing in my head that I didn't like at all.

I placed a bill on the counter between us and slipped the photo from my breast pocket. He hung up the phone and showed me an insouciant smile, looked me in the eye, but didn't acknowledge the currency.

"Have you seen this girl?" I asked.

His eyes brushed across the photo and came back to mine. "No."

"I don't think I believe you."

"I'm sorry you feel that way, detective."

"Why did you call me that?"

"You came in with the Asian guy, and he's got cop written all over him. Not you so much, but I can tell you are carrying a weapon."

"This girl is seventeen years old," I said.

"She's lovely. I wouldn't have guessed."

I have a recurring nightmare. I am in a small plane, and it is going down over a remote stretch of mountains. There is one parachute and I help strap it onto the back of the only other passenger. He balks when he reaches the open doorway, too terrified to jump, but I push him out through the opening. In the aftermath of the crash I am left alive, but the body of the passenger I had attempted to save is never found. All the shrinks in the world who work with firefighters or cops will tell you they've heard that one a lot.

"Seventeen years old," I repeated. "There will be eyes on you."

"I don't know whatever for, but I do appreciate the warning."

Hans was standing beside the passenger door of my rental car when I stepped outside. I tipped the valet, slammed the door and headed for the exit.

I missed the light at the intersection and stared out through the windshield at the landmark Hollywood sign pressed into the relief of purple hills in the near distance.

"If she wasn't in the wind before, she is now," I said.

"It's possible your brother didn't know, Mike."

There are times when words hold no value. This was one of those times.

We made our way back across town, back toward Vonda Franklin's house. I wanted her to tell us whether the ID numbers on the disk I'd just lifted from the Mandalay Plaza matched the one that had been used to threaten my brother. I punched her number into my phone as I drove. After letting it ring seven or eight times with no answer, I tried her office. The forensic lab was always open.

She was there, and she was busy, as usual. But Vonda said she'd clear the deck for me. She told me it wouldn't take long. I took the next right and headed for her office instead.

I caught Hans watching the rearview, but didn't say a thing.

I parked the car a block or so from the lab and told Hans I'd be right back. He shot me a look that left little room for argument and followed me down the sidewalk and in through the glass doors.

Vonda was waiting at the front, preventing the need to flash ID. I wondered if she knew about Hans's present situation as we followed her past the reception area, and back to her cubicle. She made a move to pull chairs over for us, but I waved her off.

"We don't want to be here that long," I told her.

"I hear you," she said. "You got the disks?"

Hans gave her the one I'd gotten from Valden, and I handed her the hotel copy. She took the first one and loaded it. As Vonda punched the keypad, the screen in front of her began to scroll through an array of numbers and characters that were completely unintelligible to me. She'd study the screen for a moment, then her fingers would dance across the keys again. Less than two minutes later she found what she'd been looking for: the twenty-one digit alphanumeric characters that put a positive ID on the video burner. The one that had recorded them both.

"So, what're the chances they're running this scam out of the hotel?" Hans asked.

"Using the hotel server as a host for the blackmail site?" Vonda said.

"Not very likely," I said.

"Because?"

"Because they don't have one," I said. "And it would be an act of weapons-grade stupidity even if they did."

We were drawing away from the curb when Hans dug into his pocket for his phone.

"Gimme the personnel list," he said as he held out his hand.

"You've done enough already, Hans. I got this."

He didn't speak.

I pulled into traffic and pointed the car toward Figueroa, cut him a sidelong glance.

"You're flying a little close to the flame as it is," I said.

His jaw was set, but his eyes were coming back to life. "In for a penny, in for a pound."

I smiled slowly, reached into my pocket and handed him the list.

I drove in silence as Hans studied the paper, flipping back and forth between pages, making notes on a small notepad.

"So?" I said.

"Seven people are scheduled to be off on both Sunday and Monday. I'm calling Roger Gaines."

I drummed the wheel with my fingers as the signal changed. I shot a glance down Exposition Boulevard, a line of demarcation that a few years earlier might as well have been the DMZ.

CHAPTER TEN

Memories are a sinkhole.

At least mine are. I can't drive five blocks in this goddamned city without it dredging something out of the sewage of my subconscious. In this part of town, for me it would always be the last day of April 1992.

The sun was the color of blood, unfocused and grainy behind the smoke thrown into the late afternoon sky by ravenous tongues of flame. Black funnel clouds ascended from dozens of fires burning out of control in every direction. It was finally happening. The city was immolating itself in one furious eruption of outrage.

My uniform was tight around the collar, and the streams of sweat that ran down my back beneath the Kevlar vest felt like a trail of ants on my skin. I hated the damn thing. It restricted my movements and made me vaguely claustrophobic. There were five of us crammed into the patrol unit, shoulder to shoulder wearing uniforms we hadn't worn in years, mothballs mixing with cop-car smells of body odor, tobacco smoke and vomit.

By the time I reached my post that night, my lungs and eyes had been burned raw by the effects of tear gas and fire, my hair already soaked beneath my helmet, my gas mask fouled by the smell of my own heavy breathing. Corrugated silhouettes danced behind the flicker of flames, backlit by the rippled reflections mirrored in the store windows that hadn't yet been smashed by rocks and bottles or shattered chunks of cinder block. Looters darted from every corner with whatever they could carry away from the wreckage, returning again and again until stock shelves and floor displays were laid bare.

A lone Korean man stood in the doorway of his tiny bodega, a sawed-off length of two-by-four clutched tightly in his trembling hands. Four teenage boys were slowly closing in on him, threatening, slapping lengths of metal pipe and hunks of concrete brick against their sweaty palms. Three of us went after the boys, our nightsticks drawn, but they scattered and disappeared into the roiling haze, the sounds of feral laughter and a city suffering the wounds of its own cruelty at our backs.

I pulled to a stop in front of a mom-and-pop liquor store off Normandie, not far from the intersection at which a lone thirty-six-year-old truck driver named Reginald Denny had been forcibly dragged from the driver's seat of his vehicle and beaten nearly to death as bystanders chanted, laughed and danced on the sidewalk only a few feet away.

The store sat alone between two vacant lots that had remained undeveloped in all the time since the riots. I could still smell the lingering anger in the streets, hovering like the smoke from a grease fire.

Hans had called in the names of the seven hotel employees we wanted background information on. Roger Gaines had agreed to lean deep into the strike zone in order to sneak the request through the system. There was nothing left to do, at the moment, but wait.

With another hour and a half before I was due to call Rex Blackwood, I had a personal matter that needed doing.

We got out of the car and walked toward the metal security gate that served as the store's front door. The cloud cover had finally burned away, and the sky overhead was a cloudless gray-blue. Two black men leaned against a cinder block wall tagged with graffiti and posted with handbills that had long since faded and peeled away at the edges. They gave us the mad-dog glare that contained a unique blend of animus and ambivalence that was reserved especially for cops. I held the gaze of the one closest to me until he broke it off, and muttered something that sounded a lot like motherfucker.

Inside, behind the counter, was a Korean man whose face had been carved into my memory, but to whom I would always remain unknown. He had only one arm now, the other having been lost to that pointless rampage back in the spring of '92. He had rebuilt his store in the same spot he had made his futile stand, losing his wife, his son, his limb and his business in the process. I wasn't sure if that made him a paladin or a fool. Regardless, in my eyes it made him one brave and brazen son of a bitch, and I admired him for it.

I paid for a fifth of Cutty Sark and a carton of Marlboros at the counter and Hans and I headed back out to the car. The wall leaners were gone, but the stink of their menace hung in the doorway like a fuel-soaked rag.

We drove the streets in silence until we reached the main gate of the cemetery. We passed beneath a stand of tall cypresses and onto the narrow lane that threaded its way through the head-stones and benches and monuments. I pulled over and parked in a turnout that overlooked a pond so green with algae that it didn't reflect the sun.

Hans got out and took a seat on a city bench not far from where I parked the car. I walked alone up a gradual incline to a headstone I'd visited only one other time since I had left the mainland. It was well-tended and a rusted coffee can that served as a vase still held a clutch of flowers that looked no more than a few days old.

I recalled my training officer's funeral, a cold, gray morning swollen with the threat of rain. I had been assigned to mid-P.M. watch all week, home just before dawn broke, most days. But I was not going to miss Reginald Carter's final honors. As far as I am concerned, missing the funeral of a friend is a supreme act of selfishness. It has become popular to espouse the opinion that attending a funeral never brought the deceased back to life, or the equally cynical view that the decedent won't know you were not there, but I hold those views to be self-serving in the extreme. One attends a memorial for the same reasons one goes to a dreaded company party, or participates in the pancake breakfast sponsored by your child's sports team. You attend as a show of support for human endeavors, to stand and be recognized as a dues-paying member of a club whose membership you don't fully appreciate until they retire your number and show you the door.

"I brought you something, you bastard," I said as I looked down at the bronze marker half-buried in the sod.

I squinted out toward the downtown skyline as I cracked open the Cutty Sark, took a swig from the neck of the bottle, and poured some out on the grass below the stone. I was grateful that his grave was being tended, even if only by a stranger. He'd left no family I knew of when he'd taken his service revolver and painted his name all over the wall behind his favorite chair.

"You were right," I told him. "The shit never ends."

The piquant scent of whiskey rose up from the lawn and mingled with the breeze that riffled the leaves inside the magnolia tree whose branches stretched out over my head.

Dark patches of shade crawled toward the stone in the shifting light and smelled of wet clay and cut grass.

I tried to remember his face, but it wouldn't come. It's how it goes when people die. They disappear over time, one feature at a time, until there's nothing left but a shadow. All that remained were the things he'd said, the things he taught me as a rookie.

I felt my throat close down around my words, so I drank a silent toast, stood and poured the rest of the Cutty out for him. The empty green bottle felt strangely heavy in my hand as I crossed to where Hans stood waiting for me, leaning against the hood of the car and staring up into the trees.

I tossed the bottle into the trash bin where I'd parked and walked back to the car.

"How's he doing?" Hans asked.

"The same." My voice came out hoarse.

Hans allowed himself a brief smile. He'd known my field training officer, too.

"You can always count on Carter," he said.

On the way out, I pulled to a stop in the gravel lot beside the maintenance shed, parked behind a John Deere tractor and left the car running. I grabbed the carton of cigarettes off the backseat, opened the end and folded three $100 bills inside, resealing the box as I walked.

"Carl?" I called out. "You in here?"

There was no answer when I shouted his name again. So I wrote a quick note, put it with the Marlboros and left them on the metal chair that was tucked underneath a workbench strewn with garden tools and catalogs.

We drove by the Lennox estate on our way back to the hotel. Anybody who read a newspaper, a magazine, or watched the news, knew the name Phillip Lennox. And anybody in Southern

California could tell you where he lived with a reasonable degree of accuracy.

Lennox had made his first fortune in the pharmaceutical business. Now in his early seventies, he spent most of his semiretirement appearing on television and investing in real estate. He acted as the self-appointed spokesman for the free-enterprise system, and was always good for a sound bite when politics or profit margins didn't cooperate with his notions of right and wrong. My brother had latched on to Lennox when he'd been invited to speak at one of Valden's Young Presidents' Organization chapter meetings and now sat beside him on the board of one of Lennox's spin-off companies.

The estate occupied six acres in Holmby Hills, an enclave of super-affluent society that occupied both sides of Sunset Boulevard, between Beverly Hills and Bel-Air. Like most homes in the area, the Lennox estate was sheltered from the prying eyes of the curious by imposing stone walls and electronic surveillance. An intercom box had been welded to steel poles and set in concrete, and stood sentry at each of the two gated entrances: one for the residents and invited guests, the other for the help. Both drives opened onto the same tree-shaded street and were separated from each other by a one-hundred-foot strip of finely manicured lawn. I pulled to a stop at the curb between the two gates and parked.

"They say he's got a seven-thousand-square-foot garage just for his car collection," Hans said.

It was rumored that Lennox owned Dashiell Hammett's Duesenberg, and had it garaged here. I intended to have a look at it, one way or another, the next day.

A grove of old-growth trees was plainly visible beyond the high walls, the steep angle of the slate rooftop of the main house barely visible in the gaps between the limbs. In my rearview was a clear shot of the driveway that led to the main entry. Before us was the service entrance, clearly marked by a sign crafted from copper that had streaked green by years of rainfall and coastal moisture. A dozen people or more busied themselves off-loading tables, chairs, barware, liquor, tent poles, and awnings from a pair of large panel trucks.

"Remind you of your childhood?" Hans said, the hint of a smile at the corner of his mouth that did not make it all the way to his eyes.

"You know what people like Lennox fear the most?"

"They don't fear anything, Travis."

"They fear that they won't be needed. They're confused when others don't want what they're selling, and don't envy what they've got; they don't trust the self-sufficient and they secretly hate them for it."

I was having a difficult time comprehending the lives of people who lived like Lennox, people whose biggest problems were the punctuality of their service personnel and the noise the gardener made with his Weed Eater. From the corner of my eye I could see that some part of Hans was still deep inside his own thoughts, and I was reminded that loyalty had been the battle standard under which I had placed myself—Hans, Rex and possibly others—at risk for the sake of sparing my brother from the wreckage that would be the natural result of his own actions.

In the end, it is the innocents who bear the greatest loss, and I had agreed to come here and do what I could to lean on the scales for their sake. I wanted to believe that there would always be someone watching the perimeter in defense of the people I cared about. I did not wish to contemplate a life lighting tapers for my failures.

"You're going to want to be parked about here," I said.

Hans ignored me. He was staring into the side-view mirror and watching a young woman wheeling a stroller pause at the corner to warm herself in a patch of sunlight that shone down between the trees.

"I've done this before, Mike," he said. "You're aware that you're a control freak, right?"

I threw the car in gear, pulled from the curb and made a U-turn back toward Sunset.

"I'm not a control freak, I am a planning enthusiast."

CHAPTER ELEVEN

Hans grabbed a bottle of Stella Artois from my minibar and stepped over to the window that looked out over the Hollywood Hills. I checked my watch and saw that I had another thirty-five minutes before I needed to place my next call to Rex Blackwood.

"What did it feel like when you did it, Mike?"

He had spoken so softly that it took me a moment to realize he had addressed his question to me.

"What are we talking about?"

"I've never given much thought to what I would do when I left the job and retired."

He hadn't turned away from the window. The low angle of the autumn sun cast the contours of his face in thin yellow light.

"My father was career air force. Did I ever tell you that? He was a tough sonofabitch, but he was a good father. He didn't hand out beatings or discipline without good reason. We moved a lot; every couple years, whenever he was reassigned. He taught me how to fight when I was eight or nine. We were stationed in Germany at the time. I'd gotten my ass whipped by a couple of older kids at the American school, came home with a busted tooth, a black eye, and a purple bruise on my eyebrow that swelled to the size of an egg. He died two days before my twenty-first birthday."

"Don't allow other men to make your choices for you, Hans."

"I've lived in seven countries. This one's the best. Even when it's fucked up, it's still the best there is."

He took a pull from the bottle and ran his fingers through his hair.

My cell phone rang and I slipped it from my pocket. It was Valden.

"Where are you?" he asked me when I flipped it open.

"At the hotel. In my room."

"You've got to get up here. Now."

We took the fire stairs rather than wait for the elevator.

My brother had taken a suite on the top floor of the Mandalay Plaza, four flights up from mine. But his opened onto an expansive view that, on a clear day like this one had become, allowed you to see all the way to the coast, to the Malibu castles that were occupied by Hollywood actors and professional athletes. After sunset, the neon colors of the Ferris wheel twinkled at the foot of the pier, and the contrails of private jets inbound to Santa Monica would streak the sky with shades of orange and pink.

Valden pulled open the door and gestured toward a laptop that sat open on the coffee table, without uttering a word. His shirtsleeves were rolled up to his elbows and the fabric deeply creased with wrinkles. His expression looked as though it had folded in on itself, and he gave off an energy that reminded me of a guitar string that had been wound to the point of snapping.

"What's he doing here?" Valden asked, jabbing a finger in Hans's direction while avoiding contact with his eyes.

"You might want to show him some respect," I said. "He's here of his own accord."

"You said you would keep this quiet."

Hans registered no emotion as he moved across the room and took a seat on one of the stools that fronted Valden's bar.

"When you've got zero time on the clock, Valden," I said, "you need all the help you can trust. You'd rather I start busting down doors and kicking over tables by myself? You get one shot with a strategy like that and you'd better be 100 percent right. If you're not, you just telegraphed your only punch."

Valden shot a glance in Hans's direction and turned back to me. He stuffed his hands into the pockets of his slacks and resumed pacing.

"I just received an e-mail," Valden said, his back to me. "It's got a video attachment."

"How bad is it?"

"Bad."

I sat on the sofa and cued up the video. It lasted about ninety seconds, but that was more than enough to make its point. It had been taped from inside Valden's room.

"You've swept the room since this video was taken?" I asked.

"Of course. I had it done while you were on the plane on the way over."

"You might want to start sweeping your hotel rooms *before* you sleep in them," Hans said from his seat at the bar.

"Thank you, Detective Yamaguchi," Valden replied.

"They found the transmitters?" I asked.

"Three of them."

"Show them to me."

"My security people took them when they left. I didn't think you'd need them."

The room was silent, but for the whisper of the air-conditioning as it cycled on. My brother's eyes looked as though they were vibrating inside of his skull. I took my notepad from the breast pocket of my jacket and wrote down the e-mail address from which the video had been sent to Valden. There had been no further message other than the attachment.

"The girl was underage," I said. "She may or may not have been a pro, but she was seventeen years old. You lied to me."

"I didn't know."

I pulled a handkerchief from my back pocket and tossed it to Valden. "You've got a little bullshit there at the corner of your mouth."

It was coming up on three o'clock and we still hadn't heard back from Hans's partner regarding any background we could gather on the seven hotel employees not scheduled to work on Sunday.

"Not to look a gift horse in the mouth," I said, "but where the hell is Gaines?"

Hans shook his head and leaned heavily against the wall as we waited in the elevator lobby.

"I gave him your cell number."

"I've got to make a landline call," I said. "Let's see how the Bengal Room operates on a Saturday afternoon."

"Why not," he said. "I've tried sitting on my ass and that hasn't worked."

As we waited for the elevator, I felt the weight of a million small choices; the ones we'd each made that put us where we were. One or two small changes and Hans would still be at his desk in Homicide, I'd be on my yacht in Kona bay, and Valden would still be playing politics-for-hire and concealing his assignations from his wife.

A bell rang softly and we stepped into the empty car. When

the doors sighed closed, the space grew crowded with troubles that had no solutions and the sound of time ticking away.

The Bengal Room hummed with an energy that was both manic and somehow perceptively desperate. Women with expensive shoes and high-maintenance hairdos sat in knots of two and three, while the men wore too much jewelry and spoke of business matters in voices that were far too loud. A lone blonde at the far end of the bar pretended to ignore the rest of the room, toying with the ice that floated in her cocktail glass, while some kind of formless European lounge music filled the empty spaces.

Hans and I took two low-back stools at the corner of the bar opposite the apathetic blonde, and well away from everyone else. The bartender, a different one than Hans had interviewed earlier, straightened his black bow tie and sidled over to us, flashing a courteous, insincere smile. We each ordered a Kirin and I asked to use the phone that was tucked against the back shelf beside the cash register.

Moments later, he returned with two frosted pilsner glasses and our two bottles of beer, and placed the phone in front of me.

"Dial nine for an outside line," he said, and stepped discreetly away.

I punched in the number Rex had given me earlier, and watched the waitress work the room. She was a tall, elegant Asian girl dressed in a tight black dress with a mandarin neckline. Her face was bathed in reflected yellow lamplight and jet black hair which had been pulled into a tight knot at the back of her head. Watching her glide between the lamp-lit tables made it easy to imagine a scene much like this one, in Shanghai or Mandalay, perhaps, at the turn of an earlier century.

As he had before, Rex picked up on the third ring.

"Who's calling?" he said.

"It's me," I answered. "What've you got?"

"Making progress. But he needs more time."

"I've got an e-mail address for you," I said, and spelled it for him to make sure he got it right.

He repeated it back.

"How much longer do you need?"

"I don't know. They're bouncing servers through China, Russia and the Maldives. Now that he's identified the route, the e-mail should help."

"I don't mean to sound ungrateful here—"

"He's working on his own," Rex said. "Without access to all the toys. I'll call you when I've got something."

"I don't know if I can tell you where I'll be."

"I'll call your cell. The next time you hear from me, it'll be with a name and address. Short and sweet. What happens after that is up to you."

It sounded like he had something else to say, but had edited himself. I wondered again how much of Rex Blackwood's official file had been permanently redacted.

"Something else?" I asked.

"I'm going to tell you two things you already know."

"Go."

"You've been skeet shooting before?"

"Sure."

"Then you know that you don't shoot where they are, you shoot where they're going to be."

"And what's the second thing?"

"Don't let the bad guys get behind you."

Hans waited silently while I passed the phone back to the bartender. He raised his glass and drank, but I could see my former partner took little pleasure from it. I took a long pull from mine and sat my glass on the bar top. Hans was about to speak when my cell phone vibrated in my pocket.

I flipped it open, still expecting Roger Gaines. It wasn't. It was my brother.

"I've thought about it," Valden said without preamble.

"I've already lost the thread of this conversation, Valden."

Long seconds contained only the sound of his breathing, the rattle of ice against crystal.

"I'm not doing it," he said finally. "They can go to hell."

"You are in a dangerous state of mind."

"I could say the video's a fake. That it's been doctored."

"Get some sleep, Valden," I said. "Scotch makes a poor partner in a strategy session."

"I can get out front of this thing, make a preemptive statement to the press."

"If you try that, they'll be sponging pieces of you off the walls."

"Mike, just listen . . ."

"Don't even think about it," I said again. "The girl is underage. At a minimum, that's statutory rape."

"She was a hooker, for God's sake."

"I'm not having this conversation."

There was heavy silence on my phone and a trill of phony laughter from a table in the back of the Bengal Room.

"Good-bye, Valden."

I snapped the phone shut and watched a man in a well-tailored suit crash and burn in his attempt to charm a pair of young women who were seated in the shadow of a potted palm along the wall. His skin was so salon tanned he was nearly purple. Hans tossed down the rest of his beer and pushed the bottle to the edge of the table. The Bengal Room was beginning to fill with the afternoon crowd, so I signaled the bartender for our tab.

On the way out the door, my phone rang again. This time it was Gaines, but I was tired of talking. I handed the phone to Hans.

I drove Hans back to his house.

I pulled up and parked behind a gray sedan that was parked across the street. A pack of school-aged kids on bicycles pumped down the sidewalk, dodging in and out of the pinkish pools cast by the sodium lights. Hans pushed open the car door, and hesitated as he got out. He turned after a moment and invited me in for dinner.

I watched the kids until they turned the corner, and followed Hans across the street and into his house.

It was a little past nine thirty in LA by the time we finished, which put it around seven thirty in Kona. I dialed Lani's number and waited through a recorded greeting. I hated leaving personal messages on her answering machine, so I kept it short.

I joined Hans outside on a lawn chair while Mie did the dinner dishes, wanting to leave us to ourselves for a while longer. I shoved my hands deep into the pockets of my jacket as Hans lit a cigar and stared up into the stars. Warm light glowed inside yellow windows, and the muted sounds of running water and the ring of silverware being placed into the machine was domestic and uncomplicated and made me feel even farther from home.

"What time tomorrow?" Hans asked.

"Noon. But you should be set up no later than ten or so, take your position before the guests start to arrive."

The night sounds of crickets and a distant barking dog mingled with a faint murmur from a neighbor's TV. We both leaned back into our chairs, neither of us speaking for what seemed like a very long time.

"I'll be there," he said.

An errant gust carried with it the scent of chimney smoke and fallen leaves and tore at the plume rising from Hans's cigar. My mind drifted back to Kona, to Lani, and I felt a momentary stab of something that might have been envy at the life Hans had built for himself.

"Hang on to this for me, will you?" I said, and slipped the Stoeger he had lent me out of the holster at my hip. "Keep it in the car with you."

I stood and said good night to Hans, who followed me into the kitchen. Mie dried her hands on a dish towel and offered her cheek for a kiss. She smiled, and in spite of my former partner's disquiet, I thought I saw gratitude there.

They walked me to the door and saw me out, stood together on the front porch as I got into my car. Hans laid a protective arm across Mie's shoulders, and she tossed me a little wave. A translucent cloud of autumn fog glowed inside the halo of the streetlight as I pulled away, to the empty hotel suite that waited for me.

PART THREE

The Delicate Sound of Thunder

CHAPTER TWELVE

At first, May Ling had tried to resist, but the punishment was always swift and severe.

Her lips had been split, teeth tinted pink by a fresh flow of blood, her torso and buttocks beaten unmercifully with socks or pillowcases stuffed with oranges or bars of soap, which left her aching and broken, but largely unmarked.

May Ling was confined to a locked room not much larger than the closet she used to have in the apartment she once shared with her brother, Tai Man Duk. A rusted metal bucket had been placed in the corner in which to take care of her personal needs, and three ragged blankets sat in a pile atop a gray tick mattress, which she used for a bed. There were no windows, so she was only able to keep track of the passage of days by using the light that showed through the crack at the bottom of the door, and did her best to sleep only when the daylight faded to dark. She scratched a tiny mark on the wall with her thumbnail each morning when she awoke. There were hundreds of them now.

After that first time, Joey Soong had kept the big man away from her. But the memory of her brother bleeding out as she herself was being so mercilessly violated returned to her often during the long nights, carved into her mind like an untended wound that had grown mephitic. Those first nights it was all she could do to fall asleep without feeling those callused hands on her again, the burning inside of her, and the sight of Duk lying helplessly while his life drained into the cracks along the floor. Her brother had died with his eyes open, and something in that knowledge made it that much worse for May Ling.

She recalled the time, back when she had made only sixty-seven marks on the wall, having already lost track of all the faces whose foul breath filled her nostrils and had left their stink on her: The day that Joey Soong released her from the closet that was her cage and gave her over to the care of two other girls who took her out and bathed her. They dressed her in fresh clothing and brushed the filth and grease from her hair.

May Ling had stayed with them for two full weeks while they tended her, fed her, and waited for the blue-black bruises to lose their color and finally fade away. The girls talked very little, but they were gentle with her, something that filled May Ling with foreboding. She had seen the dead eyes of opium addicts, but these girls were different—so beautiful, yet somehow all the more diminished and vacant because of it.

She was given a real bed on which to sleep, but sleep rarely came in anything more than short fits interrupted by the nightmare recollection of where she knew herself to be. She grew stronger over those days, left untouched by men, even Joey Soong. She was young, but not so naive anymore to believe that this would last. In that she had also been correct.

At the end of the second week, at the hour just past midday, she was informed of Soong's arrival, overheard him talking to one of the other girls. May Ling could not clearly make out their words, but the tone told her all she needed to know.

Moments later Joey Soong entered the room and stood before her. His appraisal was so cold that she had to avert her eyes when he ordered her to remove her robes. She knew better now than to consider anything but compliance, loosened the knot at her waist, and let the red silk gown drop to the floor. Tiny lines formed at the corners of his mouth as he took stock of her naked body, the smoothness of her skin, the shape and firmness of her small breasts. He reached out a hand and caressed her as he would a ceramic sculpture. May Ling's eyes remained fixed to the floor, and she felt the rush of heat in her cheeks, consumed by shame.

He turned abruptly, snapped his fingers and headed into a private room. May Ling knew she was expected to follow him, and left the robe where it lay on the floor.

When he was finished, he ordered her to shower, to dress and wait for his call. As she had earlier learned so well, she did as she was told, and by the time the sun disappeared behind the tall buildings of Kowloon, she had been delivered inside the gates of a high-walled villa near the foothills and given over to the Dragon Head himself; a gift from Joey Soong for as long as she was able to maintain the old man's interest.

It had not proven to be long.

Now, as she found herself once again seated on the hard floor of the closet from which she had been so temporarily freed, she could not avoid her recollection of the revulsion she had felt at the sight of the old man's pale and sagging skin. His hideous, hairless little staff, and the things he made her do. Once he had grown bored with her, he sent her back to Soong, who in turn sent her back to the dank and fetid rooms in which she was again forced to lie with the dockworkers, dealers and common White Orchid soldiers. Joey however, was preparing to accept his promotion as the new head of the Tong's activities along the western territories of the United States. The Golden Mountain. Los Angeles, San Diego, San Francisco, and Honolulu.

The faint light of another morning stole through the crack beneath May Ling's door, and she awoke again only to be enveloped by the salt musk odor of copulation that constantly surrounded her. She scratched another mark into the wall, counted them all once more, from the beginning, and she began to weep.

CHAPTER THIRTEEN

I floated slowly upward, out of the cavern of my sleep.

I threw back the soft hotel sheets, rolled out of bed and pulled on a pair of boxer shorts and a white T-shirt, and padded into the living room to boil a pot of water for tea. I stood before the window and gazed out to the west, toward the sea and the pastel ribbons of cloud floating on a sky that was blooming into sunrise. The streetlights of LA winked inside the clear atmosphere of predawn and stretched all the way to the limits of my vision.

I steeped a bag of Mango Ceylon in a steaming mug, took it over to the couch and switched the television to a cable news network. Unnatural light flickered from the screen and against the walls of the room as I sat there in the dark, watching the world wake up to a newly sanctified second term for George W. Bush, the pending confirmation of Condoleezza Rice to succeed Colin Powell, a war that continued to rage in Iraq, and the price of oil jumping to forty-eight dollars a barrel.

I muted the sound and watched the crawl as I felt myself come more fully awake. A commercial for Mel Gibson's *Passion of the Christ* gave over to an advertisement for a film called *Mean Girls,* and I knew I had already seen enough. I clicked off the

TV, tossed the remote onto the cushions and wandered back to the window.

The sunrise had erupted in full now, and the soft pastels of minutes before had burst into eye-searing shades of crimson and gold, and a purple so deep that it appeared to bruise the sky. My mind went to the old sailor's admonition about a red sky at morning. This was not a day whose responsibilities afforded me any semblance of pride or satisfaction, or to which I looked forward to executing. In fact, I would have been utterly indifferent to the events my brother had set in motion were it not for the irreparable harm that would come to his family, and indirectly, to me and Lani.

At bottom, it was nothing more than a blood obligation, but blackmail is a coward's crime that tracks filth across the lives of the blameless. And I should probably have tried harder to do something for the seventeen-year-old girl whom my brother had bedded, except for what experience had repeatedly taught me: that she was engaged in exactly what she wanted to be doing, and nothing was going to prevent her from continuing to do so for the year that it took for her to reach the age of majority. With some degree of accuracy I knew who she was, perhaps not by name, but I knew who she was. Collateral damage.

It was only a matter of hours before I could either rectify the chaos that Valden had caused, or fail in the effort. I drank cold tea dregs from the mug in my hand and cast one final glance at the rising sun. Red sky at morning, indeed.

I turned away, tired of rehashing the same mental terrain, probing it like a tongue in an empty tooth socket. It was done. Decided, and set in motion.

It was just past eleven o'clock as I idled in the car, adjusting the air-conditioning and waiting my turn at the valet stand. The driveway leading up to the Phillip Lennox estate was already crowded with cars occupied by well-dressed couples clutching party invitations that ran $2,000 a pop. The official start time was still nearly an hour away, and cars lined the street behind me for a full quarter mile, turn signals blinking and brake lights flashing.

On my way in, I'd spotted Hans parked along the street, already in position and not a moment too early. Catering vehicles lined the curb in front and behind him. There wasn't an empty space to be had for blocks.

In my rearview, a woman in the passenger seat of a burgundy Porsche busied herself with a fresh coat of lipstick while the driver gestured broadly as he spoke on his cell phone. In front of me, a gray-haired couple in a canary yellow Cadillac stared vacantly through their windshield. They hadn't spoken to one another once in all the time I'd been waiting behind them. Now and then I caught the old man's bushy eyebrows as he glared at me in his rearview, no doubt disapproving of the no-frills Pontiac rental that had no proper place at this event.

The day was bright and uncharacteristically clear. The blue sky was now dotted with puffed-up clouds and the sun hadn't yet beat the last of the autumnal chill from the air. Even so, I bumped the AC up a notch and twisted the vents toward my face, uncomfortable in the suit and tie I was wearing.

The lawn between the driveway and the house had been trimmed to the precision of a putting green, bordered by a long, meticulously manicured row of Italian cypresses. As the procession of cars inched closer to the main house, I watched a team of red-coated valets open doors, deferentially hand out claim tickets, then squeal off behind the wheels of rides that—most of which— probably cost more than all of theirs combined. It reminded me of the auto thief that worked Melrose for an entire night back in

1999 dressed as a valet, his victims literally, simply handing him their keys without a thought. Trust can be a remarkable beast.

I pulled up under the porte cochere and stopped, opened my own door, and got out. I handed a neatly folded hundred-dollar bill to the head valet and told him to leave my car parked up front. He eyed the make and model of my rental, and after only a brief hesitation to glance at the denomination of the bill, agreed. I tucked the claim check into my pocket and walked in through the double doors.

The mansion was an antebellum knockoff with a vaulted gallery entry, complete with a *Gone with the Wind* staircase and the obligatory cut-crystal chandelier. A flower arrangement that was the approximate size of a Volkswagen Beetle occupied a pedestal table just inside the door, and permeated the space with the sweet-heavy scent of roses and lavender.

Three young women sat behind a registration table at one side of the foyer checking invitations against an alphabetized guest list. I stood in the S through Z line and waited my turn. I told them who I was and they handed me a pin-on name tag, and directed me outside toward the back lawn.

My footsteps echoed along the marble parquet floor as I followed the yellow Cadillac couple through the gallery and toward a pair of french doors that opened onto a garden that could have been Versailles's. Rectangular ponds constructed of stacked stone marked the periphery of a smooth gravel path that opened onto a collection of canopied tables situated around a vast lawn. Tiered fountains flowed gently, and dripped a melodious rhythmic counterpoint to the swing band that was just lighting in to Ellington's "Take the 'A' Train."

I reached into my breast pocket and withdrew my sunglasses, unconsciously patting the empty place where the Stoeger should be, but wasn't. There wasn't a chance in hell I was going to risk carrying a weapon around this place, especially not with a United States congressman on the premises. Political times having become what they were, I wouldn't have even risked carrying a walkie-talkie.

A waiter in a white coat approached and offered me a flute of chilled champagne off a gleaming silver tray. I took it with thanks and began to wander the grounds, returning the curt nods and tight-lipped smiles of the people whose eyes met mine. I wanted to get a sense of the place, and more importantly, get a feel for possible escape routes the blackmailers might use after making contact with Valden. I had arrived there early enough to preempt the arrival of the main body of guests, so I used the time to wander a bit more freely than I was supposed to.

The band segued into "String of Pearls" as I strolled toward a building at the far edge of the lawn. I stopped momentarily and sipped the champagne. It was cool on my palate, dry and not too sweet, something French, pink and expensive. I took a swift glance around me before I stepped over the low swag of painted chain that was intended to designate the area as off-limits to guests, and headed for the open door of the auto garage.

The inside was cooled by the gentle swirl of ceiling fans, and lit by overhead fluorescents dim enough that I had to take off my shades. The exterior had the appearance of a horse stable, though the inside was occupied by some of the finest automobiles I'd ever seen. I was drawn first to a 1927 Mercedes touring car. Long, slender and sexy, the design had been used as the basis for the Excalibur that would make its debut many decades later. Beside it, incongruously, a Shelby Cobra, deep metallic blue with the unmistakable twin white stripes running the length of its body; and a 1946 Ford Woody station wagon—forest green with flawlessly maintained woodwork, a third bench seat in the back—that looked as though it had just been driven off the showroom floor. There was a white Mercedes gullwing; a two-tone Morgan Plus-Four; and at the far end, the car I'd most wanted to see: the Duesy that had once belonged to Dashiell Hammett. I had heard that the car had been wrecked in an accident back in the forties, but couldn't remember if that was true. Regardless, Phillip Lennox had the resources to restore it if anyone did, and whatever the real story was, there it sat.

I stood there for long minutes imagining her in her heyday, how that engine must have sounded, and the flirtatious laughter of the women who had ridden inside. I walked around to the driver's side, peered through the window into the backseat and imagined the tall man making the rounds in a far different Los Angeles than I had ever experienced.

"You're not supposed to be in here."

I startled and turned toward the voice behind me. The sun was bright, streaming through the doorway behind him, so all I saw was a silhouette. It was a damned short one. I shaded my eyes to get a better look at what turned out to be a little kid.

"I'm sorry," I said. "I was just looking at the cars."

"You're not supposed to be in here," he repeated. "My grandpa said."

I stepped toward him, half expecting him to run off, but he stood his ground.

"What's your name," I asked him.

"Randall," he said. "Randall Lennox."

"Is Phillip your grandpa?"

The kid nodded and brushed a lock of hair off his forehead.

He backed out into the sunlight, which was uncomfortably bright to my unaccustomed eyes, so I put my RayBans back on as I approached him. He couldn't have been more than eight or nine, but he was dressed in a perfectly tailored suit and tie, with brown tasseled loafers on his feet.

I offered him my hand.

"I'm Mike Travis," I said.

Randall took a step toward me and gripped as he had been taught. He looked me in the eye and squeezed as firmly as his little hand could.

"I see you've met my son, Randall," another voice said from behind me.

I turned and faced a man in his midthirties, dressed in the same double-breasted Armani as the little guy, same tasseled loafers, same tie. His face was lean, he had a healthy tan, and brown hair, the first hint of gray showing at the temples.

"Mike Travis," I said as we shook hands.

"Phil Lennox," he said.

I nodded. "A pleasure to meet you, Phil."

"Call me J.R.," he said with an easy smile. "Everyone does."

"J.R.?"

"Junior," he said. "Phillip Lennox is my father."

There was something in his voice that I recognized, something that sounded like an apology, and I was pretty sure I knew what it meant.

"I was just admiring the Duesenberg," I said.

"Hell of a car, don't you think?"

"A piece of history, a work of art."

J.R. appraised me for a second and glanced at the Patek Philippe on his wrist.

"You appreciate art?"

"I can appreciate almost anything with historical value," I said.

"Come with me," he offered. "Let me show you something."

The boy took J.R.'s hand and walked between his father and me. The sun was behind us, high in the noontime sky, and young Randall made a game of trying to stomp his shadow. I remembered being a kid, having to dress up and make appearances at adult functions a great deal like this one, wondering what the grown-ups had so much to talk about, wondering when they'd finally shut up and go home. In those days, I had Valden to pal around with, but Randall looked to be very much alone.

"Got any other kids, J.R.?"

He shook his head.

"No," he said. "Randall's mom died just after he was born."

"I'm sorry."

"Don't be," he said to me, then looked down at his son. "We get along all right, don't we champ?"

Randall nodded his head and kept on stomping his shadow as we made our way to the main house.

I've known some very wealthy people in my life—my father for one—but I'd never seen anything like the Lennox place.

In another era, the room would have been called a drawing room, or perhaps a study—dark wood paneling on every surface and a fireplace at the far end. The mantel was enormous and appeared to have been carved from a single block of stone. Instead of books, however, the shelves and display cases that lined the walls were filled with artifacts that would have been the envy of a well-endowed museum.

"My father is a collector," J.R. said. The understatement of the day.

"Apparently so," I said.

He smiled and moved toward a glass case at the corner of the room. In it was a uniform that looked like something from the seventeenth century, faded white pantaloons and a blue waistcoat. A black leather belt held a scabbard and sword.

"Know what this is?"

"No idea," I said.

"It once belonged to Napoléon Bonaparte."

I looked at it again. "It looks like the one he wore in the portrait with his hand stuck between the buttons."

J.R. smiled. "It is."

Randall had trotted off to a corner where a row of old flint-lock guns hung on pegs, individually illuminated with warm yellow light. He breathed on the thick glass and drew shapes in the condensation with stubby fingers.

J.R. stood in the center of the room, motioned to an antique desk in one corner. "Belonged to Ulysses Grant," he said.

He moved down the wall and pointed to an old tommy gun, the kind with the circular ammo feed. "This was used by Eliot Ness," he said.

"Your dad backs the big dogs," I said.

"He likes to think so," he said, moving to another glass case. "Now, these are fascinating." Inside were about a dozen Plexiglas stands, atop each was perched some kind of leathery orb about the size of a large apple. Each orb was adorned with tufts of what appeared to be hair. "Shrunken heads."

"That's a first," I said. "From where?"

"All over the world. Asia, Africa, South America," he said as he drifted down the length of the wall. "You wouldn't believe some of the things my father has accumulated over the years. Take a look at these. They're some of his personal favorites."

I followed J.R. to a case that contained an assortment of pedestals in a variety of shapes and sizes, each one individually lit by a pinspot built into the ceiling. The one nearest me held something that looked like nothing more than a chunk of wood roughly the size of my fist. On another rested an ornate box covered with fine Oriental etchings.

"I'm sorry," J.R. said. "I'm being rude. Would you like a

drink?" He was pouring himself a healthy amber dollop of something from a decanter on an old-fashioned bar cart. God only knew who that used to belong to.

I held up my empty crystal flute.

"Better hold off awhile," I said.

"Suit yourself," he smiled, sipped. "I hate these damned things."

"Parties?"

"Fund-raisers," he said. "Political fund-raisers in particular."

It appeared we shared a common opinion. As far as I am concerned, politicians are pole dancers, showing you only what they want you to see, only enough to persuade you to tuck money into their G-strings.

"I hear you," I nodded. I turned back toward the display.

"What am I looking at here?" I asked. "What are all these things?"

"You'll never believe me when I tell you."

"Give it a try," I said. "What's this piece of wood?"

"That is a piece of what is said to be the true cross."

"Jesus," I whispered.

J.R. laughed. "Precisely."

"That scrap of paper there," he pointed, "is a piece of the original manuscript of the Gospel of Matthew from the New Testament. Authenticated and dated to about AD 67."

I'd seen plenty of rich men's toys in my life, but never anything like Phillip Lennox's collection. My awe, though, was being overtaken by a creeping disdain that things like these would be locked away from the rest of the world, for the sole purpose of bragging rights.

"What's in the clay pot?"

"Are you familiar with the Bible?"

"Well enough."

"That urn was found in a cave about six miles outside of Jerusalem. Inside is the letter written to Pontius Pilate from his wife, warning him not to get involved in the trial of Jesus Christ."

I remembered the story. The Roman procurator's wife had become a believer and had been warned in a dream about the Nazarene's trial. She had tried to convince her husband to set him free, but of course, he didn't. I couldn't begin to imagine the letter's value, or if a value could even be placed on such a thing.

"And this is one of my father's particular favorites," J.R. smiled. He was pointing to the Chinese box.

I looked at it again. It was deep burgundy in color, engraved with a fine filigree of golden waves and flying herons, so small it could have fit in the palm of my hand.

"That dark red dye is made from the application of layer upon layer of pigeon's blood," he said. "Inside it is one of the Buddha's teeth."

My mind was spinning at the value of the collection Lennox had accumulated. More than that, it was almost unfathomable to imagine their historical significance. Most of all, it spoke of the self-image of a man who could justify keeping them locked in his study for his own pleasure.

What did a collection such as this say about someone who needed to acquire such things? Did he own them as a reminder of his own humanity, or did he gaze into these cases with a sense of kinship, believing himself to be in possession of the kind of grace that enticed the people who surrounded him to draw power from a touch of the hem of his robe?

"Your father," I said, "must be an interesting guy."

His face took on a strange expression. "As in the Chinese curse, 'May you live in interesting times'?"

"Not exactly what I meant," I smiled. "You work for the family company, then?"

J.R. took the last swig from his tumbler, placed it back on the bar cart. "Yes, in fact I do. I'm president of the marketing and distribution divisions."

"Congratulations."

"Your glass is empty, Mike," he said. "We'd better join the party before Daddy has a fit."

I nodded and followed him out through heavy paneled doors, Randall's loafers clapping noisy echoes behind us as he ran to keep up.

I didn't know if J.R. had been kidding about the Daddy thing, but I couldn't help thinking that that was exactly why I had chosen to use a different name, and never had joined the ranks of Van de Groot Capital. I hadn't wanted to be Daddy's lapdog, or to be a thirty-something-year-old man who would be known as "Junior" all his life. And something about J.R. told me he hadn't truly desired it either. People often mistook my choice as rebellion, where in fact it had been intended as exactly the opposite: to make my way without having to leverage off the accomplishments of my antecedents. Their victories and vices belonged to them, and mine to me. I would like to believe they would respect that choice.

CHAPTER FOURTEEN

Valden was standing at the bar with Phillip Lennox the elder when J.R., Randall and I emerged from the house. I don't know how long my brother had been there, but he looked like he'd had a couple of stiff pops even before he arrived. I felt the younger Lennox tense as we approached them.

Valden was the first to speak.

"Phil, this is my brother, Mike," he said. "Mike, meet Phillip Lennox, the gracious host of this soiree."

"A pleasure," I said as we shook hands. As expected, his grip was firm and commanding. In my peripheral vision, I saw J.R. eyeball me.

Lennox senior looked at Valden. "You never mentioned a brother," he said.

"He rarely does," I said with a smile.

"You're not with VGC then, I take it," he said.

"No, Mr. Lennox. Not actively, anyway. Only a shareholder."

"Mike's a retired police detective," Valden offered.

Lennox's bushy brows shot skyward and formed furrows across a suntanned brow. A sudden gust ruffled his thinning white hair. He combed it back into place with his fingers.

I shot a quick glance at Valden, wondered if he'd had even more to drink than I thought.

"I operate a charter business in Hawaii," I said.

"Is that so? Whereabouts?"

"The Big Island. In Kona."

Lennox glanced over at his son for the first time and placed a hand on his shoulder. There was something patronizing in the gesture, and J.R. stiffened. They seemed more like a field general and his aide than father and son. Young Randall held on to J.R.'s hand and absently shuffled his feet.

"Well, how about that," Phillip Lennox said and jerked a thumb at Randall. "The three of us are going to be in Honolulu in a few days. Even the lad."

"Is that so?"

"Big pharmaceutical convention there, you know. Maybe we can look you up."

I pulled business cards from my billfold and handed one to each of the Lennox men.

"Call any time," I said.

The elder Lennox nodded and commented on the champagne flute in my hand.

"You're empty, Mike," he said. "Let's get that taken care of."

The bartender refilled my glass as Lennox cast a broad wave to a couple moving toward us across the lawn.

He turned to Valden, then to me. "You'll excuse me, gentlemen?"

"Of course," Valden said.

I nodded.

"Valden, I assume you know J.R.?" I asked.

"We've met," he said, as the two shook hands. His expression betrayed his obvious disinterest as he looked from J.R. to me, then off into the crowd. "You'll have to excuse me as well," he said. "Need to make the rounds, you know."

We watched my brother saunter off into the growing crowd, in search of a more fruitful conversation to drift into. I was embarrassed by my brother's insolence toward J.R., though the younger Lennox seemed to take it in stride; another of the by-products of being the offspring of a powerful man. I had to give him credit for character.

"Valden Van de Groot's brother?" he said to me. "You neglected to mention that."

"For better or worse," I smiled. "I apologize for his manners."

"No need," he said. "I'm used to it." He gave me an appraising look, and I saw the thought forming even before he voiced it. "You're a Van de Groot. You know what it's like."

J.R. had had to make his choices as a very young man, I knew. The choice to accept being stuffed headfirst into a toilet bowl, to become the kind of person who would kick his tormentors in the genitals while their backs were turned, or to stand tall and act like a man, even when your father treated you like a sock puppet.

I debated leaving his comment alone, but I kind of liked the guy.

"Don't buy into their bullshit, J.R.," I said. "They'll scratch away at your self-respect until there's nothing left of you. I go by Travis. Mike Travis. And I like it that way."

"You mean you're not in a rush to mingle with the haughty and presumptuous?"

"I'd rather use a urinal as a drinking fountain."

I couldn't see his eyes behind the tint of his sunglasses, but saw the smile cross his face. He put his hand out one more time and I shook it.

"I'm glad I got to meet you, Mike Travis."

"You, too, Phillip," I said.

* * *

The sun was crawling across the dome of sky, but a light wind was blowing in from the coast, allowing for intervals of relief from the confines of my pinstriped suit. Stands of old-growth coral trees laid patches of shadow across the manicured lawn. Pristine white tents protected lavish buffet tables. Waiters and waitresses serpentined among the guests, bearing trays of mimosas, hors d'oeuvres and French bubbly, and I watched it all from my vantage near the bar beneath a massive elm. After two glasses of Cristal, I switched to Perrier with lime and did my best to keep Valden in my sights.

My brother is an adroit schmoozer, and I found myself newly grateful that I'd chosen a life as a cop as I watched him meander among the clutches of guests, shaking hands, smiling, back-slapping, and generally working the crowd. I could corner the compost market if I could package all the bullshit being cast about among this bunch.

But I kept my eyes moving, looking for what, I wasn't completely sure: a guest who appeared out of place, an overtly unskilled cocktail or food server, anyone who approached Valden rather than the other way around. I knew Hans was out on the street doing the same thing, enduring the painfully boring reality of surveillance.

The band wrapped up with "One O'Clock Jump" and Phillip Lennox took the stage. The murmur of conversation and polite laughter drifted in the breeze as he tapped his crystal tumbler with a spoon and paused for his guests' attention.

"Ladies and gentlemen," he said. "If I may interrupt."

The tinkling of silver striking glassware rippled through the speakers again, and he waited a moment longer. The murmurs died down and everyone faced the dais. Despite my instruction to stay close to me, Valden had worked his way to the far side of the platform, at the edge of the parquet dance floor, glass in hand. When he finally glanced back in my direction, I nodded to let him know I was watching. He turned away and focused his attention on Lennox.

"First of all, let me thank you for coming out on this beautiful day," he smiled. "It's clear that God must surely be from Southern California."

Dutiful laughter rolled through the crowd together with a smattering of applause. Lennox's smile was practiced and familiar as he acknowledged individuals in the front ranks, until the noise faded away.

"The man you've come here to meet needs no introduction. Though, since it's my house, I'm going to take this opportunity to give him one anyway."

Polite sounds of appreciation and the familiar Phillip Lennox strong jaw and boardroom smile.

"As most of you probably know, I am a firm believer in American business, a firm believer in free enterprise, and an even firmer believer in the right of every American to work and to make a living without concern of losing their jobs to unnecessary foreign competition or intervention.

The guests were mostly still now, even the catering staff was moving more slowly as he spoke. At the edge of the stage, two off-duty cops working security stood beside the guest of honor, all cheap blue suits and mirrored shades.

The need for any additional protective presence was limited to a couple of men who had the appearance and demeanor of Lennox's private security personnel. These latter men would be the ones with military training, those who had moved into the private sector after tours of duty in sandpit hellholes like Afghanistan, Kuwait or Iraq.

"Catastrophic attacks on American soil have only served to underscore the dignity and strength of the American people, and the importance of maintaining the integrity of the American way of life. No one, and I mean *no one,* should ever be given the opportunity to usurp that way of life.

Applause roiled through the crowd again as Lennox continued to speak.

"So it is with great pleasure that I introduce to you today the one clear voice in American government who stands for those same values. A man who has been the subject of ridicule by certain elements of Congress who believe that America should turn the other cheek; that she should throw open our business and cultural borders for the greater 'World Economy.' Well, ladies and gentlemen, I'll say out loud what the distinguished congressman cannot in today's politically correct environment: that our first priority as a nation must be loyalty to business interests within our own borders. Any notion to the contrary is a colossal load of bovine excrement."

The congressman laughed along with the guests as he pulled away from his entourage and headed for the stage.

Sparkling rings and bracelets, Rolexes and jeweled cufflinks glittered in the LA sun as he stepped up to the microphone. A siren wailed in answer to a code-three call in the distance, unnoticed, somewhere outside the wall, on the other side of the world.

Lennox acknowledged the congressman with a slight bow and a sweep of his arm.

"Ladies and gentlemen, I give you Congressman Bill Kelleher."

Kelleher was a tall man, probably six two or so. He was dressed in the obligatory politician's dark suit, white cotton shirt, and club tie. His hair was red going to gray and he had the ruddy complexion of an outdoorsman. He waved casually and offered a broad smile to a few familiar faces before launching into his message. He was a man who spoke in italics.

"The borders of this great nation have been breached—and not without great loss of life. That we should not only condone, but actively *encourage* the further *violation* of our *economic* boundaries as well is simply unconscionable and should be deemed *intolerable* by the American people.

"In particular, to allow the *flood* of low-cost goods, assembled by a *non-US workforce,* by the very country that is home to the largest population on the planet—one that has demonstrated an attitude of *tolerance* toward the *terrorism* that rocked our shores, one that has repeatedly violated human rights and advanced untold political and religious *oppression* within its own borders—should be deemed *wholly unacceptable* to the people of the United States."

This was the shtick that Kelleher had become famous for and he wasn't letting anyone down. The congressman was a charismatic speaker and he held the group in the palm of his hand. The two-grand-a-seat crowd was lapping it up, and I got the distinct sense he was using his newfound fame to test the waters for a presidential bid.

"We've seen what happens when unscrupulous Chinese manufacturers were nearly successful in poisoning our children with lead-based products contained in the *toys* we buy from them. Yet we continue to deceive ourselves with the promise of working together as *trading partners* in a free-market economy."

I used the cover of Kelleher's speech to wander closer to the stage, eyeing each guest as best I could along the way. Not surprisingly, there were a number of faces I recognized—TV personalities, actors and the like, but I ignored them, cautiously weaving my way to the area nearest where Valden stood, alone and as captivated as the rest of them.

"Remember this well," Kelleher said. "A healthy and safe

America begins with a healthy American *economy*. We've seen what happens when the threat of terrorism drives us from the skies and results in the devastating impact on our businesses. We've seen what happens when Americans are afraid to travel, afraid for their very lives and livelihoods."

I was reaching the limits of my tolerance for political chatter. Our halls of government had devolved into a fraternity house full of tenured windbags who held views that were, in reality, far more elitist, oligarchic and condescending than the populist and egalitarian line of crap they kept trying to sell us. I would feel far differently if I knew that these people had real jobs to return to once their duty in Washington had been fulfilled.

"But my question is this: What about the *American* worker? What about *American* business? What about our own brothers and sisters, fathers and mothers? What about our *children*? I say enough is enough. It is *time* to tighten up our economic borders and turn up the heat on *China*."

There was a burst of spontaneous applause.

I had heard much of it before. But he had clearly ramped-up the rhetoric to new and potentially volatile levels. I was sure this was the last speech he would make without the presence of hordes of protesters. Nevertheless, there was no doubt that he was gaining momentum and he was stumping like hell to get his new trade bill passed.

I looked to the sky and saw a lone hawk gliding in easy circles as he rose on unseen thermals. Kelleher's voice was reduced to background noise as I watched the bird's silhouette grow smaller, and wondered how long he'd been watching us.

By the time Kelleher finished his speech, I had positioned myself behind Valden and off to one side. My brother hadn't seen me, so his body language gave nothing away. It was a fine line we were treading. Valden's entire world would be turned upside down if anyone got a whiff of the trouble he was in. It was a damned small circle of those of us who knew. Only Valden, Hans and me. And we were on the very short end of the clock.

After talking it through with Hans, we agreed this would be the best moment for the blackmailers to make contact. If it were up to me, I'd use the post-speech commotion to cover my move. Now that I was here, I knew we had likely guessed correctly.

I scanned the crowd, every face in Valden's vicinity, raked my eyes across the group that swamped the congressman for handshakes. When I looked back at Valden, I saw it: a waiter with a yellow coat passing something to my brother that did not come in a crystal glass. The waiter's manner was casual, a sharp contrast to that of my brother's. His face lost its color as he swiveled his head quickly from side to side. I willed him to keep his cool, but knew how brittle and edgy he had become.

I had no choice but to leave Valden on his own while I tailed the waiter, and swung a wide arc through the crowd to flank him. He wasn't moving overly swiftly, and neither was I, just enough to catch up without drawing attention.

I cut him off as he rounded the corner of the house, toward the rear where the largest of the catering trucks were parked. A number of other employees in matching jackets milled about in various stages of disorganization, none paying much attention to either of us.

He was too surprised to make any noise when I grabbed him by the elbow, forced him back into an alcove that led to the main house's kitchen, and out of anyone's direct line of sight. I yanked one arm up between his shoulder blades and slammed him hard against the wall, heard his head thud heavily against the stucco.

"What the—"

I bounced him off the wall again and watched him blink back his bearings.

In an interrogation, you have to act quickly. The quality of the information you get is only as good as you demand.

"I don't have time for bullshit," I said. "You just handed something to a man standing next to the stage. What was it?"

"I don't know," he said. "An envelope."

"What's your name?"

"Tim."

His free hand came up to rub his face. I looked out to the staging area to see if we'd attracted any attention, but nobody appeared to see us in the shadows.

"Put both hands against the wall, Tim, spread your feet." I patted him down swiftly. Nothing.

"I'm asking you again: what did you give that man?"

Tim was trembling with adrenaline rush and alarm.

"I told you, I don't know. Just an envelope."

"Where did you get it?"

He started to turn around and face me, but I shoved him back where he was. When he answered, his voice came out muffled.

"Some guy gave it to me," he said. "Gave me a hundred bucks if I'd just hand it to the fat guy."

"When?"

"When what?"

"When did 'some guy' give you the envelope, goddamn it."

"I—I don't know. Just a little while ago. When the dude in the suit started his speech."

That had been ten, maybe fifteen minutes earlier. Shit.

"Who was he?"

"Who?"

I smacked Tim on the back of the head.

"Don't be an asshole. The guy who gave you the envelope. What did he look like?"

"Ow," he said. "Damn it, that hurt." The initial rush of fear was wearing off.

"Talk to me," I said again. "I am not fucking around. One last time. Who was he? What did he look like?"

"I don't know, man. I've never seen the guy before." His voice was rasping, a little shaky. "He was medium. Like medium height, short hair, not too heavy, not too old."

Fuck. Great. Medium. I grabbed an arm, swung him around to face me.

"How old was he? My age?"

He looked me over real quick.

"No, not that old. Maybe twenty-five or thirty. Brown hair. A little taller than me. He was wearing a blue jacket. Like a sport coat."

"Where did he go after he gave you the envelope and the money?"

Tim picked pellets of stucco from his cheek. "He just walked off toward the street, like he was leaving. He was walking fast."

My cell phone hummed inside my suit jacket and I fished it out with one hand as I planted my other hand on Tim's chest to make him stay put. I didn't recognize the number on the incoming call screen.

"Go," I said into the receiver.

"I have an address for you."

"Wait one," I said to Rex while I plucked a ballpoint pen out of Tim's pocket. "Ready."

Rex recited a name and address to me twice, then hung up. I scrawled it across the palm of my hand and handed the pen back to Tim.

He stared at me with a glazed expression as he dusted the stucco off his uniform and straightened his bow tie.

It would take too long to retrieve my car, so I turned and jogged my way down the long driveway and out toward the street. Hans fired up the car and popped the passenger door as soon as he saw me coming.

CHAPTER FIFTEEN

Hans slipped the car into gear. We were already moving as I slammed the door behind me, breathing hard, feeling sweat snake down my back.

"I missed him," I said. "You see a guy in a blue sport coat leave the party in the last ten, fifteen minutes?"

"Saw him. Burgundy Celica," Hans said. "Too far away to get the plates."

"Rex came up with a name," I told him.

I read the name and address off the palm of my hand.

Hans nodded. "I got it."

Hans pulled away from the curb and spun a U-turn back toward Sunset. I wiped at the perspiration that burned as it dripped into the corner of my eye and reached over to turn up the air-conditioning. I was adjusting the vents until they blasted straight at me, in an attempt to dry my damp shirt.

Hans read my expression.

"What? No fun with the beautiful people?" he said to ease the tension. We were moving fast through the relatively light Sunday surface street traffic.

"Tools. The lot of 'em," I said. "They think they're power brokers, but they don't even realize that the game's being run on *them*."

I reached into the glove box and withdrew the Stoeger that Hans had kept for me.

Hans's head was on a swivel as we turned onto Sunset and back toward the freeway. Ten, twelve, fifteen minutes since we'd left the Lennox place, and it felt like an hour. I finally broke the silence when we made the curve off the main arterial boulevard and into a residential neighborhood that looked like it had been developed in the early sixties and had immediately begun running to seed. The streets were all named for flowers—Poppy, Marigold and Rose—but were narrow and pockmarked, sidewalks humped up by earthquakes, water runoff and the roots of trees.

"The burgundy Celica's parked in front of that house," I said.

"He's probably inside."

"Probably. But he could also be hunkered down in the seat, waiting."

"Let's circle the block, see what we've got. If he's not holed up in the car, we'll come back here and park."

Hans nodded and aimed the car toward the next intersection, made a right turn onto Aster Street.

"You'd better get down, too," he said. "Nothing says 'cop' like a pair of guys like us driving around in a car like this."

He had a point. I made myself as small as I could, crouched down into the footwell and felt the car decelerate to a slow glide. I watched Hans's face as he scanned the street.

"Bingo," he said without turning his head. "That's our address. Nobody in the car."

My pulse began to quicken.

I felt Hans turn onto the next street and circle back to where we had started. I unfolded myself from the floorboards and dusted off my slacks. A minute later we were parked back at the spot where we'd first noticed the Celica.

"The house is a box," Hans said. "Three stairs up to a landing, then a solid slab front door. Only window is on the right hand side, probably the living room."

"Side doors?"

"Nothing I could see, but there's a narrow yard on each side."

"Okay then," I said. "I'll walk. Give me couple-minute head start and stay with the car. Keep it running in case he bolts. We lose this guy, we're fucked."

Hans nodded as I clipped the Stoeger's holster to my belt for an easy cross-draw if I needed it. I saw him reflexively hand-check the automatic in his shoulder holster as I got out of the car and began walking up the block.

I buttoned my jacket as I went, patted it down so the gun bulge wasn't too noticeable, taking in the neighborhood with my peripheral vision. My first impression had been accurate. The houses had probably never been considered much to look at, but I guessed they had been cared for at one time. Maybe a couple of decades ago. Now their plaster and paint had begun to crack, fade and peel, lawns had gone to weed, and the scuffed sedans and pickups in grease-stained driveways were in better condition than the dwellings were.

I knew these neighborhoods. Places where shattered bottles would punctuate unpleasant conversations on a typical Friday night—where dogs got kicked and wives wore dark glasses even when they washed the dishes or picked the morning paper off the stoop.

I looked sidelong up the street and eyeballed the Celica that the guy with the blue sport coat had been driving. I studied the address numbers painted on the curb and knew I was two houses away. I felt that first push of adrenaline about the same time I heard Hans's car idling up the street some distance behind me.

As I came up beside the burgundy car, I placed the palm of my hand on the hood, felt the radiating heat of a car recently driven, then heard the pops and ticks of a cooling engine. This was our guy.

All the sounds of the day disappeared as I stepped off the sidewalk and onto the narrow concrete path that led to the front door, my attention spinning down to a point. It was a familiar feeling, where my mind and body connected completely, preparing for anything, primed for the shit to blow up.

Heavy curtains, or maybe an old blanket, I couldn't tell, covered the single window that faced the street. That was probably a good thing, I thought to myself, as I unbuttoned my jacket and touched the pistol grip with the tips of my fingers.

I knocked twice and stood to one side.

I waited long seconds.

Nothing.

I thought I heard movement on the other side of the door, and waited a few seconds more. When nothing came, I rapped again, harder. It flew open so fast that I went for my gun.

The man at the door was late twenties, early thirties, medium height, brown hair cut short. He wore a dress shirt with a tie pulled loose at the collar, poorly pressed khaki slacks, no shoes on stocking feet. Medium, just as described.

His matte black automatic was partially concealed inside a fist that dangled behind his thigh.

I pushed through the door, and kicked it shut with my foot.

My Stoeger was aimed at the bridge of his nose.

"You're going to want to drop that, son," I smiled.

"What the hell—"

"Did you see that guy in the car parked outside at the curb?" I hooked a thumb over my shoulder and back toward the street. "If you even think about swinging that gun on me, he'll have two slugs parked in your brainpan before that gun hits the ground."

I have to admit, his reactions were surprisingly quick. But not quick enough that he didn't catch most of the gun-butt blow that I leveled at the center of his forehead. It didn't quite knock him over, but it took enough of the wind out of his sails to buy me a second shot at him, a swift kick to his kidneys as he tried to spin away. He'd be pissing blood for a couple days. The pistol slid from his hand and fell to the floor.

The commotion at the front entry brought a second person down the hallway at a run from a room toward the back. I turned the Stoeger on the new guy, and he stopped like he'd hit a wall. His hands were in the air before I could even tell him to put them there, and he danced from one foot to the other like a school kid who has to take a leak.

"I'm cool, man," the second one said to me. "Don't shoot. Everything's cool."

"Lie down," I said. "Face on the floor. Hands behind your head, bend your knees, feet in the air."

He did what I said while the young man who answered the door began regaining his composure. Before he got too courageous, I gave him another kick, this one in the ribs, and had him coughing and spitting and crawling on all fours.

"You too, asshole," I said. "Lie down and stop moving."

"It's cool," the second one said again, wishing it were true. "Seriously, man, everything's chill."

I picked up the automatic off the floor and slipped it into my coat pocket.

"Is anybody else in this house?"

"No, man."

I stood over the first guy, listened to his breath catch inside his throat while I spoke to the second one. I lowered my pistol, held it firmly in one hand, but no longer had it pointed at either of them.

"Which one of you works at the Mandalay Plaza?" I asked.

"The what?"

Perps get a quick sense of how much they can get away with, which is as much as you let them. I leveled another kick to the ribs of the guy who was lying at my feet.

"Jesus," the second one yelped. "C'mon, man."

"Answer me," I said. "Which one of you works at the Mandalay Plaza?"

"He does."

"What does he do?"

"Don't—" the punching bag started to say, but my third kick cut him short. I was sure I heard a rib crack that time.

"Security!" The second one yelled, his words spilling all over themselves. "Security, man. He works security at the hotel. God *damn* it."

I glanced around the room; it was sparse, a bachelor pad in the lowest-rent sense. On the table beside a lumpy brown couch was a phone with a thin gray cord that stretched across a faded shag area rug to an outlet behind the TV. I yanked one end of the cord from the wall and pulled the other end out of the phone. The first guy was still rolling around on his stomach, but the talker was craning his neck, watching me from over his shoulder.

"Look at the floor, asshole," I said.

He mumbled something that I'm sure had something to do with being cool, but I was too busy hog-tying his buddy's hands and feet.

"The more you struggle, the tighter those knots are going to get," I told him. "So sit still."

He didn't believe me at first, but he found out I was telling the truth quickly enough.

I stood and trained the gun back on the talker.

"What's this shitweasel's name?"

"Harrison. Ken Harrison."

I recognized the name from the employee list.

"Yours?"

"Brian Cates."

"We need to talk," I said. "Who else is in this with you?"

"I don't know what—"

"Bad start, Brian. I asked you who else is in this with you."

"What are you talking about?" he said.

I pressed the barrel of my pistol against his cheekbone in a way that was sure to leave a bruise.

All perps lie. One of the real challenges isn't so much about determining the truth, but rather telling the relevant lies from the impulsive ones.

"Do you believe I'll hurt you?" I asked.

"Yes."

"That's the first smart thing you've said. How many people are involved in this thing?"

"What thing, man? I don't know what you're talking about."

I leveled the Stoeger at the bridge of his nose and thumbed the hammer. "Brian," I said.

His eyes glazed with fear. "Nobody. I mean just the two of us. Just Ken and me."

I slipped a copy of the photo of my brother's little girlfriend from my pocket and held it in front of Brian's face.

"Who is this girl?" I asked.

"I don't know."

I turned to Ken Harrison, on the floor at my feet, knelt and showed him the picture.

"Who is she?"

He didn't say a word.

"Am I going to have to shoot you in the knee, Ken?"

"I don't know her name. She comes to the hotel sometimes. Some of the guards know her."

"Why?"

"We watch her pick up guys."

"Want to know what I think?" I said. "I think you used a seventeen-year-old girl as bait to place a wealthy mark in front of your cameras. That makes you a pimp as well as a thief. And I think you and everybody associated with you needs to be hosed out of the bowl."

He looked away.

"Last time, now: Who else is working with you?"

"Just the two of us."

I turned, pinned his partner with my gaze.

"Is he telling me the truth, Brian?"

He licked his lips, swallowed dryly. It looked like he was working up a hairball.

"You've got to stop making me ask everything twice."

"Yeah. He's telling the truth."

"Show me your computers, Brian, and do it now."

He led the way down a short hall that terminated at a bathroom that separated two small bedrooms. He turned left into one of the rooms.

The overwhelming stink of stale cigarettes and pizza assaulted my nostrils before I entered the room. There was something else, too: an animal smell, like dried meat, mildew and sweat. It was so pervasive it seemed painted on the walls.

In one corner was an unmade bed, sheets gray and tossed to one side. It was strewn with dirty clothing; a plastic milk crate at the foot of the bed contained an outfielder's mitt, a couple of scuffed baseballs and an aluminum bat.

Along the wall beneath the window was a folding table that

supported two computer terminals, CPUs humming beside keyboards and screens that danced with fractal screen-saver images. A stack of electronic gear that looked something like a stereo system occupied the space between the two computers and winked green lights in an oblique kind of rhythm.

I tapped one of the keyboards and a screen came to life. It was the log-in page for the Royal Bank of Mauritius.

Brian Cates was looking at me, his expression betraying his anxiety as to what the hell was going to happen next.

"Give me the video disks," I said.

"I don't know—"

I backhanded him in the mouth.

"Give me the video disks."

My knuckle throbbed in time with my heartbeat, and I watched a ribbon of bloody saliva drip down his chin. He made no move to wipe it off, only stared at me with the look of a feral animal.

"Give me the disks."

He went to a small plastic box, flipped the lid and handed me six or seven shiny CDs, the entire contents of the box.

"Pop the trays on both computers. I want them all, everything. Put 'em in that crate over there."

He did as I asked, dumping over the crate, and the baseballs rolled across the carpet. He was shaking now, entering the first stage of Victim's Shock.

"Are you hosting the website from here?"

He didn't answer me, just stood there, his shudders growing more severe. I was fairly sure I wouldn't need to cuff him around anymore.

"Talk to me."

His eyes darted, looked at the wall like he could see through it, like he could see the look on his partner's face.

"It's over," I said. "Answer me straight, and you both might walk away. Nod if you understand me?"

He took a few more seconds, then nodded.

"Which one?" I asked, jerking my head in the direction of the computers. "Which one of these is the server?"

He pointed to one of the machines with one hand while he used the other to smear drool and blood across his chin. He never moved his eyes off me.

"Turn around," I said. "Put your nose against the wall."

He opened his mouth to speak, his lips stained red, but nothing came.

"You got ADD or something, Brian? I told you to turn around. Do it."

He watched out of the corner of his eye as I parked the Stoeger Cougar back in its holster and picked up the baseball bat. He screwed his eyelids shut, and I knew what he was thinking.

I swung hard.

Sparks flew, and the room filled with gray smoke and an electrical odor as I smashed the two machines to pieces. Brian cringed with the impact of every stroke, but I kept swinging until there was nothing but a pile of bent and smoldering plastic, glass and metal on his filthy carpet.

"Pick up the crate," I said finally. My breath was coming hard. "Get back out there with your buddy."

He turned from the wall and did as I asked. His eyes were red and wet.

When we returned to the living room, Ken Harrison was lying still. He'd struggled and found out how a phone cord feels when it digs so deeply into flesh that it cuts off circulation. His hands were red and puffed up like rotting fruit. There was one last chore before I made the computer geek lie down on the floor next to him.

I reached into the back pocket of Ken's trousers and removed his wallet. I slipped his driver's license from behind the plastic liner and tossed the wallet on the floor in front of his face.

"Your turn. Give me your wallet," I said to Brian. He did it without hesitation, and I liberated his license as well:

"Game's over," I said. "Completely. Nod if you understand what I'm saying to you."

They both nodded vigorously.

"I tracked you down today," I said. "I can do it again. I can find you any time, anywhere you try to run. Nod if you understand."

More bobbing heads.

"I'm keeping your IDs. I have your names, your DOB. I have the number of your offshore account. I have everything I will ever need to hunt you down again. This shit is over. Do not call anyone. Do not speak to anyone. Not the police, not your doctor, your priest or your poker pals. If there is anybody else involved that you did not tell me about, I will come for you. Do not utter the name Valden Van de Groot, even in your sleep. Any trace of any image from that video or those disks ever appears on this planet again, I will know, and I will come back for you. Both of you. You do not want that to happen."

I crouched down low and faced them.

"Look at me," I said. "Do you ever want to see me again?"

The air inside the vestibule was sour with the fetor of urine. One or the other of them had soiled himself.

"No," Ken said. "No, sir."

I was certain he spoke for both of them.

"Congratulations," I said. "You two knuckleheads have just become your own hostages."

Hans was seated behind the wheel when I came outside.

The afternoon sun was following its low autumn trajectory

across the cloudless sky. The ambient low-frequency hum of the city filled the atmosphere and throbbed like a living thing inside my ears.

I had packed the milk crate with shattered hard drives and circuit boards, and two dirty pillow cases with disks and electronic implements whose names or uses I had no idea of, and brought them out to the car. The whole operation had taken less than fifteen minutes, but I knew I'd made a hell of a racket. Hans popped the trunk from the inside and I tossed the crate in, slammed it shut and jumped into the passenger seat.

"It appears we came to the right place."

CHAPTER SIXTEEN

It took us more than three hours to properly destroy the gear I had liberated from the house.

We worked methodically, using the tools Hans had in his garage. I ran every disk through a crosscut shredder while Hans removed the motherboards and hard drives from the battered computer housings. He crushed them between the steel grips of a table vise, tossed the flattened parts into a metal garbage can and doused them with lighter fluid.

I emptied the contents of the shredder into the can, and we doused the whole pile again. I scraped a wooden kitchen match along the strike-strip of the box and dropped it in.

A blue flame danced inside the container while we watched it all melt into a blackened, malodorous lump. Hans opened the garage door to clear the air as it burned itself out. The stink of burned plastic lingered in the space, and we stepped outside into the late afternoon.

Hans drew a cigar from his pocket, trimmed the end and tucked it into his mouth, unlit.

I phoned Valden and told him it was over.

A few minutes later, Hans and I went back inside, thoroughly stirred the burned shards inside the can with a hardware-store yardstick, and divided them into two equal piles. This we placed into a pair of black plastic garbage bags, talking little during the process, each of us intent on seeing the evidence of Valden's indiscretion rendered useless and scattered to the wind.

I took Mie's car, and Hans drove his own. We departed his house in opposite directions, stopping every five minutes or so to scoop a handful of computer debris from the trash bag we each carried and dumping it into a different public garbage receptacle.

Hans was already home by the time I returned, so I parked behind him in their narrow driveway and brought the keys inside.

"I started without you," he said. He was sitting alone at their kitchen table drinking an Amstel from the bottle. The pistol I had liberated from Ken Harrison lay there like a centerpiece. "Help yourself."

I grabbed a beer from the refrigerator, cracked it on the under-counter bottle opener, and took a seat in the chair across from him.

I slipped the Stoeger from the holster at my hip, dropped the clip and ejected the one in the chamber, and placed it all on the table. Hans didn't even give them a glance.

"When're you heading back?" he asked me.

"Soon as I can," I said. "Tomorrow morning, if possible."

Hans nodded pensively, trying to put something together in his head. He frowned and looked out the window over the sink.

"You had my back today," I said finally. "I appreciate it, Hans."

He sat there for a moment, shrugged. "Like old times."

We stayed there like that for a little over an hour, polished off a six-pack and watched the evening slide away. He offered to take me back to the Lennox estate to retrieve my car, but I called a taxi instead.

The valets were gone, tents and tables folded and trucked away, the gathering long over. Soft lights illuminated the trees and the ivy that climbed the stone walls of the house. I stepped up the stairs to the front door and rang the bell. Half expecting a servant of some kind, I was surprised to find J.R.— still wearing his tan Armani and carrying a drink—there to answer the door.

"Aah, Mike Travis," he said. His smile had been loosened with the assistance of an extra cocktail or two.

"Evening, J.R. I'm sorry to bother you, but I left my rental car here. I just came to pick it up."

"So *you're* the culprit. My father was afraid we might have an intruder, an interloper, you know." He said it with a hint of mockery, a twist of sarcasm on the rim. "We were about to set out the dogs."

The November sky was clear, long since having faded from gray to black. A vague halo of city lights bleached the distance, and blotted out the stars that floated above the heart of downtown. Around the compound, more landscape lighting began to flicker on inside the foliage.

I looked at J.R. Lennox again and saw what might have become of me. I was overwhelmed in that moment with a need to be home, aboard *Kehau*, with the sun-warmed deck beneath my bare feet. I needed to feel Lani's warm skin against mine, and the roll of the sea beneath us. I wanted nothing more to do with meaningless collections of people and artifacts, estates and politics, illicit desires and greed.

I was silent a moment too long, and J.R. cleared his throat. "I'll go see about your keys."

I turned and studied the rows of floodlit cypresses, and listened to the indistinct drone of traffic. A moment later, J.R. returned to the door, made his way down to where I waited. He stood there for a few seconds, following the slow progress of a jet passing across the sky, then handed me my keys.

"Still have my card?" I asked him.

He patted his jacket, his pants, then dipped into his shirt pocket and came up with the one I'd given him.

"Take care of yourself, J.R.," I said.

He smiled in a far-off way, looked like he was about to say something, then thought better of it. He shook my hand before I turned to collect my rented Pontiac, and I saw him walk back into that big, empty house with the stiff-legged gait of a semi-inebriated man, a man who had been pressed into service to bear burdens that belonged to someone else.

Valden was seated on the couch in my suite when I opened the door. His tie was pulled low from an open shirt collar, his suit jacket thrown casually over the back of the sofa. Three airplane bottles of Chivas sat empty on the coffee table beside his stocking feet.

"Surprise you?" he asked.

"Rarely."

Ice tinkled in his crystal tumbler as he watched me shed my coat and lay my empty holster on the bar. The beer I'd had at Hans's had given me a headache, so I poured myself an Absolut on the rocks and let it chill while I went to the bathroom for an aspirin.

"You gonna say it?" Valden called to me from his place on the couch.

"Say what?" I called back from the bathroom.

"That I'm fucked?"

I walked back into the sitting room and picked up my drink before I answered. "Okay. You're fucked."

His eyes were glazed, but he kept his focus on my face. His slack expression went hard momentarily, followed by an equally rigid smile.

"My brother, Mike," he said. "Such a comedian. Such a wiseass."

I looked at him sitting there, spread out on the sofa, feet resting on the table, dim overhead lights reflecting off his shiny face. We drank at the same time, neither of us taking our eyes off the other.

"You can thank Hans Yamaguchi next time you see him," I said. "He hung his ass way out in the wind for you."

"Hans Yamaguchi hung his ass out for you."

"Valden, when you hear yourself say shit like that, don't you just want to grab those words and jam them back in your mouth?"

It took an extra few ticks to sink in, but he chose to ignore it and move on. His face morphed into a mask of victory.

He pumped his clenched fist in the air, splashing a dollop of expensive whiskey across his chest. "It's over."

For a brief moment I thought he was going to hug me.

"I'm leaving tomorrow on the early flight," I told him.

"The hell you are," he said. "I'll send you home in the Gulfstream."

"You need to go now, Valden," I said.

He sat his glass on the coffee table with exaggerated care and approached me, working his expression into something like sincerity. I moved toward the door and reached for the handle as he placed a hand on my shoulder. He gave me one of those political handshakes, all firmness and eye contact and honesty, like you're all that matters in the world.

"We did it," he grinned. "We fucking *did* it!"

A fog of Scotch vapor hung in the doorway as I watched him navigate the hallway to the elevator, pumping his fist like he'd just made the Final Four.

And I wondered who the hell he thought "we" were.

PART FOUR

Hard Latitudes

CHAPTER SEVENTEEN

May Ling had not seen the light of the sun for days. Her pupils had dilated to the extent that they all but obscured the deep amber of her irises.

At the beginning, there had been only seven or eight of them packed into the truck's nearly airless cargo compartment, but the group had grown to more than a dozen, as they had augmented their numbers at various stops along their route.

The vehicle traveled only by night, bouncing across narrow rutted passes and dirt roads that did not exist on any map: these roads were known only to the smugglers and racketeers who owned her now. The only thing that distinguished day from night was that the truck remained still during daylight hours, though to its occupants it made little difference. They remained imprisoned inside that putrid metal box without regard for the time—or the oppressive heat—of the day, dipping handfuls of rice from a covered communal pot that had been strapped to D-rings embedded in the floor, or relieving themselves into a receptacle just a few feet from the source of their food.

She often went days now without dreaming of her brother Tai Man Duk, or her parents, or the time she had spent working for the produce vendor. Each of their faces had grown hazy and indistinct over time, until they had all but disappeared from her memory. But on those occasions when she did dream, they came to her like a soft cloud or a filial kiss, so lifelike, authentic enough to make the waking reality of her life all the more difficult to bear once her eyes came open again.

She attempted to peer through the darkness at the others. She had seen them only briefly as they were passed through the half-open doors and into their places in the cargo hold. She had judged in those short moments that most of them were refugees who had paid for the privilege of illicit transport, but it was impossible to know, especially since the guards had forbidden them to speak to one another. Only the day before, an old man of seventy or more had been severely beaten when he'd spoken to May Ling. After that, the group had maintained an unremitting and anxious silence.

She turned her head in the direction she knew the old man to be. He was still suffering the effects of his injuries, huddled into a damp corner. She listened helplessly as his musculature periodically seized and shuddered—spasms that were punctuated by the phlegmy rattle of his breathing. He could no longer lift his chin from his chest, his head lolling in unison with the motion of the van, emitting an occasional groan as the road grew particularly rough.

Most of them wore the telltale uniform of the exile: two, sometimes three or four layers of clothing on their backs, and nothing more; no baggage or personal effects, no belongings of any kind apart from what they had enfolded about their bodies. When they reached the final destination, wherever that was to be, each would shed that filthy outer layer like dead reptilian skin, leaving them something, at least, that might be presentable enough to wear while seeking some sort of employment.

May Ling tried to discern the shapes of the young couple who had brought along the little boy aged no more than five or six. Though it was impossible to distinguish individual faces, her eyes had adjusted enough to identify shapes inside varying degrees of darkness. It had been some time since she had found herself in the presence of young children, and she'd never considered herself very good with them. The boy had soiled himself some hours earlier, but the reek of sweat and urine and bodily functions already hung in the compartment like a visible fog, so his contribution mattered very little, really.

She had no idea of their destination, only that she had been swiftly and suddenly removed from the cell she had occupied under the supervision of Joey Soong, and packed shoulder-to-shoulder into the cargo compartment of a transport truck whose outward insignia suggested its contents to be farm produce. She had etched nearly three thousand marks into the wall of her cell by the time she had been sent here. More than eight years as the property of the White Orchids. The one thing for which she remained grateful was that in all that time she had never been subjected to the needle. There had been days early on when she might have welcomed it, but she had witnessed the damage it had done to the others. May Ling could scarcely imagine the added horror that she would be suffering at this moment if she had been forced into addiction. She had learned to find gratitude for the things that she could.

No one had mustered the courage to ask if any among them knew where they might be going, though May Ling reminded herself that their destination was of little consequence to her. By now, each had been subjugated to the extent that their vacant, submissive expressions resembled one another as closely as did their crusty layers of soiled garments.

So May Ling slept. Or attempted to.

And she prayed that she would not dream.

She was awakened by an odor.

It was a damp and musty scent, the kind she had long associated with Hong Kong harbor during slack tides. In that other life, on special days, her brother, Duk, and May Ling would take the bus to the floating city at Aberdeen to browse the fish market. Brightly colored canopies flapped in the limpid breeze that wafted between the merchant stalls, canvas tents held aloft by lengths of rusted metal pipe that sheltered broad tables from the sun. Tables were laden with whole fish, some with bulky tubs in which live creatures still crawled on spindled legs or swam in listless patterns, or rolled onto their sides and seemed to watch her with their lidless silver eyes. Sometimes, when they had set aside enough money, Duk would bargain with a fishmonger and they would carry one home, wrapped inside a parcel made of soggy newsprint and held together with rough twine. Most times they would merely browse, and savor a day spent inside the ebb and flow of commerce at the market as others might treat a trip to an amusement park.

The odor she encountered now was distinctly, impossibly similar. But that memory seemed so distant it might just be a tale she'd once been told, a story she had heard but involved someone else altogether.

The screech and hiss of the air brakes echoed inside the cramped compartment, and anyone fortunate enough to have found sleep was jarred awake at once. The wounded old man groaned from his place in the corner, and the little boy began to speak. The boy's mother moved swiftly to cover his mouth with her hand. The rumble of the truck motor coughed and went silent, and seconds later the metal doors swung open.

A small cadre of men dressed as soldiers stood outside,

and the quality of the light outside told May Ling that it was morning. Wet fog rolled across a field of broken tarmac strewn with gravel and broken glass and clots of dying weeds, the atmosphere cast in pale blue.

The leader of the men spoke to them in words May Ling could not make out, but his orders had left the unloading of the truck to two of his charges. The remainder of the troop followed when he stalked away.

The two he left behind bore no resemblance to the White Orchid men she had known in Hong Kong, so distant from the mold that she doubted they could be affiliated with the Tong at all. Though they were dressed as the others in the unit, in military style, clearly none of them were official army personnel, either. They possessed only the barest semblance of military bearing, but even from a distance May Ling could see that these men had been broken from the inside, as if they had once been trained as proper soldiers, but their minds and souls had gone rogue.

"Up and out, all of you," the taller of the guards ordered.

The darkness inside had been so complete for so long, that even the diffuse morning light had them blinking back the pain that stabbed behind their stuttering eyelids.

"By God," the short one said. "They smell like the latrine in a Korean whorehouse."

Both guards shook their heads and backed away from the stale putridity that roiled out of the truck.

"Get out. Now," the tall one said. "Your trip is over."

"Climb down," the short one echoed. "Move along."

Without taking his eyes off the people who remained cowering and blinking against the light, the tall guard moved his rifle to his shoulder, passed his arm through the olive-green web sling that held it in place, and tugged the elbow of the woman nearest the door. He pulled her sharply outward, off the elevated bed of the transport truck and onto the ground. She landed awkwardly on her hipbone and cried out as she struck the pavement. The guard paid no attention, except to shove her away with the sole of his boot as he made a grab for the person seated in the space beside where the woman had been only a moment before. Almost as one, the rest unfolded themselves from their positions and began to leap from the vehicle before the guards could yank them down. In the end, only the old man remained.

"Don't make me climb in there," the short guard said.

After a moment of hesitation, he leaped into the hold and went to gather the old man. He touched him with his boot, not so roughly at first, but with growing aggravation. Rolling the old man onto his back, he called out to his comrade.

"This one is nearly gone."

"Then toss him in the river."

May Ling looked on in silent dread as a frail woman approached the taller guard. She was nearly the age of the old man, and moved with the mincing and uncertain steps of the elderly. Her eyes remained focused submissively upon the ground. May Ling wished she had the courage to reach out to her, or at least, the ability to look away. Instead, she stood as transfixed and helpless as all the others.

"Please," the old woman begged, never lifting her downward gaze. "He is my husband. Let me help him."

The guard turned to her, his expression one of contempt.

"This is your husband?"

Her eyes remained as they had been, her attitude one of utter entreaty.

"Please," she pleaded again.

The guards eyed one another, then the old woman. The short one spoke again.

"I understand," he said.

The tall one leapt inside the container, pulled a face at the foul odor and moved toward the far corner, nearly enveloped by shadow. He secured his rifle with one hand as he used his other to drag the semiconscious body to the opening. As he emerged from the shadows, May Ling could see that both of the old man's eyes had swollen shut. A deep gash on his temple had scabbed over during the long drive, but had begun to bleed freely again, coursing over the line of his brow and down the side of his face.

"I will make you a deal, grandmother," the guard said. He looked down from the truck bed and into the eyes of the old woman. "If you can get him down by yourself, he lives."

She was small and far too weak to move her husband from the raised platform, and she looked to the guard again, her eyes seeking something, anything that might resemble compassion.

"If not," he said, "he goes into the river."

The old man's head lolled near the edge, and a sound emanated from him that was more animal than human as she tried to work her hands beneath his shoulders, to grasp onto his clothing, but she failed to get a grip, couldn't budge him from where he lay.

"Pull harder," the guard said, and watched the old woman struggle as they all looked on. May Ling felt ill, but could not move, as immobilized by revulsion as by dread.

What happened next happened quickly.

The shorter guard leaped down from the truck and, without warning, took hold of the old man's collar and lifted, dragged, and pitched the inert body at her. The force of contact threw the old woman off balance, her bony fingers still threaded inside a knot of her husband's clothing.

His skull struck the ground with a hollow thud and his body fell across hers, pinning her to the tarmac. There was an elongated vacuum of utter silence that preceded the piercing shrieks that were either the product of pain from the bone that protruded through the parchment skin of her femur, or the realization that the viscous ruby pool that was rapidly spreading beneath her husband's skull marked the moment of his death.

The old woman's cries glanced off the walls, and shattered May Ling's eardrums as well as her heart. It was the tragic and mournful sound of a great wounded bird, and the image refused to fade from May Ling's mind: the likeness of an ancient, gray heron, elongated neck and skeletal legs, vainly flailing its wings in its powerlessness to rise from the earth. Her wails grew louder and louder, until there was no woman at all, only a helpless, frightened bird.

From the corner of her eye, May Ling saw the little boy's father lunge for the guard, a belated act of courage or compassion, but he was momentarily hampered by his wife's clutching grip. The guard rewarded him with the administration of a swift stroke to his face from the butt of his rifle, and sent an arcing spray of blood across the boy, his mother, and May Ling. The father flew backward and landed on his back, semiconscious. The wife crawled to a place beside her husband while the little boy held fast to May Ling's leg.

The old woman was screaming uncontrollably now, and the guards, agitated and disturbed by their sudden loss of control, vented their rage on her. The first blow crushed her orbital bone and silenced her, but they were acting with unchecked animal aggression, and their vicious assault did not cease until the two aged bodies had become little more than a heap of raw meat and soiled clothing.

The great gray heron had fallen silent, just blood and feather and bone, and the final spastic clutches of dulled claws in the empty air.

May Ling felt the little boy's fingers dig deeply into her flesh as he worked to bury his face against her, attempting to disappear. She wrapped a protective arm around his narrow shoulders and watched as the boy's mother cradled her husband's shattered head in her lap. The remaining refugees stood with their backs pressed against the wall, stunned into silence as the guards backed away, their chests heaving from exertion. The empty echo of savage cruelty hung in the damp, pale light of the rising sun, the first of many mornings they would spend as captives of an unknown militia, housed inside a decaying metal warehouse on the banks of the Yangtze River.

CHAPTER EIGHTEEN

Monday morning traffic moved slowly over the surface streets as we wound our way from the Mandalay Plaza all the way out to the Burbank airport. The morning had broken cold and gray, with a high overcast cloaking the whole of the LA basin.

Valden and I sat together in the rear seat of his limousine, the privacy divider scrolled up between ourselves and Jimmy, his driver. We had words with respect to what my brother needed to do next in order to best ensure that all of this crap was concluded with prejudice, as well as what he should do for those innocent parties who had been caught in the fallout. Valden had been predictably defensive, but following a brief and ineffective tirade, it had been a predominantly silent ride.

We pulled to a stop at the curb in front of the private aircraft terminal and I faced my brother one last time before I exited the car.

"Just so we're clear, you'll do what I told you, right?"

He straightened his tie and drummed his fingers on the leather seat in the space between us. "You're assigning my Acts of Contrition?"

"Transgressions have consequences, Valden. They don't require punishment. Thanks for the ride."

He remained in the car as I gathered my briefcase and bag off the jump seat and got out.

I stopped off at the driver's side window and waited for Jimmy to roll it down. He masticated his Dentyne and stared at me through a pair of opaque sunglasses.

"I'm sure I don't need to tell you never to discuss what happened here," I said.

He moved his eyes off me and gazed through the windshield.

"You are a very difficult man to like," he said. "I can see why Mr. Van de Groot has issues with you."

I smiled and tapped the doorframe.

"Keep the shiny side up, Jimmy."

The woman standing behind the counter at Executive Aviation appraised me with a cool once-over as I passed through the door. Her obdurate gaze reminded me how tired I was of this particular brand of Southern California bullshit.

I gave her my name and she informed me the VGC Gulfstream was fueled and nearly ready for boarding.

I took up a place in the lounge, steeped myself a cup of tea and looked out the window at the line of hotel and rental-car buses making the crawl around the commercial end of the airport loop. I was tired. Bone tired. Tired of petty people, and tired of their scams and petty plans, tired of their pretension and their lies, and the politics of self-interest. I was sick to death of objects and things, sick of shops and storefronts filled with objects and things, and of the perpetual quest to accumulate more and more and more. I was revolted by the notion of hearing any more speeches, disgusted by recycled opinions—I'd heard every goddamned one of them before, as though everything worth saying had already been said a thousand other times by a thousand other people, any one of whom was probably a thousand times smarter than the ones who were saying them now.

It was time to go home.

I was ushered aboard the jet and took a seat near the cockpit. I was traveling alone, but for the flight crew. An attractive attendant offered me a drink, which I declined and looked out the window as the engines ran up.

My mind wandered back on the twenty years I spent on these streets. How the victims were still victims, the robbed were still robbed, the raped were still raped, and the dead were still dead.

We pulled out onto the active runway and awaited permission for takeoff.

Son of a bitch, I thought, every time I come back to this town, it slithers back inside me. I had never intended to be a cynic, never imagined I would feel such contempt, and especially had never wanted to lose hope. I wanted to believe in greater things, like grace, like justice, like integrity; I wanted to believe in heroes or a higher purpose, for Christ's sake.

As we gained altitude and banked toward the western horizon, I could see the flicker of flames that ornamented the tips of the exhaust stacks at the refinery near Signal Hill. I turned away and pulled the window shade down.

Good-fucking-bye.

It was three o'clock in the afternoon by the time I landed in Kona.

Fifteen minutes later, I had retrieved my Jeep, paid the parking lot attendant, and was heading down Queen Kaahumanu Highway with the wind in my hair. The vog had been cleared from the sky by a steady southern breeze, so the ocean met the sky in a line that was as sharp as a razor, and I tuned the radio to the Hawaiian music station just in time to catch the beginning of Kaikina's *pau hana* drive time show. The Makaha Sons were playing their version of "Hopoe." I cranked the volume and let the warm wind bring me back to a reality I understood.

The parking lot behind Jake's Diving Locker was jammed with cars by the time I got there, so I parked in the dirt between the Hard Rock and the Yacht Club, stashed my briefcase and carry-on in the lockbox welded to the back of the Jeep, and picked my way across the rocks and gravel.

The air was sweet with gardenia and salt spray, the sky blue and cloudless. Traffic was brisk along Alii Drive, but the boisterous racket of a volleyball game being played on the sand court between the buildings blotted it out. I cut across the freshly clipped grass and stopped at the ice cream place on the corner, the one that Lani and I like to go to after dinner in town, before making the long walk back to the pier, or back to her apartment.

I waited in line behind a pair of middle-aged tourists and their two spoiled kids. Stop throwing napkins, okay, sweetie? Okay, honey? Say please. Say thank you. Don't step on the nice man's toes.

A double scoop of *haupia* ice cream had dripped a thin, white trail down the cone and across the hairs on my wrist by the time I got upstairs to Lola's. Lani had her back to me—busy making change for a group at the far end of the bar—so I slipped onto a stool on the shady side and waited for her.

A minute later, she turned around and spotted me. She made her way over and showed me a smile that didn't quite reach all the way to her eyes.

"You're back," she said.

"I brought you lunch."

The corners of her brown eyes turned downward and looked like she might burst into tears. Lani took the cone from my hand and licked around the soft, melted part near the bottom.

Lola's was fairly quiet, between customer rushes, and it was not quite time for happy hour, so I just sat there watching her, seeing that girl as I had seen her, the girl at the beach with the sand dusting the tops of her feet. She was wearing a red hibiscus tucked behind her left ear, long hair falling free, now and again catching a gust that blew in off the bay.

"You're staring at me," she said, and brought me back to the bar at Lola's.

"I know."

Neither of us had been happy with the way I had left for the mainland. I had amends of my own to make.

"Listen," I began, "I'm sorry I wasn't—"

Lani held up a hand, glanced hastily around the bar.

"I'll buy you a beer," she said.

I watched her step back toward the cooler. She returned a minute later with a bottle of Asahi and a tall glass filled with ice. Her eyes never left mine as she poured it and put the bottle down softly as the beer foam met the rim.

"Threads, Mike," she said softly. "I've been thinking about threads."

I watched her search my face for understanding, not finding it.

"Like a knitted sweater," she said. "Most times, if you pull one of those loose threads, the whole thing starts to come apart."

"And you think that's what's happening here? With us?"

She gazed out toward the bay and frowned as she collected her thoughts.

"No, not exactly. It's more like . . . It's like you miss a flight you were supposed to take. You forget to set your alarm, and you suddenly wake up all panicky. You're late. You throw all the stuff you had lying on the bathroom counter into your suitcase, and you race around the house locking the doors, grabbing your car keys and rushing to the airport. You park your car, run through the lot to the ticket counter and when you get there the ticket agent tells you your plane already took off. You're all upset, right? So you take the next flight, like three hours later, and you sit around the airportangry and upset, kicking yourself for not setting the alarm clock."

She hesitated then, only for a moment, waiting for me. I nodded, watching her tie her story together.

"But then you finally get to where you were going," she continued. "And you find out that the plane you missed—the one you were supposed to be on—crashed and killed everybody on board. It's like that. It's as though you're alive just because you forgot to set your stupid alarm."

I sat in silence for a long moment, looked past her, looked past the tourists seated along the railing, out to the *Kehau* as she lay on her moorings. I took a deep breath, held it a little too long.

"Mike?"

"I'm sorry," I said. "I really am."

"It occurred to me," she said,. "While you were gone."

I felt a knowing anger then. Not a hot-skinned, burning anger, but the kind that moves in like frustration's abusive stepfather.

"You're upset that I left the way I did," I said.

Her smile was patient, a little sad. "No."

"Then what?"

"It's your priorities, Mike. You're just so damned independent, so *God* damned self-sufficient. I want to be *needed*."

It sliced straight through me, that bit of truth. For most of my life, I'd desired independence more than anything, had even changed my name to attain it. But I never imagined that independence carried a downside, never thought it would exact a price. And then I thought that maybe it wasn't independence at all.

I thought about how I had felt when I was a cop. There had been times I was so consumed by the job I was sure if it were ever taken away, I'd completely disappear. I wasn't that man now, didn't want to be.

"There's nothing I need more than I need you, Lani," I said.

It appeared in her eyes at that moment. That thing I'd grown to love about her. The dim reflection of whatever hope she still allowed herself, and the kind of wisdom of experience I knew she had never asked for.

I started to say something, but she waved me off. She dabbed her eyes with a cocktail napkin and tried to smile.

"I have to go," she said.

I leaned across the bar and kissed the soft skin behind her ear.

"I love you, Mike," she whispered. A tear escaped along her cheek and she hugged herself tight. She turned away before I could ruin it with another word.

I stopped in at Jake's Diving Locker to see if Yosemite was working.

The place smelled of wet suits and newly printed T-shirts. Framed photos of manta rays and tropical fish and Jerry Garcia wearing an aloha shirt hung along the walls. An eel hunkered down among the rocks inside a huge aquarium and I watched some kids tap on its acrylic walls. Yellow tangs and Moorish idols swam in aggravated circles seeking escape from the attention of the irritating little bastards.

"Good God, Mike. You all right?" It was Teri, one of the owners. "You look like something my cat coughed up."

"Just a little tired," I lied. "Dave around?"

Teri rolled her eyes. "Your boat's been a floating party for the past two days."

Perfect.

I thanked her and called Yosemite on the cell phone as I walked back to the Jeep. Yelling to make himself heard above the music that blasted in the background, he told me he'd pick me up at the pier in ten minutes. I jumped into my Jeep, cranked the engine and headed out, leaving a rooster tail of gravel dust floating across the lot.

I came to a stop at the corner and waited to make the turn onto Alii. I cast my eyes up between the palms and into the shade of Lola's bar, feeling void and sodden. A loud honk from a rented convertible behind me sent a sudden rush of adrenaline straight to my brain, and I felt something untamed threaten to breach the wall and cut loose in a kind of nameless, pointless hostility.

I'd had enough. Enough Valden Van de Groot and limo drivers named Jimmy. Enough Phillip Lennox and congressmen named anything, and enough mainland attitude to last three lifetimes. Then it all drained away, leaving only that bone-deep fatigue I had awakened with that morning.

I threw the big Jeep into gear, pulled out onto the street, and did something I swear I will never do again: I wondered what the hell else could possibly go wrong.

CHAPTER NINETEEN

I parked near the foot of the pier, in the late afternoon shade of a banyan tree that was alive with the rustling of mynah birds that roosted deep inside its branches.

There was no sign of Dave yet, so I took a seat on a weather-beaten railroad tie that served as a parking bumper and waited.

I tried to watch the line of customers clambering up the boarding ramp to the Oceanic Dive boat, or the kinetic preparations of the crew aboard Captain Bean's booze cruise, but I couldn't stay focused, kept drifting back to Lola's.

My relationship with Lani had always been one of silences. From the beginning, it had been those long, quiet moments that we fell into, a nearly tangible thing we indulged ourselves in as we learned to know one another. They were sensual silences at first, but they had lately begun to change into something different, stretching into lapses that demanded interpretation as they grew deeper.

I could see she was searching for me inside those widening silences, but that's not where I could be found. I was in the spaces between, on the uncharted islands I constructed for myself where there was no police work, but perhaps very little else. I had sailed away from that other coast so I could begin again, start over; there were so many things I didn't want to bring into this new life. But despite my strongest intentions, those things had begun to seep between the cracks and fissures, into the spaces and silences like smoke, and stained everything they touched.

I looked *mauka,* past the steeple of the Congregational Church, to a mountain dotted with rooftops, the evidence left behind by intermittent surges of economic development. In between lay expanses of lush green coffee, papaya, mango, and the untamed and untended soil grown over with philodendrons, tall native grasses and heavy vines. My eyes played across familiar landmarks until I located my coffee plantation, certain that Tino was still up there working.

I was pulled back by the spontaneous musical laughter of a gathering of little girls in the distance. They were preparing for a hula class, and their noises rippled across the narrow throat of the channel from Hulihee Palace, where ladies wearing oversized woven-straw hats waited on the wide swath of lawn for the show to begin.

"Hey, Mike," Snyder said, startling me. He had strolled across the street, on the way to his bar, and seen me sitting there. I hadn't heard his approach. "How was LA?"

"The same," I said. "If that's the center of our cultural universe, we're fucked."

"I've got your mail over at the bar. You want it?"

"I'll grab it later on."

Snyder stepped into the shade beside me, placed one hand across his brow to block out the glare as it flashed off the rippling chop, and looked out toward the *Kehau.* Wafts of rock music carried over to us on the wind.

"Been going nonstop like that since you left. I assume Yosemite is boat-sitting."

"Good guess."

"You're a hell of a good host when you're not on the island," he said and clapped me on the shoulder as he began to walk away. "Come by and get your mail once you've hosed the puke out of the gunwales. I'll have an Asahi waiting."

I watched him walk away, past the children as they played in the lagoon that bounded the hotel.

When I looked back again toward *Kehau*, I saw my skiff, the *Chingadera*, ripping toward me, and for no reason at all, felt the first trace of respite from my toxic mood.

"I wasn't expecting you 'til tomorrow," Yosemite said. "I thought that's what you told me when you called."

"It is tomorrow," I said, and tossed my bag and briefcase on the deck of the skiff.

An expression that almost passed as embarrassment crossed his face. It disappeared as quickly as it had come. He was wearing a T-shirt that said BEAUTY IS ONLY A LIGHT SWITCH AWAY, and he smelled of beer, fresh fruit and rum.

"Time's a motherfucker," he said and pushed away from the dock with the sole of his bare foot.

He smiled and pulled a cold beer from a covered cooler, handed it to me.

"I stopped by Jake's on the way over. Teri said she hasn't seen you in a couple days."

He tossed off a loose shrug.

"Taking care of your boat, bro," he said. "Can't leave *Kehau* out here by herself. That's not why you're paying me the big bucks."

I took a pull off the beer, smiled and shook my head. "You smell like a party."

"It's a 'Welcome Home' party."

"For who?"

"For you."

Dave kicked up the throttle and sent a flume of white water across our wake.

"Thought you weren't expecting me until tomorrow," I reminded him, shouting over the roar of the twin Evinrudes.

He took on a pained expression, explaining something to a dim student. "Getting an early start, man. You've met me, right?"

Five minutes later, I was climbing up the aft ladder and boarding the *Kehau*. There were at least thirty people in various stages of inebriation and undress on deck, about half of whom I recognized. No telling where the others had come from. Dave collects people like others collect loose change.

The stereo was blasting out something from the eighties, while a pair of sturdy-looking girls danced with one another on the foredeck, naked to the waist. A tall, skinny guy I had never seen before leaned against the chrome railing and watched the two girls dance while he puffed on a hand-rolled cigarette that cast a dubious odor in my direction. If he was any higher he'd need to paint numbers on his tail.

"Yosemite," I said. "I'm going below to stow my gear."

Dave nodded and made for the bar. I grabbed his arm and pulled him close enough so I didn't have to shout.

"When I come back topside, I don't want to see anything illegal happening up here." I shot my eyes across at the skinny guy poofing the bone. "Okay?"

Dave appeared alarmed, as he should have been. The Coast Guard takes a dim view of the presence of controlled substances found aboard commercial vessels. I could lose my license, maybe even my boat.

"God*damn* it," he said. "I *told* everybody about that."

"I don't see a thing," I said. "Just get it the hell off my boat."

I shouldered my way through a galley full of people and

into the narrow companionway that led to my stateroom. My eyes strayed across the new doorjamb, at the place where the old one had once absorbed the brunt of a shotgun blast that had been meant for me. I opened the door and walked into the master stateroom, which was mercifully devoid of party guests, and closed out the noise wafting down from the galley. Bass notes reverberated through the hull and the footfalls of dancers bounced off the ceiling as I unlocked the drawer beside the bed where I had stowed my Beretta Tomcat. It is a sweet little .32 caliber with an overall length of about five inches, weighing in at just more than twelve ounces. Fifteen in the clip and fit perfectly in the special pockets I'd had sewn into my shorts. It was almost completely undetectable when I carried, and packed more muscle than the Bobcat model I used to carry.

Now that I was back home, I would put all my weapons back where I usually keep them: one in the galley, one in the wheel-house, and one in the nightstand. Despite the distance from my old life, I never liked being too far from firepower.

After putting in my papers with the LAPD, I had studied medi-tation for a while in an effort to provide a bit of yang to balance the yin of the violence that represented the other aspects of my life. So I sat for a moment in the relative quiet of my stateroom, and focused on an imaginary spot on the wall, trying like hell to regain my center. As I attempted to empty my mind, the images of the past seventy-two hours flashed through: images of airports and flight lounges, limousines and rental cars and hotel bars. I saw Hans and Mie, Valden and Lennox and Kelleher, cocktail parties and blackmail schemes until they all ran together into an unruly abstract triptych that demanded I either hang it for display right there on my wall or burn the bastard to a crisp and flush the ashes.

I opened my eyes and decided a hot shower and a change of clothes would more effectively help adjust my attitude.

When I came back topside some time later, Yosemite was busy ferrying a batch of people back toward the pier in the *Chingadera*. I asked his girlfriend, Rosie, what he was up to. She told me Dave didn't think that that particular group had a proper appreciation for the house rules.

"Hell with 'em," she said. "The party's more manageable without 'em anyway."

Rosie was a redhead with a full-throttle brain and a temper to match, and a fierce loyalty to the people she considered friends. Dave had fallen for her the minute he met her. Their roommate, Melinda, was another story.

"So, is Lani coming?" Rosie asked me.

"I don't think so," I said.

She looked puzzled. "Working?"

I shook my head.

Rosie spoke in a tone that was part assurance, part condolence. "She'll be okay."

We stood there for a few beats, allowing the breeze to blow the awkwardness away. She tossed a glance over my shoulder toward shore, toward Lola's, then back to me.

"Let's get you a beer," she said. "This is supposed to be a party, goddamn it."

By midnight the only remaining sounds in the air were the rush of waves as they broke against the seawall, snippets of bad karaoke from one of the bars along Alii Drive, and the animated conversation taking place in the stern cockpit of my yacht. There were only five or six of us left by then, each just a little more drunk than we were letting on.

The coals from the barbecue grill cast a throbbing glow on the faces gathered around the banquette, and I watched from my place in the captain's chair, bare feet propped on the wheel, as

Rosie got up a bit unsteadily and handed Melinda the bottle of Jack Daniel's she'd been drinking from. Dave held out a hand to support her, and then she disappeared down the stairs. Melinda was the third roommate in the house Dave and Rosie shared upslope, in the Palisades. She was a dark-skinned brunette who was long on opinions that were short on research, and who harbored a simmering dislike for me whose origin I had never understood. In deference to the obvious absence of Lani, she was taking it uncharacteristically easy on me.

Melinda took a pull at the whiskey bottle that was being passed from hand to hand and chased it with a beer. She convulsed with a belch, and her eyes went momentarily glassy. Dave took the bottle from her, wiped the neck with his shirttail and took a pull for himself.

I heard Rosie rummaging through the CD drawer below as I looked up into the clear night sky. The southern wind had kept up for most of the afternoon, and the moon had disappeared. The atmosphere was crisp and flooded with stars.

A minute later, Janis Joplin's voice wailed from the stereo. Rosie was singing along with her and gyrating her way back topside, and Melinda had popped back to life.

The whole thing suddenly felt like a wake. I must have had an odd expression on my face, because Rosie came up behind me and began massaging my shoulders, as if to take all my pain away. I shot Dave a questioning look, and the one he gave me back told me to shut up and roll with it.

"C'mon, Mike," she said. "Try to relax."

I wasn't in the mood for this anymore.

"I'm going to bed."

Melinda rolled her eyes and took a sloppy pull from her beer.

Nobody else seemed to notice when I stood up, stretched, and lobbed my empty Asahi into the cooler.

I left Rosie, Dave and the rest of them. Melinda was rocking slowly back to sleep as she sat on the deck, her head resting against the bulkhead. I descended the stairs with their voices at my back, climbed into my bed, and tried to fall asleep to the lazy rhythm of water slapping the hull, the draw and strain of *Kehau*'s mooring ropes, and the hint of Lani's perfume on my pillow.

CHAPTER TWENTY

I was up before the sun, preempting the inevitable hangover with a pair of Aleve and a bottle of Asahi.

I stood there beside the stove, waiting for the teapot to boil and gazed out the window at the shimmer of the ocean and watched as, one by one, the streetlights that traced the shoreline cycled off.

I dropped the empty bottle in the bin beneath the sink and carried a steaming mug of Mango Ceylon topside to survey the damage from Yosemite's two-day *pa'ina*. A cold offshore wind blew down the slope of Hualalai and ruffled the pennant that flew from the mainmast. My eyes swept across the deck. Apart from the stains from a few spilled cocktails on the teak, the only real damage was a nasty cigarette burn along the gunwale. I'd have to strip, sand and refinish it. All in all, not as bad as I had every reason to expect.

I took a seat on the decking, dangled my feet over the side and leaned my head against the brightwork. The chrome railing retained the chill of the night air and sent a brief shiver down my spine. Through the porthole below, I could hear Yosemite snoring and wondered how Rosie ever got any sleep. A few minutes later, I got my answer.

"Dave wake you, too?" Rosie asked as she took up a seat on the deck beside me. She was wearing white shorts and a red halter, her hair pulled back in a loose knot. She set a mug of coffee between us as she tucked a renegade strand of hair back behind her ear.

"I try to get up with the sunrise," I said.

"First one I've seen in a long time," she said. Her voice was husky from the late night. "What the hell day is it anyway? I've lost track."

"Tuesday."

She nodded and sipped from her coffee. "You're a patient host."

"Not always."

Rosie turned and looked at me, took in my features like she'd never seen me before, or like she thought she might never again. "Dave really needed this, Mike. I think we both did."

"I heard about his trouble with the navy."

"Assholes," she spat. "I don't know why the hell they have to chase the goddamned whales anyway. They're killing them, Mike. They say the tests don't do any harm, but just look out there." She waved a hand out toward the horizon, across the expanse of open ocean. "I haven't seen a normal-sized pod in two years."

"It's early in the season yet," I offered.

Rosie scowled at me. She was nothing if not passionate about environmental issues. Some might call her militant. Many did.

"You heard about the CO_2 testing they want to do now?"

I shook my head. "The navy?"

"No," she said. "Some scientists from an east coast research outfit. They want to release a huge cloud of compressed carbon dioxide into the ocean to see if it will dissipate before it reaches the surface."

"What's the point of that?"

"A theory that it might be a method of disposing of unwanted greenhouse gases from the environment."

"What, are you kidding? They want to take toxic gases from the air, and put them in the ocean instead? What kind of horseshit is that?"

She nodded. "Right?"

"Has it been approved?"

"They've been through every agency but one, and so far, they've all given it a green light."

"Where do they want to do the tests?"

"You'll never believe it."

"Try me."

She looked off to the north, toward the mouth of the bay. "Off Keahole Point."

"Are they fucking nuts?" I said. "There's living coral out there."

She nodded slowly.

"Jesus."

"See what happens when you don't pay attention?"

Blasting whales with low frequency sonar, taking poisonous gas from the atmosphere and intentionally releasing it next to a live coral reef? Who the hell was running this idiot carnival?

"Whatever I can do," I said.

Rosie reached over, placed her hand on my knee. We sat there like that for a long while, wordlessly watching Kona stretch, yawn, and stir itself awake for another day.

"You doing okay?" I asked finally.

"The usual threats and name-calling," she said. "Ignorant assholes writing newspaper editorials about things they know nothing about, that sort of thing."

"Any more bomb scares?"

"Only the odd unsigned piece of hate mail."

I started to say something, but she interrupted, me with a wave, dismissed the whole thing.

"Goes with the territory, Mike. I've been there before. Some people get alarmed by granola-eating, tree-hugging, whale savers, afraid we're going to upset the status quo. But the sex? The sex has never been better."

Two hours later I was working up a sweat sanding spilled-liquor stains out of the teak deck. The earlier breeze had died down to a whisper, the pennant on the masthead hung limp over my head, and the heat of the morning sun was at my back as I moved the belt sander in slow circles. I blew the fine dust from the patch I'd made, and caught the first whiff of the breakfast Rosie was preparing down below. The smell of onions and grilled meat filled the air. It mingled with the sounds of Dave's gravel voice and Rosie's playful giggle when he smacked her on the backside.

I wiped the sweat from my brow and pulled a little more slack from the electrical cord, about to start in on a new stain when I heard my cell phone ring. I knew I wouldn't get to it in time, so I called down to the galley for someone to pick it up. A few moments later, Dave came topside and handed it to me, his face unshaven and unusually humorless.

"Your partner," he said.

"Hans?"

"Yeah. He sounds pretty grim."

"He always sounds grim," I said, and heard Dave mumble something about how goddamned hot it was as he headed back down to the galley.

"Travis here."

"We've got a situation, Mike." In the background I picked up the sounds of traffic.

"Where're you calling from?"

"Doesn't matter."

Alarm bells went off. "Go on."

"The two guys we visited on Sunday?"

"Yeah," I said. "What about 'em?"

"How were they when you left the house?"

Some type of large vehicle passed near wherever Hans was calling from, something like a bus. He cursed under his breath and I could almost see the exhaust billowing across the sidewalk and engulfing him.

"What the hell're you talking about?"

He clearly did not want to be too specific, even on a public phone. He only repeated himself. "How were they when you left? Health-wise."

I wasn't liking the direction this was taking. I especially didn't like the idea that Hans and I were reduced to speaking in euphemisms. But I trusted him like I trusted no one else on earth.

"Shaken, maybe," I said. "One of them was, uh, encumbered."

"Encumbered."

"Yes. Encumbered. Bound. Secured. Trussed." A rush of anxiety was eroding my patience with this.

"Okay, pard," he said. "Take it easy."

"What the fuck is this?"

There was a heavy silence on the other end. "I'm just asking you: were they *okay* when we left?"

I thought back to that afternoon, pictured it. "A cracked rib, a fat lip, a bruise or two."

"Roger Gaines phoned me a few minutes ago," Hans said. "There were two people found dead in that house yesterday afternoon."

"How?" I said. Waiting for the other shoe to drop.

"Two shots each. To the head. Twenty-five caliber. Execution style."

"Shit."

He didn't speak for several seconds, like he was framing what came next. "They found your prints inside the house."

At a minimum, I knew they'd be on the baseball bat and the cord I'd used to bind Ken Harrison's hands. What else had I touched?

"You hearing me?"

His words hit me like a hammer. "I'm a suspect."

"Not yet."

"Not yet?"

"Roger has it on pretty good authority that there could be photos. You and me in front of that house. He called me with a heads-up."

Fuck.

"Kemp," I said. "IAD."

I could almost hear Hans nodding on the other end.

My knuckles went white as I clutched the phone. I held it away from my ear and stared off toward shore, feeling the blood-heat run up my neck. I kicked the rubber bumper that hung from the railing.

"You still there?"

"Yes, I'm fucking here," I said. "What about you?"

"I'm all right," he said. "I was already ass-deep in alligators before any of this came down."

My mind raced, made a beeline of blame to my brother. A distinct wave of nausea came over me as I thought about how this would probably play out for Hans, and for Mie. Then the ifs. If only I had turned off my cell phone that day at Snyder's, or just let the fucker ring; if I had simply told Valden that his vagabond penis was his own goddamned problem.

"Are they bringing you in for questioning?" I asked him finally.

"Haven't come for me yet," he said. "But they will."

"I'll catch the next flight, Hans. I'll tell them you didn't even get out of the car."

"I don't think so, pard. Bad move."

"I'm not—"

"Right now, you're in a lot worse shape than I am. If Kemp wants my job, well fuck him, he can have it. My prints are nowhere near that house. But you?"

He didn't have to finish. He was right. If Kemp wanted to work out his long simmering hard-on for me and Hans, he might be able to get an indictment for murder. Retribution for his career-long dance with mediocrity. If they could indict a ham sandwich, they could sure as hell indict me given that my prints were all over the place, at the scene of an execution.

It would be a stretch, circumstantial at best, with no murder weapon linked to me. But if they somehow also had photos that could prove I'd been at that house anywhere near the time of death, it wouldn't be good at all. Even if Kemp's case ultimately fell apart, he'd have accomplished what he'd wanted to accomplish for a long, long time. He could take Hans down on appearances alone, and might just fuck me up enough that I could lose everything I'd ever built for myself. Setting aside the matter of monetary expense, the personal toll of defending against a capital indictment was astronomical. I knew Kemp, and the depth of his vindictiveness.

"There's no warrant out on me?" I asked.

"Not yet. And you need to hear me on this: it would make things much more difficult for them if they couldn't find you for a while."

"I've never run away in my life, Hans."

"It's not running. You live on a sailboat. So, sail."

"This is seriously fucked up."

"Let me reframe this for you in a language you might find more acceptable: If they can't find you for a few days, you'll actually be *assisting* in the investigation. You give IAD and Kemp nothing to grab hold of while the Homicide cops work the leads. No Travis, no distraction. You need to let Homicide build a case that does not include you. You hearing what I'm saying?"

He had a point. If I weren't around, Kemp wouldn't be able to drum up a circus that would obfuscate a useful investigation. They'd have to concentrate on actual cop work. Like ballistics and forensics and physical evidence. Like finding the actual fucking shooter.

"And what about you?"

"They were looking at me before you ever got here. It all has to play out one way or the other. It either goes away or it doesn't, know what I mean?"

Yes, I did. "You've got my e-mail address."

"Probably be better than phones for the time being," he agreed. "But let's keep it to a minimum."

I was reeling at the prospect of having betrayed my friend in the pursuit of my brother's interests. My visit to LA had been brief, and I had managed to squeeze in the commission of about ten felonies, but they hadn't included murder. I had never feared treading close to the line—or crossing it from time to time—but this clusterfuck had the potential to escalate into orders of magnitude I had no desire to contemplate.

"Goddamn, Hans."

"We'll push past it."

"Keep in touch. One word from you and you know I'm there."

"I know."

"Hans—"

"Gotta go, bud. Have a nice trip."

I stopped in at Snyder's bar to pick up my mail and to let him know I'd be gone for a while. Given that I live on a sailboat, Snyder allowed me to use the bar as my permanent address rather than renting a post-office box. It was a short walk from the pier, and it offered table service.

"Frosty beverage?" Lolly offered as I pushed through the saloon doors. Lolly Spencer was Snyder's right hand, and looked like she'd just stepped out of a Swedish fashion magazine.

I shook my head and she faked a pout.

Snyder came out from his office in back with a bundle of mail neatly wrapped inside a rolled-up magazine and tied with a rubber band.

"What's the rush?" he asked.

"A last-minute thing," I told him. "I don't know how long I'll be gone. Just toss my mail in a box."

I could see the wheels working behind his eyes.

"You look like ten pounds of bad news in a five-pound sack. I'm familiar with the look."

"No worries."

He seized my elbow in a grip that could crack macadamia nuts and pulled me into the back room. It was empty of customers at this hour, chairs still stacked on the tabletops. He slid the glass door shut behind us.

"Talk to me."

"I stepped in a turd on the mainland and tracked it back here."

"I know what it looks like when a man's ready to run, Mike. I've been that guy so don't bullshit me. That's all I'm saying."

I gave him the digest version, but didn't bother to sanitize it much. There was nobody I knew who was more closed-mouthed than Snyder, and that included Hans. It was all he needed to hear.

"Well your life just keeps getting more interesting all the time," he said. "They ought to put a fence around you."

"They just might."

"If you're taking off, I'm going with you."

"Yosemite's already aboard. I need to lay in a few groceries and we're gone. But thanks anyway."

Snyder pursed his lips and squinted into the glare as he looked out the window toward my mooring.

"I like Dave as much as the next man," he said. "But you know that guy is a bent arrow."

"He's a licensed boat captain."

He turned his attention back to me as he spoke. "He throws a good party, too, but that's not exactly a skill set that's real useful right now. You need somebody on your six, Mike."

My focus spun inward as I considered his words.

"Why are you looking at me like that?" he said. "I can still hump my own weight up a hill and back down again, and I can shoot the dick off a lizard with the firearm of your choosing. And by the way, I sailed solo all the way from Baja to Palmyra and on to Rarotonga before I ever met you. I know how a boat operates."

Sometimes Snyder said things that reminded me how little I really knew about him.

"You know I'm right," he pressed. "You do not defend the perimeter with a third-string squad. Been there before, too."

"I'm not defending anything. Only putting some space between me and a potential problem. A precautionary move."

"A distinction without a difference," he said, and showed

me a lupine smile. "I'll grab a few things and throw some groceries together. Meet me at the pier in thirty minutes and we'll go tell Dave he gets to stay home."

CHAPTER TWENTY-ONE

It was the time of day that May Ling had learned to dread most.

The pinpricks of light that shone through the tiny holes that years of rain and sun and neglect had eaten through the metal corrugation of the ceiling—would crawl ever so slowly across the floor with the changing angle of the sun, and ultimately disappear into darkness. This was the time when whatever semblance of order that existed among the soldiers eroded into anarchy. These were the terrible hours.

She had learned the names of the young family on that very first night, whispering to one another in the dark, fighting off the damp chill and the constant lurking terror. The father, a man she guessed to be about thirty, was called Jiang, and came from a village not far from Beijing. Together with his wife, Siu, and Djhou, their six-year-old son, Jiang had bribed petty officials, and endured hardships he would not have been able to imagine before, just for the chance to get to this place, and the prospect of transport to America. The smugglers' fees had been exorbitant, but Jiang had been promised they would be worked off, a little at a time, once they arrived at the Golden Mountain. He and Siu had communicated in hushed whispers for months, late into the night. The risk was enormous, and discovery—let alone capture—meant death for them all. Even the boy, Djhou. Ultimately, the choice became obvious, and the gamble had to be made. Anything was better than the future they faced in China. Jiang had been politically outspoken one time too often.

But the blind hope that had provided them the strength to get this far was draining away. May Ling could practically feel the despair that emanated from them all. Jiang fell in and out of consciousness. His eyes no longer focused properly and he slept almost constantly.

Now, as May Ling looked over at him, lying motionless on the concrete floor, she knew he wouldn't live out the day. Maybe with proper medical attention, but certainly not here. Not like this.

But that was far from the worst of it. May Ling was also aware that the guards had their eyes on the boy.

She looked on as Siu gently cradled her husband and envied the natural beauty of their affection. Though she judged that Siu was at least five years older than she, May Ling knew that whatever softness or comeliness she herself might have ever possessed had long since been abraded by the hard use she had suffered at the hands of Joey Soong. She was under no illusions as to what she had become.

May Ling had seen so many other girls come and go during her confinement in Hong Kong. Most of them had either been misused so badly that they died of their mistreatment, or contracted some vile disease that slowly, inexorably claimed their lives. Those that hadn't perished had been sold off and never heard from again. This, May Ling knew, is what had now happened to her. She had grown too old, too hard, and probably too unattractive, and she, too, had been sold. To whom, she didn't know, and it really didn't even matter.

But the boy, Djhou, needed her. He needed her strength, and if there was one thing May Ling had accumulated in her life, it was strength. He had reached out for May Ling in the aftermath of his father's injury. She could feel his fear through the tiny fingers that grasped onto her in the night, when the soldiers outside grew intoxicated and unruly. It felt good to be needed; it was a feeling she'd never truly known, and Djhou's mother was grateful for any help May Ling could provide.

Over the past three days the original band of refugees had been joined by a number of others. They had come in small groups of three to five, until the shed to which they were all restricted now housed two dozen or more. Mainly, the others were men, of an age similar to Jiang's. The old couple who had been so savagely murdered that first day were an oddity, and the few women remaining were either wives or sisters of fellow refugees, as was the case with Siu, or they were the wives of men who had gone before. Djhou was the only child—among them.

Now, as dusk faded to night, she studied the features on pathetic faces that slumped against the walls of the warehouse or wandered, stoop-shouldered, in aimless circles. The stink of their collective bodies, and the uncovered hole in the floor that served as their toilet, suffused the air with a gauzy haze that, together with the mist that floated in off the river, hung inside that space like a rank and fetid dream.

A metal door at the far end of the building opened with the squeal of rusted hinges, and woke any who had been fortunate enough to doze off. The flicker of a bonfire along the bank of the river framed the silhouettes of the same two thugs—May Ling refused to believe they could be legitimate soldiers—who had brutalized the old couple. Each carried a lantern fueled by kerosene, trailing a swath of heavy smoke, as they meandered through the enclosure.

Their eyes passed across May Ling's face, registered something that resembled contempt, but something else, too, before their attention focused on Siu. Jiang's head was nestled in Siu's lap as she ignored their leering stares, stroking her husband's blood-encrusted hair. A knowing look passed between the two men that left little doubt as to their intentions.

"Come," one said as he wagged his fingers at her, as one would to call a dog.

When Siu refused to look up from the face of her unconscious husband, the other arched back and planted a kick to Siu's foot.

"Come along."

May Ling willed Siu her strength, and pulled Djhou close as she watched the scene unfold. She knew well that to speak was to consign all three of them to a thrashing.

"I have my husband to care for," Siu said. There was curiously little fear in the tone of her voice.

The two men appeared surprised at first, but reverted to that same ugly expression they wore when they first stepped through the door. Their eyes were edgy and restless, limned in pink and wet with an alcohol shine.

"Then we'll take the boy," the guard said simply.

May Ling had no time to prepare herself for the sting of the sharp slap that stung her face, and echoed in the stillness of the room. Yellow lamplight reflected inside the expectant, cowardly eyes of the other refugees, and she knew they wanted nothing more than for this to be ended, for someone to surrender and give the overseers what they wanted.

With a kind of dignity that caught May Ling by surprise, Siu gently moved her husband's head from her lap and stood. Jiang lay immobile on the concrete, mercifully oblivious to his wife's willing sacrifice. Beside her, May Ling felt Djhou's fingers dig more deeply into her flesh.

The two guards shared a predatory smile, each holding fast to one of Siu's arms, and turned toward the door. She marched out between them without a backward glance. Their lanterns drew shadow patterns along the far wall as they departed, all eyes fixed to the floor but for May Ling's and Djhou's. May Ling could not decide who she hated more in that moment: these pirates that held them captive or the cowards who sat in their own filth and did nothing at all.

As the metal door slammed shut, May Ling began to sing, softly at first, only for Djhou—her eyes passing between the boy and his father who lay beside them unaware—then louder so that she might drown out the unbearable noises that began to drift in from outside.

CHAPTER TWENTY-TWO

It was after five o'clock in the afternoon, and I had a choice to make: either put in for the night at Kawaihae Harbor, or brazen it out and remain on a heading for Maui.

Snyder and I talked it over and decided to let common sense prevail; it was too long a leg to risk running through the darkness in the unpredictable seas of the Alenuihaha Channel. So we trimmed the sails and put in at the harbor on the northwest end of the Big Island.

I had spent the last three hours tossing everything I could think of that I might have taken with me to Los Angeles over the side. Every fifteen minutes or so, I thoroughly shredded every shirt, my jacket, and even my shoes, into pieces no larger than a stick of gum and let them sink into the sea.

Out of fairness to Snyder, I had filled him in on my situation, omitting only the elements of detail that could still compromise my brother. It wasn't as much about protecting myself as it would be better protection for Snyder if he knew as little as possible when the shit came raining down.

The last thing to go under was my cell phone. I crushed it beneath the heel of my deck shoe, extracted the memory card and tossed the whole mess overboard.

Snyder watched me without judgment as the last of the evidence of my trip to the mainland slipped beneath the surface and disappeared into our wake.

"You're feeling like a chickenshit right about now, aren't you?" he said.

"Yes, I am."

"Well, stop it."

I leaned on folded arms against the railing and watched the harbor grow nearer off the starboard beam. I was thinking that perhaps the greatest illusion in our lives is that we have control over anything.

"I wish it was that easy, Snyder."

"It is that easy. You want to know how a person quits smoking?" he said. "He stops putting cigarettes in his mouth."

It had been several hours since I'd left my last message on the old-school answering machine Lani still had connected to her landline at home, and I was beginning to grow concerned. I debated, but only for a moment, sending an e-mail so that she would at least know I was okay. But that would likely only make things worse. I logged off the satellite feed and watched the screen go blue. I checked the strength of the cell signal on Snyder's phone. Still nothing. Cell service had been nonexistent since we'd rounded Kaiwi Point.

"No bars on the phone?" Snyder asked as I handed the phone back to him.

I shook my head and went inside to the cooler to grab another beer. I dug around in the ice until I got one by the neck, dragged it out, dripping cold water all over my feet. I used the opener that was screwed to the bulkhead and caught the cap as it fell away. I tossed it into the Coleman.

"Need to put another case in there," I said. "More ice, too."

Snyder went below and came up a couple minutes later with more beer, and took a chilled one for himself before he dropped in the new ones.

I was sitting in the captain's chair, my feet propped on the wheel and the bottom of a cold bottle imprinting wet circles on my shirt. I watched the blinking lights at the crown of the cargo crane as it loomed over the container ship that was pressing its bulk against the commercial pier and tried to figure why anyone other than Valden would want those two blackmailers killed. Still, Valden had known it was over, he'd practically skipped-rope down the hallway of the Mandalay Plaza when I had told him as much. But no one needed to remind me that fear is the human emotion that could drive the most extreme and bizarre of behaviors. It was unsettling to entertain the idea that my own brother might have actually ordered the hit, and in the process placed us both in the crosshairs. Despite the tension that existed in our relationship, Valden was anything but a fool. He had proven himself to be vicious when he felt threatened or backed into a corner. Having someone killed was not entirely out of the question. It was also not something I wanted to contemplate. The next few days would tell, and all I had to do was to stay off the radar.

"Nice night," Snyder said as he reclined on the stern banquette and looked heavenward. I swiveled the chair toward where he sat, and nodded.

"I checked the weather for tomorrow," I said. "Looks good to make Maui."

Snyder shifted his focus to the weather vane on the mast, then back down the coast toward Kona. "South swell. A nice cross if it holds."

"Things going to be okay at the bar?" I asked.

He waved it away.

"Fuck it, Mike. Lolly knows what she's doing."

We sat for long minutes in the quiet night, not speaking a word; the only sounds were the slap of the tide along the waterline and the popping of taut ropes against the masts. My mind drifted. To the south of us, down the coast, was nothing but darkness. The crenellated outline of the point displayed itself in silhouette against the blue-black sky, the lights of Kona town only a dim incandescence in the distance. To the north, a dusting of stars hovered over the wide channel that separated the Big Island and Maui, and the moon was a silver crescent hovering over the horizon.

Kehau swung around on her anchor and a breeze cast a lock of hair into my eyes. I swept it back with my fingers and looked over at Snyder.

"So, what now, Travis?" he asked.

Damned if I knew.

Later that night we were in *Kehau*'s salon, watching *Apocalypse Now* on DVD, tired of thinking, tired of talking.

The last thing I remember before I nodded off was Duvall's voice coming down from the chopper, calling out over the bullhorn for Lance to give his stolen surfboard back. By the time I opened my eyes again, they were dropping Frederic Forrest's head in Martin Sheen's lap.

I blinked my eyes into focus and located Snyder, asleep on the couch with a book propped open on his chest. I yawned, stretched myself out of my chair and worked at a kink in my neck. I let the movie run while I inspected the length of the boat, and made my way to the bow for one final check on the lie of the anchor. It struck me then, as it happened sometimes, when my subconscious went to work on a psychic knot. I looked down into the black water, where the anchor chain disappeared into the darkness, and I knew what the first of the big questions was, and where I needed to start.

I went below and fired up the laptop. I had a new target in mind.

I punched up the Mandalay Plaza on my browser, read every word of every page that came up, but still didn't find what I was after. A few keystrokes later, I was logged on to the site for the *LA Times,* working my way through the archives until I came across the first of several articles that mentioned the opening of the new hotel.

I scrolled back in time, through datelines some three years earlier, about the same time I had begun my retirement in Avalon, and I found what I had been seeking. It was an article written by Bob Childers, a *Times* staff writer. The headline read, "Luxury Hotel Breaks Ground Near Music Center," and there below the bold type was the obligatory photo of a chorus line of businessmen wearing suits and spotless construction hard hats, and clutching the handles of ceremonial shovels in their fists. But it was the sidebar piece that caught my attention:

A BRIEF CONVERSATION WITH
PHILLIP LENNOX

By Bob Childers, Times Staff Writer

It is a quiet spring day at the Lennox estate, the kind of day that could make you believe Phillip Lennox controls even the weather. I am greeted at the door by a uniformed butler straight out of Central Casting, and led to the "Lower Garden," where Mr. Lennox awaits me. He is dressed in a fawn-colored linen suit, a yellow-on-blue Parisian tie, and a starched shirt the color of the sky. There is a predictably firm handshake and a brief exchange of pleasantries before I am reminded I have been granted only fifteen minutes.

"I'm a self-made man," he begins emphatically.

"You built your company on your own," I repeat.

"I didn't say that," he answers with a smile in his gray eyes. "I've had many people assist me in very meaningful ways over the years. What I said was that I was self-made. Nobody gave me anything. Everything you see around you, I created out of nothing."

These are the sorts of statements you'll hear often from biopharmaceutical magnate Phillip Lennox. He is quick to point out his humble upbringing, and the absence of a university degree. He is a proud—though mainly benevolent—dictator in the corporate world he has created, and he does little apologizing.

"I do a great deal of work for both charitable and political causes," he states in a tone that suggests you'd better do your own homework to understand the magnitude of the understatement. And when you do, you discover the tens of millions that have been spent on political concerns, and amounts of a similar size to establish the Lennox Foundation, a charity whose primary concern is the fight against communicable diseases. But Lennox makes no bones about his feelings on capitalism.

"I have always stood behind the right of every American to make a dollar. To make as many dollars as one's desires may determine. That is the American way, and anything that undermines it should be fought tooth and nail."

As for politics, he is nothing, if not equally direct: "Congress must be made to act in a way that is consistent with the intent of the architects of the constitution, and to defend ourselves on the battlefield of the global marketplace."

A great deal of military allusion peppers any conversation with Lennox, an army veteran. "Everything is war," he says seriously. "To imagine one's daily conflicts in any other terms will ultimately undercut the probability of success. It is far too easy for complacency and lassitude to creep into a culture, whether a social culture or a corporate one; so every conflict is war, every war a call to reinvigorate your commitment to the cause: and my cause is success."

Which compelled me to ask the question: Isn't there more to life? Is financial success really everything?

"Success is who I am. To paraphrase Lombardi," he says with the now-familiar Lennox smile, "it's the *only* thing."

My heart was beating faster as I finished reading. I checked my dive watch for the time; a little after one o'clock in the morning. Even with New York five hours ahead of me, I knew it was still too early to catch Thel Mishow—the only attorney I've ever met that I actually trusted—at his office, so I banged out an e-mail and asked Thel to get back to me, first thing.

I turned my attention back to the movie that was still playing on my TV screen in time to see the ox as it gets slaughtered from five different angles. And by the time Sheen pulled away from the Kurtz compound I was powering down the laptop, knowing that sleep would not come easily.

CHAPTER TWENTY-THREE

I awakened to a sapphire sky so rich and deep in hue it invited me to rethink my views on the subject of infinity. It was a fleeting moment in the islands that sometimes preceded false dawn. The slopes of Mauna Loa rose steeply from the coastline and were cast in shallow relief, like a child's scissored cutout held before a duvetyn backdrop.

I carried my mug of tea up to the afterdeck, where I found Snyder seated in the captain's chair, lost in thought. He looked as though he had been there for some time already. He acknowledged me with the briefest of nods as I took up a place on the bench, and returned his attention toward the heavens.

"The blue hour," he said, under his breath. I wasn't sure if he was talking to me or to himself.

"Say again," I said.

"The blue hour," he said again, softly, as if not to disturb the morning. "L'heure bleue. That's what they called it back in Indian Country. It never lasts long."

I watched him as he squinted into the distance. The breeze coming down off the volcano was gentle, but cold, and I wrapped both hands around the mug to collect the heat as Snyder spoke of having stood watch along the wire in the jungles of Vietnam.

"It was the only time of morning when things seemed still, the line of demarcation between the nightly flop-sweat terror you spent staring into the dark while you waited for Chuck to pop up out of the elephant grass and light up your shit—between that and the beginning of another day. But the Blue Hour was peace. No promises, man. Just peace, if only for a few fucking minutes."

I left him alone with his thoughts, went below to the galley and brewed a fresh pot of Kona coffee. It looked like he could use it. The mystical azure had already leeched from the sky by the time I came back, and the haunted expression that had inhabited his features was fading away along with it. But his eyes remained hollow and bloodshot, like those of a man who had emerged from a house fire, as I handed him the steaming cup.

We were midway through Alenuihaha Channel, halfway to Maui, when a call came through on Snyder's phone. He glanced at the number on the screen and passed the phone to me. Snyder took over at the helm and I went below, out of the wind and sea spray, to talk.

"Travis," I said. My own voice bounced back to me a full second later, a familiar long distance echo as the signal reflected off the satellite somewhere far overhead.

"Mike? This is Thel Mishow." His voice was warm, and exuded paternal competence. "I'm returning your call."

"Thanks for getting back to me," I said.

"Haven't heard from you lately."

I thought back to my retirement party, the last time I had seen him face to face. "It's been a long while."

There were several seconds of silence, and I thought I'd lost the connection. "You still there?"

"Yes, yes," he said. "Sorry, Mike. Just thinking how I've lost track of you boys."

My father had been one of Thel's first clients. Thel had been a young hotshot attorney with a highbrow New York firm specializing in mergers, acquisitions and corporate law. As Van de Groot Capital had grown, so had Thel's practice, and on the twin strengths of VGC's business and my father's friendship, Thel had taken a leap of faith and gone out on his own. As far as I knew, he had always been the family's attorney, so I was surprised to hear him say he'd lost track of my brother.

"You haven't spoken to Valden?"

His laugh was dry, humorless. "Not since he fired the firm."

"I don't—"

"Your father was a good man, Mike," Thel interrupted. "How you must miss him."

I thought about my father then, the way he had been before my mother drowned in the bay at Hōnaunau. Everything had changed after that, something missing in him as if my mother had taken it with her. He never looked at me or my brother the same way again. I had been thirteen that terrible summer, and Valden two years older than I.

"Yes, sir, I do," I said. "I miss him a great deal."

"Listen to you," he said. "Still with the 'sir' business."

"Old habits," I said. "Can't seem to get used to calling you by your first name."

"Well, we don't need to reminisce. What can I do for you?"

"I need some information on a piece of real estate in Los Angeles."

I heard New York City noises from the other end of the line, the whoop of sirens on the street far below his office window. "What kind of information?"

"Ownership. Title. That sort of thing."

"You know it's most likely owned in the names of

partnerships, corporations, LLCs. You want a title search all the way up the line?"

"As far as you can go until you bump into actual human beings," I said. "I need names."

Kehau rolled under my feet and I reached out a hand for balance, the other continuing to press the phone firmly to my ear.

"Could take a bit of time, Mike," he said. "These things can get pretty tangled. How soon do you need it?"

"As soon as possible. Hours, not weeks."

"I promise you that we'll move as fast as the paper trail allows," he said. There was a moment's hesitation, and the shuffle of papers on his desk. "Fire away."

"The Mandalay Plaza Hotel," I said. "Los Angeles."

"I know the place, fairly new?"

"Three years plus or minus."

"I'll get back to you as soon as I have something. Shall I use this same number?"

The wind caught the crest of a breaking swell and sent a cloud of white spray across the bow. Mist floated through the open window.

"I appreciate it, Thel."

"I know you do," he said. Then, almost as an afterthought, "You are your father's son, Mike." Melancholy laced his voice.

"Thank you." I smiled. There had been times when I wasn't sure either of us—my dad or I—would have considered that a compliment. I took it as one now, as it had been intended.

"Any time," he said, and the line went dead in my ear.

The boat yawed and I felt her roll at an odd angle. I went to the stairs and called up to Snyder at the helm. "What's going on up there?"

"Wind's shifting on me."

I ascended the stairway and got my visual bearings. We had almost made it into the lee of the island, and I knew that until we did, the wind would whip around from the east and give us a steady chop for the next few miles. Once we got through it, the smoother southern swell would carry us straight up the coastline.

"Keep your heading," I said. "I've got another couple calls to make."

"Take your time, Hoss. I got this."

I dialed the New York number for VGC's head office, looking for my brother. After working my way through the various barriers of bullshit that it took to get through to his desk, he finally came on the line.

"Can we make this quick?" he began. "I've got people waiting."

"There's been a complication," I told him. "Two people connected with that situation in LA have been found dead."

"Dead? How?"

"Shot in the head, execution style."

"What's this got to do with me? I certainly didn't kill anybody."

"Can you think of a reason why anyone would? Other than you."

"What? Are you kidding? Those people are—were—criminals."

"Not all criminals take a bullet to the back of the head in their own homes, Valden."

"They damn well should."

I waited a few seconds and concentrated on my breathing.

"I'm concerned about blowback."

The line hummed with silence. I could picture him there at his desk with the view facing out over the river, processing the threat. "How do you mean?"

"I mean that both Hans and I had been at the scene beforehand, Valden. My prints are in there."

"Well, you're not going to mention why you were there, are you?"

I tried to remember back when we were kids, to a time when he didn't put every situation into a context that placed himself at the center of it.

I felt the heat rising again.

"I need you to listen carefully to what I'm saying," I said slowly. "It's very conceivable that Hans could lose his job. It's also conceivable that I could be implicated, even formally charged, with the murders."

"We'll need to get you a good lawyer, then. This whole thing is absurd."

"I don't want a goddamned lawyer, Valden. What I want is for you to think about whether you know of any reason, any possible reason, that someone would kill the very same people who were blackmailing you. You can see how this looks, and I will choose to continue to believe in your innocence. Just know that this could blow up into an All-Universe Goatfuck in the time it takes you to wind your Rolex."

"You think there's a risk the details could still come out?" His voice had gone an octave higher.

It was well within the realm of possibility that the investigation, particularly if Homicide elected to focus on my presence at the scene, would uncover the blackmail attempt. If that happened, the motive component would look like a slam dunk. Means and opportunity were already in the bag.

"I'm doing what I can to prevent that, Valden."

"Jesus," he sighed. "I thought this thing was over."

"There's more at stake here than your reputation and marital status, now."

"The shit never ends," he said.

I had to hang up soon. My brother's self-absorption was

pissing me off. "Please give it some thought, Valden. If you come up with anything, or think of anyone else who might have had a similar problem. Anything at all, you call me." I gave him Snyder's number.

"Jesus, Mike, what a day. What a fucked-up day."

The conversation was over.

Outside the galley window, off to starboard, was the Maui shoreline; to port, and slightly northwest of us, was the island of Kahoolawe. As we sailed a reach farther into the island's lee, the wind grew more orderly and the disorganized swell diminished to that of a mountain lake. The low rumble of waves that broke along the sun-bleached coast drifted back to my ears, driven by the breeze. The smell of salt brine and the white smoke ascending from heaps of smoldering sugarcane slash laced the air.

Snyder was standing shirtless at the helm as we made the gap between Molokini and Maui. The wide mouth of Kihei Bay carved deeply into a valley planted with cane fields that stretched like green velvet all the way from the beach to the base of Haleakala. I was working the belt sander again, in an effort to remove the last remnants of the cigarette-burn souvenir that had been left on the gunwale and the conversation I'd had with my brother.

Having finally sanded my way through the worst of it, I heaved myself up off the deck, my knees popping audibly. I rolled up the electrical cable and stowed it below in the engine room, brought up a can of teak finish and a rag.

The wind whistled through the rigging and pulled the ropes taut with the whine of stretched linen.

Snyder looked up into the sails as they billowed against a crystal sky, then back toward the hazy purple shadow of Mauna Kea in the distance.

A lone gray dorsal broke the surface off the port bow. Several seconds later, a dozen more appeared close behind. A pod of spinner dolphins. I went to the railing and leaned over, watched as they sliced through the crystal blue water where the *Kehau* cleaved and displaced the sea with her hull.

"In another life," I said.

"I know what you mean."

"Beautiful. Damn."

He nodded, and a tide of something bitter washed through his eyes. "Rosie's working to get some restrictions on the tuna boats."

"The seiners?"

"Yeah," he said. "Mostly Japanese and Korean net boats working outside the limit. They scoop up entire pods of dolphins when they get mixed in with the tuna schools."

"They're supposed to let them loose."

"You know that's bullshit, Mike," he said. "They kill 'em more often than not. Most of the time, they're crushed under the weight of a net full of tuna anyway. Or drowned before they're ever hauled in."

I looked back over the side, watched a juvenile dolphin break the surface and execute a playful airborne spin. It was said their intelligence was superior to humans', and that scientists had actually made progress deciphering their communications among one another.

"I don't know, Snyder," I said. "I don't know why the hell we do the things we do."

"Who?"

"People," I said. "All of us. Everything we touch, we fuck it up or try to kill it."

"What's the old saying: 'They know the price of everything, but the value of nothing.'"

We both watched in silence, saw the dolphins weave in and

out of the wake we created. Then, on some cue unheard by Snyder or me, the dolphins peeled off from beneath the bow and headed back toward the bay as one.

I looked at Snyder, his eyes still tracking the pod as it moved off.

"You gotta do what you can, though."

I watched their dorsals grow smaller in the widening distance, until finally, I couldn't see them at all.

"Roger that, brother," I said.

CHAPTER TWENTY-FOUR

The bar smelled like low tide.

The odor of mildew and stale beer clung to the air inside, but the drinks were cold, and it was relatively quiet compared to the inebriated tourist chaos out on Front Street.

I had originally intended to heave-to in some little noname bay on the leeward side a few miles south of town. Then I thought, to hell with it, sometimes the best place to remain invisible is in plain sight, a needle in a stack of needles. Besides, I believed that both Snyder and I badly needed some distraction from the storms that were gathering strength inside our heads. By the time the sun had descended to a point just over the yardarm, I'd made arrangements to tie up at the guest dock in Lahaina Harbor, locked up the boat, and walked the few blocks along the seawall toward the Lahaina Beach Club.

A couple of Absolut-on-the-rocks later, I felt better prepared to face the crowds and sample some of the barbecued ribs whose smoky aroma had been drifting across the lanai from the restaurant next door.

There was a twenty-minute wait for a table, so we took the last two seats at the bar and listened to the bartender make personal calls between bouts of ragging on his wait staff. In the far corner, a puffy-looking guy wearing a faded black T-shirt strummed a guitar and sang an endless stream of Gordon Lightfoot, Seals & Crofts, and Air Supply; a selection of seventies-lite folk/rock that made me want to shove an ice pick into my ear.

"Oh, my God," Snyder said for both of us. "That has to fucking stop."

At the opposite end of the bar, a trio of sunburned coeds sucked at straws that protruded from glassware that was big enough to soak your feet in. They laughed and flicked at their hair in that way that was both youthful and entirely self-conscious.

Snyder watched the girls play with their fruit garnish, which had been artfully impaled on long wooden sticks, one of them performing the ever-popular cherry-stem trick, using her tongue to twist it into a knot while the others looked on expectantly.

"How long ago was that?" he asked.

I shook my head. "Gets a little further out of focus every day."

"Doesn't feel like it sometimes."

"No," I agreed. "It doesn't. And at other times, it feels like it happened to somebody else."

The guitar player stopped momentarily, then adjusted his mic and launched into a particularly grating imitation of Cat Stevens. Snyder squeezed his eyes shut when the college girls began to sing along. I was surprised they knew the song at all.

"Just when you thought it couldn't get any worse," I said, and tossed some cash on the bar.

The foot traffic on that end of Front Street was heavy, so we ducked up one of the side streets and cut over to a place I knew called the Blue Max, and walked in through the back door. The riffraff hadn't discovered it yet tonight, so it was only about two-thirds full, mostly locals, and we took a deuce along the second-story rail that overlooked the street. Snyder stepped over to the bar for a couple of after-dinner beers as the sound system rolled out something old and pleasantly familiar by Steve Stills and Manassas. I just sat there and tried to forget what might be waiting for me out there, somewhere below the horizon. Whatever it was, I knew it would still be there in the morning.

Snyder returned to the table about the time the three college girls drifted in, all loose limbs and giggles, daddy's credit card doing some heavy lifting. The willowy blonde looked like the kind of trouble the two brunettes didn't even know about. She scoped the place with one pass and headed for a four-top a couple tables away from Snyder and me.

"Your girlfriends are here," Snyder deadpanned as he set the beers on the table.

"Outstanding," I said, and turned my attention to my beer.

Snyder lifted his glass, tilted it toward me.

"Better days," he said.

The beer was icy and the breeze drifting in off the water cooled my skin. I looked out across the channel, watched the torchlights flicker and the outline of Molokai roil and change shape inside the heat waves they threw off.

"I'm Anna," the voice said. The blonde appeared as if from nowhere, standing beside my chair and offering her hand.

"Mike," I said. I shook her hand and looked across the table. "And this is Snyder."

She let go, stumbled a little as she leaned across the table to shake Snyder's hand. Anna gave us a wet and glassy smile. "We saw you guys at that other place."

"The Broiler," I said.

"Right," she said with certainty, and stood there like she was waiting for more.

"Listen, I—"

"That's Trish over there," she interrupted, pointing to one of the girls at her table. "And *that* is Megan."

Her friends looked embarrassed, then waved.

"Nice to meet you ladies," I said. "Hope you girls have a nice time."

A four-piece band took the stage and began tuning up, while Snyder and I avoided further eye contact with our new friends. Snyder was about to say something when I heard his cell phone ring. He tossed it to me without even looking at it, but I recognized the number and nearly pulled it apart in my haste to pry it open.

It was Lani.

Bar sounds and the noisy laughter of drunk young girls filled my end of the line.

I put a finger in one ear, struggled to hear Lani's voice as I made my way from the table and down the stairs to the street to find a quiet place to talk.

"I got your messages," she said. "Whose number is this?"

"Snyder's."

"Do I even want to know why I'm not supposed to call you on your own phone?"

"I had to ditch mine," I said. "I need you to listen carefully, Lani. Something came up when I was in LA, and it might not be good. I can't say anything more about it. I just need you to trust that I'm doing the right thing here. I can't be at home, and I can't tell you where I'm going. But I'll be back as soon as I can."

"Why do I feel like we keep having this same conversation?" Her voice was calm, like drifting ice.

"I've got to take care of this thing," I said.

Lani made a chuffing sound as the band upstairs ripped into an old Stones song. "Where are you?"

"I'd really rather not say."

There was silence on the line then, a thick and heavy thing

that lasted too long. "You know, for a good guy, Mike, you can really be an asshole."

A part of me wished like hell that I could take the chance, to tell her the whole story, tell her now, but even half in the bag, I knew it was impossible, even dangerous.

"I'll stay in touch as best I can," I said.

"I want you to know something," she started, but her voice caught. She cleared her throat and began again. "I'm not a jealous woman, Mike. I'm barely even angry. But you scare the hell out of me sometimes. I'm not scared for myself, but for you. The shitty things people do are not your fault. They're not all your responsibility to fix. But it's always like this, always so much chaos. All this secrecy and turmoil. I don't understand what you're doing, where you're going. Or even why."

"I need you to trust me. I can't say anything more right now."

"I know. You already said that."

A young couple glanced at me, leaning there against the wall, phone pressed to my ear. Their faces were relaxed, vacation faces, reddened by a day on the sand. I wondered for a split second what it was like to feel the way they felt, to have never fired a weapon at another human being, never had the explosion of a shotgun shred your flesh, never have felt the flames of a riot at your back or the whistle of a bullet past your ear.

"I'll see you when I get back, Lani," I said.

"I don't know if I can do this."

The line went dead.

I squeezed the phone to the brink of snapping it in two, barely checked myself from throwing it against the wall. There was a strong pulse in my temples as I looked back across the street, and I felt my storm inching closer, creeping up over that dark horizon.

* * *

I made my way back to the boat, leaving Snyder at the Blue Max to fend for himself. There was no escape for me that night, not even with booze and loud music to drown out the echoes in my head.

I had knocked back just enough alcohol to feel morose, reliving every goddamned misstep I'd taken, every bad decision I'd made—a bad trip on the best of days. So I walked alone down Front Street, along the seawall, back toward the harbor. I thought about old cases, about the pedophiles and the wife beaters, the rapists and crackheads, the dealers and stone killers.

And I walked.

I looked at the faces of the civilians I passed. That's how I still thought of them: civilians. I looked into their faces and saw their lives, the kids and car payments, the mortgages and maxed-out credit cards. I saw the in-laws and the unpaid loans, tight white skirts and tennis lessons, liquor bottles and lipstick stains.

And I walked.

I flashed on that last raw conversation I'd had with J.R. Lennox—the money and the name, but an emptiness so vast it should have its own zip code. That image still haunted me, like a mirror reflection from a past that never happened, and I realized he'd probably trade places with any of the people on Front Street tonight. Even me.

I walked past the jewelry stores and T-shirt shops, past the restaurants and bars. I passed a hundred different couples: couples with kids, couples on their honeymoons, couples with gray hair, couples with red faces, chubby legs and baggy shorts.

I was almost back to the dock, alongside the Pioneer Inn, when the phone rang inside my pocket. I willed it to be Lani, calling to take another stab at our aborted conversation.

"Lani," I said. "Listen, I—"

"Travis," the male voice said. "Check your computer." And hung up.

I ran for the boat, threw open the companionway hatch, went to my nav table and fired up the laptop. I paced the floor as the computer went through its startup crap, then finally logged on to the server and opened my mailbox. It was from Hans:

> PD report available courtesy RG, copy attached. Jeff Johnston is lead. Rat photos unavailable as yet. RG will scan and send when possible. Kemp moving under the radar. Happy sailing. Talk later. H.

There were dozens of questions I wanted to write back, but limited myself to a few equally cryptic comments. I told him I was working on some background of my own, and I'd fill him in if anything started to pop.

I downloaded the file he had attached and read through the contents.

Crime scene photos were among what Hans had sent, courtesy of Roger Gaines, so it took me a minute to realize the "rat photos" he mentioned were surveillance shots rumored to have been taken of Hans and me at the victims' house. Gaines and Hans were going way out on a limb if they were willing to track those pictures down and scan them over.

I looked at the scene photos first.

They showed both victims facedown on the floor, heads lying in viscous black pools. Both had their hands tied behind their backs. They'd been kneeling when the bullets bored into their brainpans.

The photos that didn't focus on the victims themselves showed every room in the house, taken from a number of different angles. I parsed through them all, seeing that place again, room by room. It was in the same condition it had been in when I'd left, right down to the mess I'd made of the computer system in the back room.

I studied the victims one last time before I moved on to the text.

The bodies had been discovered by one of their girlfriends after he failed to show up for a coffee date Monday morning. She called 9-1-1 from the house, and had been found vomiting on the front lawn by the time the responding officers arrived.

Cause of death was listed as two .25 caliber bullets to the back of each victim's head. There were no exit wounds, as the bullets were still lodged inside of their respective skulls, and the little finger of each one's right hand had been severed.

A preliminary search of the premises showed indications of a struggle, certain electronic equipment having been smashed and/or stolen. There was no other evidence of robbery, though both victims were missing driver's licenses from wallets that otherwise still contained credit cards and cash. No murder weapon was recovered at the scene.

A canvass of the neighborhood revealed nothing out of the ordinary, other than a report of what might have been an altercation, said altercation being heard by a next-door neighbor in the early hours of Sunday afternoon. The neighbor placed the time at somewhere between one and three o'clock, but was unable to be more precise.

A number of fingerprints had been collected at the scene, and processing was continuing as of the time the report had been written. There was some additional blah, blah, blah, that I knew I'd return to later, but I'd read what I needed for the time being. This was clearly a professional hit, either perpetrated by unknown accomplices to the blackmail, or contractors associated with my brother. Or a cop.

I shut the laptop and went up on deck, looked back at the

street life in Lahaina, let the wind clear my mind. I stood there on the fantail, listening as the sounds of a bygone whaling town morphed into the commercial tumult of its own future. Masthead pennants popped and rigging sang, and the sea broke against the seawall as it had for hundreds of years. But now, amplified music blared from car stereos, and the thrum of an endless line of internal combustion engines rumbled over the same streets that had once been rutted by the narrow wheels of horse-drawn carriages. Potted ferns grew in hanging planters, nailed to the beams and rafters of saloons where drunken whalers had once exchanged musket fire and the sudden slash of knives.

I had begun pacing *Kehau*, wondering why there had been no mention of my prints at the crime scene, nor any mention of surveillance photos of Hans and me, when Snyder ambled down the ramp.

"Where'd you get off to, bud?"

"Phone call," I said. "Had to take it outside."

He weaved slightly, standing there on the dock looking up at me.

"You coming aboard?" I asked him.

Snyder shook his head, shrugged, and moved aft to climb the ladder. I held out a hand to steady him, and assisted him over the transom. He landed stiff-legged on the rear deck, and I saw that he was in worse shape than I'd first thought.

Snyder looked at me, something hidden behind his beery eyes. He backed himself up to the captain's chair and sat himself in it.

"Mind if I make an observation?" he asked.

"Why not?"

"You're stuck between worlds, my man. I know the look, and I am familiar with the symptoms. I've been there."

"And?"

"Look around," he said, gesturing broadly toward the open ocean. "There's a reason people like you and me choose to live in a place like this. A place with a two-thousand-mile moat around our houses. Hell, man, you don't even have a house. Your whole life is surrounded by water."

"What's your point, Snyder?"

"We are not the kind of people who appreciate shit sneaking up on us."

He crossed his arms and leaned back into the chair. He closed his eyes for a few seconds and smiled to himself. "How about a nightcap?"

"I can't imagine that will help either of us," I said.

"Don't see how it'll do any harm, either. What's it going to do, put you in a bad mood? You're already there, and you're all by yourself."

He had a point. I reached into the Coleman and pulled two bottles from the ice and uncapped them.

"You finished with your observations already?" I asked. "Pretty pithy for a bartender."

"I was not speaking as a bartender. I was speaking as a man who has walked a mile in your flip-flops, bud."

"Then let's hear it."

He leaned forward, elbows resting on his knees.

"You want peace in your world, but you can't handle injustice. You want a life with Lani, but you're afraid all the shit from your other life will follow you through the door. So what do you do, right?"

I took a long pull from the bottle and listened. I couldn't argue with what he'd said.

"You either stand still and let Darwin have his way," he continued. "Or you put the boots on their throats, drop the shit where it belongs and pull the chain."

"Full throttle or fuck it."

"That's what I'm saying."

We drank for a while in silence and listened to the night.

"Thanks for the use of your phone," I said finally. I withdrew it from my pocket and held it out to him.

"I don't need it right now," he said. "You hang on to it. It's making your life miserable, and I don't want it."

"We're both going to need new numbers when this thing is over."

He nodded and that faraway expression took over his face again.

"You're a good man, Mike Travis," he said. Then he nodded to himself, confirming his judgment. He stood and slow-motioned his way down the stairwell, through the galley and into his stateroom below.

CHAPTER TWENTY-FIVE

The offices of Dunross, Frankel & Wood occupied the top two floors of a modern high-rise off Ala Moana Boulevard.

It had been three days since we'd left Lahaina behind and sailed into Honolulu, and Thel Mishow had finally been able to dig up the information I'd asked for regarding the ownership of the Mandalay Plaza Hotel. Thel had always been a stickler for caution, one of the traits that my father had valued most, so he'd contacted a friend of his and set up an office for me at a law firm here in town.

The air-conditioning felt severe, coming as I had from the humidity of outdoors, so I paced the koa-paneled lobby as much to keep warm as to kill time. I was admiring a Jan Kasprzycki nightscape of Diamond Head, an orange swirl of sunset giving way to the city lights of Waikiki, when I heard high heels clicking across the hardwood floor behind me.

I turned and faced her, a green-eyed redhead with a dusting of freckles across a creamy complexion. She was in her late thirties, I figured, and wore a nicely tailored blazer over a matching skirt and beige blouse that was all business. The silk scarf she wore tucked beneath the lapels of her jacket bore an Oriental pattern, but the color set off her eyes and seemed to underscore the distance from her Celtic gene pool.

"Mr. Travis?"

I confirmed that I was, and followed her into an elegantly appointed office that offered a view out across the wide avenue and overlooked the city park that traced the edge of a long stretch of beach. Her desk reflected the red patina of cherrywood, its surface occupied by neat stacks of documents and file folders. She ignored the ringing of her office phone as she closed the door behind us.

"We sweep these offices twice a month," she began without preamble.

"Good to know."

She searched my face for sarcasm and found none.

"Still, you can never be too careful," she said. "Did you bring a checkbook?"

Always prepared for a shakedown in a lawyer's office. "Yes."

"Please make out a check for $100."

I looked at her.

"Just do it. One hundred dollars even. And be sure to note 'legal services' in the memo section."

I did as she asked, tore it from the book and passed her the check.

"Congratulations," she smiled for the first time since I'd met her. "You've just retained the services of Dunross, Frankel & Wood. Everything you say from this point on is protected, understand?"

"Attorney-client privilege."

She nodded, and held out her hand. "I'm Patricia Dunross."

Her grip was firm, but not overbearing.

"Mike Travis."

She took a seat in the black leather chair behind her desk, and I pulled up a matching one across from her. An assistant came through the door carrying a cup of black tea and placed it on a saucer in front of me, then left without a word.

"Thel Mishow speaks very highly of you," Dunross said, once the door had closed again. "Mind if I ask you a question?"

"I'll let you know."

"What's your connection with Van de Groot Capital?"

I smiled, the question being a variation on a familiar theme. "Why do you ask?"

She shrugged. "You don't look like any New York venture capitalist I ever met before."

"I'm a shareholder. My brother runs the company. Too many type-A personalities in the kitchen, and all that."

Patricia Dunross leaned back in the big chair and smiled like she didn't quite believe me. "Valden Van de Groot is your brother?"

"Afraid so."

"I never would have guessed."

"Thank you."

Her laugh was natural and erased years from an already youthful face.

"May I ask you a question?" I said.

She leaned back into the chair again. "Try me."

"What kind of law do you practice?"

"Me personally? Or the firm?"

I glanced around Patricia Dunross's office, took in the original artwork that decorated the walls, the framed law degree, the photos on her desk. Out the window behind her, late morning was moving toward noontime, casting shadows across the fescue that grew beneath the monkeypod trees.

"Both," I said.

"The firm handles all kinds of cases: corporate, criminal, civil, litigation, the works."

"And you personally?"

"Corporate law," she said. "Contracts, M&A work."

"Which is how you're acquainted with Thel Mishow." She nodded. "Which is also how I know Valden Van de Groot."

"You've worked with him, then."

"Valden?" She waved a hand in front of her. "Nobody works *with* Valden. He makes it quite clear you work *for* him."

My eyes wandered across the photos on the credenza behind her, landed on one that had caught her laughing, an arm wrapped around a tall, athletic dark-haired man wearing sunglasses and a white linen shirt. The cove beside which they were posed in the photo was turquoise and shimmering with reflected sunlight.

"My ex-husband," she said, without turning, without being asked.

"Ah," I said.

"Emphasis on the 'ex.'"

"Ah," I said again, followed by a long moment of silence that skirted the borders of gracelessness. "Yet you still display the picture."

"I have a fondness for Tahiti."

"So Thel explained to you what I needed?" I asked, changing the subject.

"We've got you set up in the small conference room. It has its own fax machine, direct phone line, secure Internet access, and a lovely view of Waikiki."

She stood, leaned across her desk and punched the speaker button on her phone. There was an electronic buzz, then, "Yes, Ms. Dunross?"

"Please show Mr. Travis to Conference Room B."

"You don't start with the easy ones, do you, Mike?" Thel Mishow said over a phone connection that sounded like he was in the next room.

"What did you find out?"

The sound of ruffling paperwork hummed down the line at me. He sighed audibly. "You have the fax I sent you?"

The machine had started ringing about the same time I dialed Thel's New York office. I'd heard it begin to print while I waited for him to pick up, but I hadn't yet looked at what he'd sent, so I turned and grabbed it off the tray. There were two pages: a cover sheet and a detailed diagram that looked like a family tree.

"Got it right here," I said. "What am I looking at?"

"That's the ownership chart for the Mandalay Plaza."

The chart showed a pyramid of boxes, layer after layer of them, each with the name of a corporation or partnership printed inside.

"Holy shit."

"You're not kidding," Thel laughed. "It took a pair of my best paralegals almost three days to put it all together."

"Where the hell are the humans? There's nothing here but corporate entities."

"We've got some of the stockholders' names already, Mike. But I've got to tell you, I don't know how fast I can get the rest to you."

I gazed out the conference room window, out toward the convention center and the Ala Wai Canal. In the distance, rain clouds hovered over green cliffs and hinted at an afternoon shower.

"Give me what you have," I said.

"Once the chart was assembled," Thel said, "I had the paralegals pull each entity apart, using data available through the Department of Corporations."

"Go on."

"I had them focus on the top two tiers, to begin with, and here's what they found: The Mandalay Plaza is owned by an S Corp called Mandalay Holdings. The Managing Partner of

Mandalay Holdings is another S Corp called LenWest. LenWest is owned equally by two separate parties."

"Who?"

"Phillip Lennox, and an offshore corporation registered in the Caicos Islands."

"Who owns the Caicos corporation?"

"There's the rub, Mike," Thel sighed again. "I'm keeping somebody on it, but you need to know that obtaining ownership information like that is a hell of a hard thing to do. These tax haven countries thrive on privacy laws."

I felt the first dull throb of a headache in my temples.

"So all we've got so far is Phillip Lennox and a bunch of corporate ghosts?"

"I'm afraid so."

I picked up my tea and sipped at it. It had gone cold, but all I really wanted was a few seconds to think. I stood and watched an outrigger glide down the undisturbed water of the canal while I tried to gather my thoughts.

"You still there, Mike?"

"Yeah," I said. "I was just thinking. Have you torn into the lower-tier companies yet?" I picked up the fax Thel had sent and scanned it. "Like this group of LLCs down near the bottom?"

"Not yet. I kept the focus on the top tier. That's where the management is going to be."

"Can you do it? Can you crack into these other LLCs?"

I could picture him then, silver-haired and imposing, gazing down from his office in lower Manhattan, watching the constant flow of cars, taxis and buses navigate the heavy rush hour traffic half a world away.

"Shouldn't take overly long," he said. "Domestic Limited Liability Companies are a hell of a lot easier to peel apart than offshore corporations. I'll start right away."

I thanked him and hung up, and paced around the conference table about a dozen times. I kept returning to the Mandalay Plaza's ownership chart lying there, kept asking myself why Lennox felt he had to create such a Byzantine structure merely to own the hotel. I knew it was common to place real estate ownership inside a corporate shell for liability reasons, or to create a partnership or two in order to keep estate planning straight. But the chart Thel had faxed me was overkill to the nth degree. And overkill usually smacks of something else.

I was about to head to the break room when the door swung inward. It was Patricia Dunross.

"Everything okay so far?"

"Fine, thank you," I said. "I was just about to get a refill on my tea."

She did that dismissive wave thing again. "I'll have my assistant brew you a pot and bring it in."

Her eye caught the fax on the table in front of me, scanned it. I could tell she was an accomplished upside-down reader. A valuable skill to master if you made a living by negotiating from the opposite side of a desk.

"Mind if I ask your opinion about something, Ms. Dunross?"

"It's Patricia," she said. "And no, I don't mind."

I slid the fax to her.

"That's the ownership chart for a hotel property in California," I said. "You're a corporate lawyer. Does that look normal to you?"

Her eyebrows knitted as she looked it over more carefully. She was lost in thought for a full minute before she tossed the paper back onto the table.

"There's really no such thing as 'normal,' Mike. But that does look a bit elaborate."

"What do you make of it?"

"In what way?"

I looked squarely into her face. Her green eyes were alive with the game.

"If you were negotiating a deal involving an ownership structure that looked like that, you'd certainly make some baseline assumptions about it. What would you assume?"

She smiled. "I see something like that, and I think one of two things: they're hiding money, or hiding people."

"Laundering?"

"Perhaps," she said. "Or the people who own the offshore corporations don't want their identities to be known."

I looked back out the window again, followed the glint of a jetliner gaining altitude on a return trip to the mainland.

"So, white-collar crime?" I said.

"It does have that aroma."

I worked in the conference room for another half hour, checking my e-mails, weather forecasts and the like, and felt my stomach growl. My watch showed 12:55, and the foot traffic on the street below said the lunch hour was in full swing.

I figured I'd catch a cab over to Chinatown a few blocks away, but wanted to make contact with Hans before I left for lunch. I typed a one-line e-mail to him and sent it off, then placed a call to his home.

"Check your e-mail," was all I said before I hung up. When he did, he'd find the number I'd given him for the direct line at the law firm, followed by the time I suggested that we make contact. Four thirty, California time; two thirty for me. Within the next hour or so, I knew that Hans would head for a clean phone and call me.

In the meantime, I intended to stretch my legs, get some fresh air and give this new information some thought. I felt a thousand disparate fragments floating around my brain, none of them coming into focus enough to point anywhere that would explain Lennox or the Mandalay Plaza's connection with Valden's blackmail, or the subsequent execution of the two fools that had been behind it. And absolutely nothing that might get Hans and me off the hook.

CHAPTER TWENTY-FIVE

May Ling could tell that something had changed. She could feel it.

For days on end, the cargo vessel had pushed through rough seas—the deck vibrating beneath her as the bow plowed through yet another enormous swell—contributing the odor of seasickness to the ever present stench of unwashed bodies and excrement. The pirates no longer checked on them, had not done so for four days now by May Ling's reckoning, disgusted enough by the condition of their charges that they no longer desired to be serviced by either May Ling or Siu.

But the ship had begun moving slowly now, pitching heavily as the rhythmic throb of the engines wound down, and hurling sacks of rice and waste buckets across the floor of the padlocked container, soaking them all in filth and spoiling much of what remained of their dwindling food supply.

May Ling peered through the dimness at Siu and tried to catch her eye. But Siu had disappeared, had not been the same ever since that night along the river. The condition of Siu's husband, Jiang, had grown increasingly worse, until, only three days into the voyage, he was gone. His body had been stacked on top of the others of the dead, piled like rotting logs in a corner of the container. Siu had clutched and scraped, held fast to his body with all her strength as the remaining immigrants pried his corpse from her arms. Her young son, Djhou, watched in silence, without understanding, from the nest he had made in May Ling's lap.

It seemed to May Ling that Siu's wailing still echoed inside that small space, perhaps the last of what had been left of Siu's humanity, perhaps all that was left of her at all. She lay in the corner, unmoving, not eating, not even attempting to reach out to young Djhou anymore.

The familiar noises of the vessel fell away into silence, a silence so complete that May Ling could no longer feel the vibration that turned the propellers far below. The din and palpitation of the engines had gone dead.

She ran her fingers through the lank and oily tufts of Djhou's hair, felt the tiny scabs and bumps that had started to appear on his scalp. He stirred slightly and she felt him look up at her, sunken yellow eyes in a face gone slack from malnutrition. She brushed her hand along his cheek, and nestled him back against her bosom. He wriggled slightly and settled there, sighed and closed his eyes as May Ling began to sing softly to him, began to sing the song she had come to think of as theirs alone. She felt him as he drifted into sleep, grateful he could not feel her as she wept.

CHAPTER TWENTY-SEVEN

The taxi dropped me at the corner of Merchant and Bethel Streets.

The sun shone brightly in the noonday sky as I walked, but I felt only a trace of humidity emanating from the rain clouds that had wrapped themselves around the shoulders of the *pali*. I took my time making my way into the heart of Chinatown.

The buildings dated back to the mid-1800s, constructed mainly of wood or brick, with facades ornamented with the faint remnants of hand lettering that had existed when some of the first Chinese immigrants had worked off their five-year labor contracts and had elected to stay in Hawaii rather than to return home. The place had been known to them as *Tan Heung Shan*, the Country of the Fragrant Tree.

I looked into the faces of their descendents now, still laboring inside the shops I passed, generations that stretched all the way back to the earliest survivors of the punishing fifty-five-day sailing passage they endured for the promise of food, clothing and thirty-six dollars a year. Many of them returned to China with whatever little money they'd managed to save, but those who remained in the islands quietly and efficiently set up shops, married local women, and indelibly placed their chop on Hawaii's consciousness.

Drifts of sandalwood incense, fresh flowers, and cigarette smoke floated across the busy sidewalk as I made my way up to Smith Street, where the racket from the mah-jongg parlors tumbled down from second-story windows. A half block later, I found what I was looking for.

I ducked into a crowded restaurant that specialized in *dim sum,* ordered a Tsingtao beer and waited for the food carts to make their rounds. I was the only round-eye in the place, which I considered to be a good sign. I sipped at my cold beer and sampled a selection of *manapua,* boiled shrimp, steamed rice and bok choy, while I looked out the window and watched the passersby. Except for the automobile traffic, there was an almost timeless quality that made it easy for me to imagine a young Sun Yat-sen and his schoolmate Ho Fon meeting together on these very streets, plotting the formation of the secret *Kuomintang* society that would set the foundation for China's revolution.

When I finally finished lunch, I paid the tab, left a few bills on the table, and wandered down King, past the sidewalk vendors, fruit stands and lei shops, all the way to River Street, where I turned and headed *mauka,* up toward Vineyard and the shrine that occupied a quiet, tree-shaded corner of the square. I purchased a handful of joss sticks from a peddler at a stall outside the gates and worked my way to the foot of the stone statue of Kwan Yin, the goddess of mercy. One by one, I lit the sticks of incense and placed them on the altar to take their places among the hundreds of others that had come before. One for safe passage; one for Lani; another for my lost partner, Reginald Carter. I lit one for Hans, and one for Mie, and so on until, finally, my bundle was gone.

I stood in silence for what seemed a long time, in the shade cast by the image of Kwan Yin, and I watched the strands of thin gray smoke, together with my prayers, tangle skyward and disappear into the wind.

It was quarter after two when I stepped back into the conference room at Dunross, Frankel & Wood. I figured I had time enough to speak with Valden before Hans was due to call. This time, I got right through.

"I've been checking into the ownership structure of the Mandalay Plaza," I told him.

"Okay." His voice sounded tentative, wary.

"But I'm running into walls."

"Such as?"

"The whole thing is a series of corporate shells, many of which are registered offshore."

My brother cleared his throat, and I could almost see him sitting straighter behind his custom desk. "Can't help you."

"You haven't heard my question yet."

"Don't need to."

"I want to know if VGC had any part in the financing or construction of that hotel."

He gave me a dry chuckle, like if I'd been there in person he'd be ruffling my hair like a kid who'd asked where babies came from. "I didn't need to hear the question. I don't do business with offshore corporations. No ifs, ands, or buts."

"Why not?"

"Because they stink to high heaven, that's why not."

It looked like my first instincts had been correct.

"Money laundering, tax evasion?" I asked.

"You name it, they're a potential shield for it. I'm not saying they're all being used for those purposes, mind you.

It's just that VGC doesn't need the business badly enough to risk it."

But you'll risk it all to dip your quill into the company inkwell on a fairly regular basis. I thought it, but I didn't say it.

"Phillip Lennox is one of the partners," I said.

"He is?"

"Yes."

"Funny."

"Funny in what way?"

"It doesn't sound like something Phil Lennox would be involved in."

"He seemed pretty slick to me."

"Maybe so," he said. "But getting into an arrangement involving offshore entities can get sticky, Mike. Just doesn't sound like him, that's all. But I suppose you never know."

No, you don't ever know. That's for goddamned sure.

"Thanks, Valden," I said, and killed the line.

I paced the room some more and considered what I knew about Phillip Lennox. In a sense, Valden was right: Lennox had a reputation as a hard-nosed businessman, with a political agenda that backed it up. Lennox Biomedical was an enormous company in its own right, not to mention the holdings that Lennox Senior owned personally, outside of the parent corporation. Nevertheless, it appeared that, at least on the Mandalay Plaza deal, Lennox had become involved with something that could have a taint on it. I wondered why.

I walked down the hall to Patricia Dunross's office, found her door was open, but knocked anyway.

She looked up from what she'd been reading and smiled. "Come in."

"I've got another question," I said. "I'm having a hard time digesting this offshore corporation thing."

"How so?"

"I just got off the phone with Valden and he pretty much echoed your sentiments."

Patricia Dunross placed a bound document on her desk, rested her chin on steepled fingers as she studied my face. "And you're wondering why anyone bothers with them at all."

"Yes."

"First off, they're not illegal," she said. "Quite the contrary, there are perfectly justifiable reasons for doing business in an offshore shell. Plenty of legitimate businesses do."

"But?"

"But, historically, they've been used to shield one's assets from seizure."

"Seizure by whom?"

"By lawful governmental agencies: the DEA, IRS, the FBI, Homeland Security. You see, Mike, when we're talking 'offshore corporations,' we're *not* talking about places like Switzerland, Germany, Austria, Japan . . . places with first-world economies, industrialized countries.

"What we *are* talking about are places like the Cayman Islands, the Turks and Caicos, the Cook Islands, Mauritius. You get the idea. These are tiny little dots on the map, little third-world havens that base an enormous portion of their economies on the registration of 'dummy' corporations—corporations that have no real assets, don't own anything tangible, yet move millions of dollars through their accounts. The banking and disclosure laws that exist in places like those make it almost impossible to track the identities of the people behind the dummy corps, nor where the money comes from—whether it's drug money, arms dealing, or genuine business income."

"And in a post-September 11 world . . ."

She nodded. "And a post-Enron world, yes, doing business with companies registered in places where bad people can easily move millions of dollars in secret smacks of having something to hide."

"But it's not illegal," I repeated. "And what if such a business predated terrorist or Enron concerns?"

"There's very little to prevent a legitimate business from insisting on a restructure," she said, though her voice was laced with skepticism. "However, if I were an investor in that hotel deal you showed me, I'd insist they collapse the whole structure and transfer it into something else. A structure that eradicated the offshore corporations, for instance. It's certainly not all that difficult, and not that expensive."

"Unless you couldn't," I said.

She leaned into her chair again, crossed her arms and nodded. "Correct. Unless, for some reason, you simply could not."

"Like what?"

"Like the real owner of that offshore corporation is flatly unwilling to do so."

"Because they actually *are* hiding something," I said.

"I believe you may have cracked the code, Mike."

When I returned to the conference room, the phone was ringing. I glanced at my watch and saw I was ten minutes late for Hans's call.

"Where the hell have you been?" Hans said once I picked up. "This is the third time I've tried this number."

There was traffic in the background that told me Hans was at another pay phone. "What do you need?"

"Two things," I said. "First, I haven't heard from you in a few days. I want to know what's happening on your end. I'm not going to keep sailing forever and leave you hanging out in the breeze."

"My IAD hearing's tomorrow," he said. "You need to stay off the screen until it's over."

"What do they have?"

Hans's laugh was empty. "Kemp's been on me like stink on shit. Gaines and Johnston can't be seen anywhere near me."

"So you don't know what they've come up with on the murders?"

"I'll know tomorrow, sure as hell. One way or the other."

I thought about the joss sticks at Kwan Yin's feet, silver smoke twisting like rope, disappearing into nothing.

"What's the second thing?" Hans asked.

"I'm working on a lead," I said. "I might need somebody to look into some white-collar stuff."

There was a moment's hesitation. "I don't think I know anybody over there anymore," he said. "Besides; I got a cloud around me like that kid from the *Peanuts* cartoons. My hearing's tomorrow. I'll know where we're at by the end of the day. At least, I'll have an idea of what they're going for. In the meantime, keep a low profile."

"Listen, Hans, I'm—"

"Forget it, pard," Hans said. "I already told you. I knew I'd hit the wall the minute Kemp put that Texas rip on me. I'll call you tomorrow. Same number. I don't know what time."

And he was gone.

It was late afternoon when I decided to call it a day. Thel's paralegals were digging further into the ownership of the Mandalay Plaza, Hans was preparing for his hearing, and I was outside the investigative loop until it was over. In short, I was left in that place I hate the most: the one where there's nothing left to do but wait. I left a message with Patricia Dun ross's secretary thanking her for the use of the conference room, and told her I'd need it again tomorrow.

Outside, I looked across the boulevard past the wide

greenbelt, and off toward the beach. People walked aimlessly through the park, dozed beneath the shady spread of palm fronds and poinciana, or read dog-eared paperbacks while they reclined in beach chairs on the white sand. The sun cast a muted rainbow beneath the clouds that had finally delivered on their promise of rain, the air still sweet and heavy with moisture.

I turned back toward downtown, toward the high-rises of Waikiki, feeling coiled and tight from a day spent indoors. As I walked back in the direction of the boat harbor and *Kehau*, I figured I had two options for relieving the tension that was gnawing my insides: either take a long jog through Ala Moana Beach Park, or settle in for happy hour at the first bar I encountered that possessed a working television set and space for my ass on a stool.

CHAPTER TWENTY-EIGHT

The place was called "The Scoop Deck," a neighborhood dive located down a narrow side street and tucked between two high-rise hotels that had been in need of remodeling since the 1970s. The place was done up with walls adorned in dust-encrusted marker buoys, fishnets, dried starfish and old life rings, a faint haze of spilled liquor and pine cleanser in the air.

But it had what I was looking for.

The TV behind the bar was tuned to a cable news channel, MSNBCNBCNN, one of the alphabet networks that were interchangeable with all the others. The talking heads were busy at work behind their broadcast desks, sincere-looking yuppies with freshly cut hair, unambiguous political leanings and stylish wardrobes who excelled at reading words from a teleprompter but didn't understand a fraction of what came out of their mouths. But that is what I'd come in for, a recap of what I'd been missing from the outside world. That, and the tall Asahi over ice on the coaster in front of me.

The bartender was a heavy-set guy in his midfifties, with a toilet-seat ring of shaggy hair around a shiny head and skin that looked like it had been applied to his face with a Spackle trowel. He busied himself stocking the cooler and the shelves of booze beside the register, then began polishing at a spot on the bar until I thought the finish would either wear off or catch fire. There were only about five of us in the place, and it was getting harder for him to ignore me since I was the only one seated at the bar.

"Where you from?" he asked me.

I didn't desire a conversation any more than he did.

"Kona."

"Nice."

"Yeah," I said, sipped my Asahi and turned my attention back to the television. The volume was low, so I used that as an excuse to appear focused and concerned as I stared up at the screen. It worked for a couple of minutes while a sportscaster on-screen reeled off half-clever puns about the day's scores.

"Whattaya do down there?"

"Charter business," I said, then pointed to the TV. "You mind turning that thing up?"

"No problem," he said, looked relieved when he went for the remote. "You want the local news, instead?"

"Sure," I said. "Why not."

He flipped through the channels until he landed on one of the local network affiliates doing its evening rundown. He placed the remote on the ledge behind him and disappeared into the back room.

I was starting in on my third beer and beginning to feel the tension dissipate from the muscles in my neck when the screen filled with the image of what appeared to be an industrial blaze burning out of control. Black smoke poured into an after-noon sky as the words "Lennox Biomedical Plant, San Diego, California" appeared underneath. The camera cut to a team of firefighters directing heavy streams of water onto the roof of the building while a voice-over said, "This was the scene earlier today when another of Lennox Biomedical's plants went up in flames. The five-alarm San Diego blaze was the second Lennox facility to catch fire today."

On screen, the image changed over to a three-story urban office building, also belching flame. "This building, in northern Virginia, is one of only two Lennox research facilities in the US. We've been informed of two fatalities, among a growing number of minor injuries that have been sustained among employees at the Virginia location, though officials have yet to provide details of any possible victims in San Diego. Both blazes continue to rage out of control at this time; a terror plot has not been completely ruled out by authorities, and local police and fire officials are investigating both as cases of arson."

A local Oahu anchorwoman appeared on screen. "We go now to Randy Manago, who is standing by at the Honolulu convention center with Phillip Lennox, chairman of Lennox Biomedical."

"Thank you, Linda," Manago said. "I'm here with Phillip Lennox, a face that is familiar to many in the business and political arenas. He's here in Honolulu to serve as tomorrow's keynote speaker at the pharmaceutical convention that gaveled-in earlier this week."

The camera panned back to include Phillip Lennox, in an open-collared shirt and business suit, forgoing a tie in deference to the tropics. His son, J.R., stood beside him. The senior Lennox had gathered himself into an expression of both gravitas and control, while J.R.'s resembled something more akin to shell shock. I flashed back to their fund-raiser in LA, only then remembering what they'd said about their plans to visit the islands.

"Needless to say," Lennox began, "we're deeply saddened by the events taking place in Virginia and California. Our prayers go out to the families that have been affected by the fires, and Lennox Biomedical is cooperating fully with the authorities in determining the causes."

The reporter nodded, pulled the hand mic back to speak. "What are your thoughts regarding the investigation of the fires as acts of arson?"

Lennox seemed to ponder that momentarily, though I was certain he'd been well briefed by his legal and public relations people long before he agreed to an on-camera interview. His brow furrowed with paternal concern.

"Randy, I think it's too early to comment on that. As you know, the fires are still, unfortunately, continuing to burn, and it will likely be several days before the experts will be able to clearly determine the possible causes."

"Are you worried that acts of terror may have been perpetrated against you or your company?" the reporter asked.

Lennox reacted physically to the question, a flinch and an expression of distaste twisting his face. "As I said before, I think it's far too early to speculate on the possibility of arson, let alone to sensationalize this tragic coincidence into something as serious as terrorism. Lennox Biomedical has always dedicated itself to the prevention, treatment and the cure of disease, so I see no earthly reason why it should be considered the target of an arsonist, much less of organized terrorism."

"Will you remain here in Honolulu, or will you be traveling back to the mainland in the wake of all of this?"

"We have no immediate plans to return to the mainland. I've made a commitment to speak to this very important gathering of industry professionals, and I intend to honor it. As I said before, my company will be doing everything in its power to cooperate with the investigation, and to minimize any impact on our employees and their families; however, there is nothing that I can add to the investigative process with my presence in either Virginia or San Diego."

The camera returned to close-up.

"Thank you, Mr. Lennox, for talking with us," the reporter said. "This is Randy Manago, at the Honolulu convention center. Back to you, Linda."

Linda was appropriately grim and severe as she took it back into the studio. "Thank you, Randy," she said, and turned to face the camera. "And in other news, a freighter bound for Mexico was discovered abandoned and foundering in moderate seas, some 140 miles southeast of Hawaii. Coastguard officials stated that every effort will be made to tow the vessel to Honolulu, where a determination—"

A song by REM came ripping through the house speakers, startling the shit out of me and completely obliterating the news story. I turned to see a pair of thirty-something vacation drunks feeding coins into the juke and punching buttons like it was a game of Whac-A-Mole.

I looked back to the TV screen, watched the anchorwoman mouth a few more words, then break for commercial. Hell with it. It was obviously time for me to go. I tossed down the rest of my Asahi, and signaled the bartender for my tab.

Late afternoon had faded into a moody plum-colored dusk, and I felt the cool breeze on my face as I neared the door while the jukebox screamed:

"It's the end of the world as we know it, and I feel fine . . ."

It was that indistinct, in-between time of day, no longer sunset and not quite dark; that time of evening when the beaches have emptied, and the streets have filled. The lights inside the city park hadn't yet come on, and the branches of plumeria and ohai spread their bent fingers and scratched at the darkening sky.

The walk back to the harbor wasn't a long one, but I didn't want to spend it shouldering my way through the dinner crowds. Instead, I took a route that led me down a concrete path that ran alongside the wide swath of beach, separating it from the manicured landscape of the park. Behind me, the lights of the hotels reflected wavy patterns on the surface of the receding tide and the postcard view of Diamond Head. Ahead of me I could hear the rhythmic plodding of joggers as they threaded their way through the park, working their way toward me, in the direction of the city lights.

There was a breeze coming in off the ocean, ruffling the palm fronds with a sound like rattling bones. My stop-off at the bar had left me feeling mellow as I listened to the city, and the last clatter of mynahs as they roosted for the night, which is probably why I didn't hear the bicycle closing in on me from behind. And by the time I did hear it, it was too late.

My guess is that it was an old-fashioned sap, the kind the beat cops used to carry, with a spring in the handle and leather wrapped around a heavy cylinder made of lead. The guy on the bike had swung it with professional precision once he glided up beside me.

He hit me at the base of the skull, and shot a bolt of blinding white light through my brain as my knees buckled and dropped me like a sack of rocks. When I opened my eyes, I found myself on the ground wrapped up in a fetal position. The rider was already fifty yards away and making for the boulevard. I placed a hand on the walkway beneath me to steady myself, and tried to get to my knees. I felt my stomach lurch and I rolled onto my side instead. Instinctively, I reached for the Beretta that I wished had been there rather than lying in the nightstand beside my bed aboard the *Kehau*.

I got to my knees about the time the joggers reached me.

I started to wave them away. "No problem," I said. "I'll be okay."

The first kick found my stomach and knocked the air out of my lungs. The second found my ribs. After that, it was a blur of footwear, grunting and the meaty thud of fists meeting flesh. My flesh. I tried to get to my feet, find my balance and land a few punches of my own, but the sap had done a number on my equilibrium and the world spun sickeningly around me. I couldn't get myself off the ground, so the joggers' job was swift and furious and complete.

"Stay the fuck out of it," one said, then grabbed a hank of my hair and slammed my head, face first, into the concrete.

They finished me with a final vicious kick to the groin that sent me headlong into a tree, where I lay curled into a ball, retching my guts out even as my world went black.

When I came to it was dark, and my attackers were nowhere in sight. My chin was crusted with blood and dried vomit, and there was a pounding ache in my ribs that marked time with the throbbing inside my skull. I sat up slowly, leaned against the tree and waited for the world to right itself. I patted my back pocket and found that my wallet was still there, looked at my wrist and still had my TAG Heuer. A few minutes later I'd gathered the strength to stand. I pulled my shit together enough to limp my way to the boat harbor, stopping frequently to recover my balance, and once to wash the blood off my face in the cool water of a drinking fountain.

"Jesus Christ," Snyder said. "You look like you went three rounds with a jackhammer and got dragged through a cactus patch."

"Which is exactly how I feel," I said. But the swelling and

the split in my lip made it sound more like *Whishiz ahzacka howa feeah.*

"What the hell happened?"

"I got jumped in the park."

"Robbed?"

I shook my head and was immediately sorry I had. My peripheral vision clouded with static and my knees felt unhinged. Snyder grabbed me under one arm and helped me down into the salon and sat me in a chair.

"Anything broken?"

"I don't think so." *Uh doan thikso.*

"That's a nasty lump on your forehead, bud." He leaned over, looked hard at my face, and studied my eyes one at a time. "You might have a concussion."

I sat there, fought down a heaving stomach.

"You lose consciousness at all?"

"Yeah," I said, careful not to move my head.

Snyder's face was solemn, which concerned me. I knew those eyes had seen combat. "You're gonna have to stay awake for a while. Can't let you sleep if you've got a concussion. I need to keep an eye on the dilation of your pupils."

"Shit," I said.

"Yeah," Snyder agreed.

An hour later I had washed myself up, changed into clean clothes, and surveyed the bruises and contusions all over my face and torso. My balls ached, my head pounded, and at least two of my ribs were probably bruised. But nothing felt like it had been broken. In the mirror, I saw a lump on my forehead that looked like I'd had half a golf ball implanted there, and my lip was swollen to twice its normal size.

"I can't believe they didn't break your nose."

"Not for lack of trying," I said.

Snyder shook his head. "And they didn't steal anything?"

"No, they just sapped me on the skull and kicked the living crap out of me. One of them advised me to stay the fuck out of it."

"Stay the fuck out of what?"

"Hell if I know."

"You get a look at these ass clowns?"

"Had a close-up view of their shoes. Adidas."

I went to the sofa and lay down on it, trying to find the least miserable position I could.

"Nice," Snyder said. "That should be helpful."

I arranged a pair of pillows behind me, and had just settled back when his cell phone rang. Snyder picked it up off the counter, checked caller ID, and brought it over to me.

"What the hell is going on, Mike?" It was Lani and she was pissed. In the background I heard the racket from the bar at Lola's, and she didn't wait for an answer. "There were people here asking for you. Cops."

"Who were they?"

"Detective Moon and some other guy. I didn't get his name."

I was grateful it was Moon. I knew I could get some breathing room if I called him back and checked in. He was one of the good guys.

"What did he want?" *Whaddiddee wan?*

"He said he was looking for you. Needed to talk to you, and asked did I know where you were."

"What did you tell him?"

There was boozy laughter in the background, and a blender cycled on.

"Are you drunk or something? You sound weird."

"I'm okay," I said, and tried to sound convincing. *I'n hokay.*

"Mike, you are freaking me out. What's happening?"

"Nothing, Lani. Don't worry about it. It's just stuff from before." I don't like to talk about my cases, and she knew it. It was a cheap move on my part, but it got her to stop asking questions.

"Well, call him at least. He said he'll be at the substation in the morning."

"Okay, Lani," I said. "I'll take care of it."

There was a long moment of silence before the blender rattled again and shook her out of it. "You sure you're okay?"

"I'm okay."

"I didn't tell him where you are," she said. "Of course, I don't *know* where you are."

"I know. Thank you."

Her voice came out like a whisper. "Son of a bitch," she said and the line went dead.

CHAPTER TWENTY-NINE

I don't claim to know much about women," Snyder said, "but that didn't sound like happy talk."

"Detective Moon was at Lola's asking for me."

"That can't be good."

I was sure that somebody in LA was finally trying to track me down, and working through the Kona department to do it. I had no intention of making contact until after Hans's hearing, as I had promised him. I knew they'd need an explanation for my fingerprints being found at a murder scene, if only to close a messy little detail that could look bad for the LAPD if it went unanswered. It was time to start thinking about developing a credible lie. Even so, I couldn't take the chance and make official contact before they were finished with Hans. I'd done enough to fuck him up, and I wasn't going to make it any worse. So Moon was going to have to wait right along with everybody else, at least for the time being.

"Probably not," I said.

Snyder eyed me skeptically, changed the subject. "How's Lani?"

"Angry," I said. "Scared."

He looked out the window into the dark, squinted at some thought inside his head. "When this is over we need to get good and drunk. We'll consider it a wake. You're obviously not ready for a woman like her."

"You finished?" I asked.

He eyed me for a few seconds, then went to the console where the TV was hidden, opened the door.

"For now," he said, and turned on the set.

We sat like that until the news came on. Snyder got up from time to time, checked my eyeballs and wandered the *Kehau*'s deck. On the news, I watched a rerun of Phillip Lennox doing his song-and-dance about the fires, watched J.R. Lennox look on uncomfortably from the sidelines, and learned that the fire in San Diego had killed three more of their employees.

By the time Conan O'Brien was over, Snyder had fallen asleep. I prodded him awake and told him to go below, that I'd look after myself for the night. He made a token protest, looked at my dilated pupils again, and reminded me to stay awake.

It was after three in the afternoon when I woke with a start. I was damp with the sweat of my dreams, my mouth dry as cotton, lips cracked and leaking blood.

I'd managed to keep myself awake until dawn when Snyder had come topside to check me one final time, and said he thought I was well enough to sleep. Despite the beating I'd taken, or maybe because of it, I hadn't expected to sleep so long, and was instantly pissed that I'd lost the day.

I took a shower, feeling the aftereffects of every blow the joggers had laid on me, aching from somewhere new every time I moved or tried to slide the bar of soap over my bruised skin. I grabbed a pair of faded surgeon's scrub pants and a long-sleeved T-shirt from the drawer in my stateroom. I put them on to cover the damage, to keep from alarming the neighbors. I looked into the mirror, decided against shaving, and saw that the swelling of my lip had gone down considerably. The lump over my eye was another story. I tied a bandana around my head, pirate-style, in an attempt to cover it, and put on my Ray-Ban shades.

I came up topside and found Snyder tinkering with the scuba equipment. He sat cross-legged on the teak deck, the parts from a scuba regulator spread out in front of him.

"Shiver me timbers, mateys," he said. "It's Doctor Bligh."

I started to smile, but winced when my lip stretched too far.

"You look like an asshole, Travis."

"I should lose the bandana?"

He picked up a small screwdriver and went back to his work. "As soon as possible."

The day was all bright light and moving shadows, the trades blowing intermittent white clouds across the sun. I looked out toward the mouth of the harbor, followed a nice looking Hatteras as it made its way up the channel.

When I turned back to Snyder he was looking past my shoulder, focused on something farther up the dock.

"Friend of yours?" he asked.

It was Patricia Dunross, taking cautious steps in her sling-back pumps as she came down the steep ramp to the dock. She wore a dark business suit, with a skirt that showed off a pair of shapely calves, one hand on the wood railing and another on a black briefcase-purse that was slung over her shoulder.

"Nice," Snyder said.

I tossed her a wave that sent shock waves down my aching back and abs, which she returned with a smile. She picked her way across the dock, careful to avoid planting a heel in the spaces between the planks and came up alongside the *Kehau*'s transom.

"Patricia," I said, offering a hand up the stairs. "I meant to call you."

Her red hair was pulled back in a ponytail, but the wind had blown a few strands loose across her cheeks.

"I thought you were coming back to—" She interrupted herself when she looked up at me. I couldn't see through the Gucci sunglasses she wore, but I could tell she'd noticed the knot on my head. "Good Lord, what happened to you?"

"Got blindsided on my way home last night."

She reached out her free hand and gently touched my forehead. "Are you all right?" She turned to Snyder, who was standing now, the regulator parts scattered at his bare feet. "Is he all right?"

"He's fine. I thought he might have a concussion, but he doesn't. Don't know why."

I interrupted him, wanted to change the subject. "Patricia Dunross, this is Snyder. A friend of mine from the Big Island."

Snyder wiped a hand on his shorts, and reached out to greet her.

"A pleasure," he said.

"Ms. Dunross is the lawyer who lent me the use of her conference room yesterday," I told him around my split lip.

"I thought you were coming back to the office today," she said to me. Her face had gone serious. "We got a call for you this afternoon and it seemed important."

A gust of wind picked at the halyards, pulling hard at *Kehau*'s dock lines. I looked up at the wind sock on the mast, watched it fill momentarily and go limp.

"You could have called," I said. "I'm sorry you had to come all the way down here."

"You didn't leave your number. Besides, it's almost five o'clock and I wanted to get out of the office."

"How'd you find me?"

"I called Thel Mishow. He told me the name of your boat."

She smiled, pushed a stray lock of hair behind her ear. "From there, it was easy, a yacht this size."

"Can I offer you something for your trouble?" I asked. "Glass of wine, maybe?"

"Beefeaters?"

Snyder smirked, but had the decency to look away, like he was concentrating on the work he'd left in pieces on the deck.

"How do you like it?" I asked her.

"On the rocks and *very* dirty."

Snyder buried a chuckle inside a noise that was supposed to sound like a cough. I shot a glance at him as he sat back down to finish rebuilding the regulator.

She followed me into the salon below. I mixed her drink, and capped a bottle of Asahi for myself. We took seats on the banquette along the port bulkhead and let the breeze drift in through the open sliders.

"You mentioned a message? "I said.

"Yes, of course," she said, as she sipped at the martini and put it on the table between us. She reached into her black leather bag, withdrew a pink phone message slip and handed it to me. "When you didn't come in this morning, I forwarded the conference room line to my assistant. She took the message."

It was from Hans and it listed his home phone number. The slip was time stamped three fifteen. That would have been five fifteen in LA. A glance at my watch told me that Patricia Dunross had called Thel at home, then come right over with it. All it said was, *Call me.*

"Thank you," I said. "I appreciate all the trouble you went to."

"No trouble," she said, and kicked off her Guccis. "Your boat is lovely, by the way."

"Thank you. She was built in Southern California."

"Your friend seems like a nice guy."

I heard the shuffle of feet above deck, and the rattle of tools being tossed back in the box.

"He has his moments."

She smiled and sipped her martini, and settled into the banquette. The equipment locker door slammed shut, and Snyder's shadow preceded him down the stairs. He pulled a beer from the refrigerator just in time to hear her ask me if I was married.

I hadn't seen that question coming.

"His lady recently broke up with him," Snyder answered for me. "But he doesn't seem to know it yet."

CHAPTER THIRTY

The day flamed out with a brilliant orange sunset that faded to pastel before dying altogether, leaving the ocean like a flat purple blanket.

Patricia Dunross had left before things grew even clumsier, but I'd managed to watch the whole light show, punching in Hans's number every fifteen minutes or so, listening to the monotony of unanswered tones.

On the fifth try, I finally reached him at home. He picked up on the first ring.

"It's me," I said.

"Hey, Mike." I was expecting the routine we'd developed, the cryptic message followed by the waiting while Hans drove to a clean phone. He sounded tired, maybe a little drunk.

"How'd the hearing go?" I asked.

"About as I expected," he said. "Room full of assholes with legal pads wearing shiny suits."

"And?"

"They gave the murder case to Townsend."

"Did they show you Kemp's surveillance shots?"

"Oh, yeah," Hans said. "They showed me the photos. I told them we had tailed some guy from Phillip Lennox's party. Hell, they knew it already, so figured I'd salt the mine with a dose of honesty. Anyway, I told them that we tailed the guy, but I didn't know why. I was just driving, you know."

"Good," I said. "What about the pictures?"

"They have one of you at the door, Mike, talking to one of the victims. Then another couple shots of you walking back to the car with a box full of smashed-up crap a few minutes later."

"They know what was in the box?"

"No. They asked, but I said I didn't get a good look at it."

I figured I knew now what the call to Detective Moon was about.

"What about Roger Gaines?" I asked.

"I was able to leave him out of it. They bought it. Didn't seem to know he'd been helping me out."

"What's the witness saying?" I asked. "The girl who found the bodies."

"Not real up to speed on details, Mike." His voice sounded like an open wound.

I told him about Detective Moon's visit to Lani.

"I think Townsend, or maybe Kemp, is looking for me."

"Probably Townsend," Hans said. "I got a sense that the case is going over to OCID."

Organized crime. Something clicked. "What about Kemp?"

A bruised laugh came down the wire. "Kemp's done. He got what he wanted. These new pictures on top of the Austin thing . . ."

"I'm going to talk to Townsend."

He thought that through before he answered. "That's probably okay," he sighed. "I don't think they really like you for the murders."

"But it's an embarrassment to have our photos and my prints at the scene."

"Yeah, that's a mess. And Townsend isn't going to turn the case over to OCID with a big fucking hole like that in it."

The rumble of luau drums blew across the water from an outdoor stage at the high-rise hotel that stood at the edge of the boat harbor. The start of the nightly show. If I closed my eyes, those sounds could've been coming from one hundred years earlier. At that moment, I wished they were.

"What about the Texas deal?" I asked him.

"Moss is in the gray-bar hotel back in Austin, but he's not saying a word."

"Not even about your not being a part of his bullshit? He didn't clear you?"

"Not a fucking peep, Mike. Nothing. I knew that guy was a shitweasel from the moment I met him."

The drums next door went suddenly silent, and the vacuum was filled with applause. The emcee's voice announced something unintelligible, more applause, followed by the lonely wail of a steel guitar.

"I don't know, pard. I'm not feeling too strong here. My advocate isn't holding out much hope, either. I think I'm fucked."

"When do you hear back?"

Ice cubes rattled inside a tumbler in Southern California, sent their music into space and beamed themselves back down to a big chunk of lava in the middle of the Pacific.

"Tomorrow," he said. "But I already wrote my letter."

"What are you saying, Hans?"

"You think Walmart's hiring? Or maybe I should start to practice saying, 'You want fries with that?'"

I called Detective Moon at home.

"Hey, Big City," he said. "Been looking for you for a couple days."

"I heard."

I had first met Moon at a crime scene my memory still can't shake. We had gotten off to a rocky start, Moon not wanting much help from a big-city homicide cop like me. Eventually, we'd forged a workable—even cordial—truce that had evolved into a friendship. He was a good cop doing a hard job in a small town, a town where everybody knew him, and he knew everybody.

"Anything you want to get off your chest, Travis?"

There was after-dinner noise at his house, two young boys fighting over a video game and the clang of dishes in the sink.

"You tell me," I said.

"You're cool on my rock, bruddah," he said. "But there's an LA cop named Townsend who wants to talk to you. Said you know him."

Maybe Hans had been right. Maybe Kemp was finished dicking around with me.

"I know him," I said. "Did he leave a number?"

"Lemme find it," he said. "I think I got it in my briefcase."

I heard him utter something to the boys and the rough-housing stopped cold. When he came back on the line, he'd found what I needed.

I scratched the number on a scrap of paper. It didn't look familiar. The office number was permanently stamped on my brain, and this wasn't it. So the one Townsend had given to Moon had to be his cell phone, or a personal line at home.

"Just a heads-up, Travis," he said. "This Townsend dude sounds heavy. Know what I mean?"

"No worries," I said, making it casual. "It's caseload. They drop a lot of bodies over there, Moon."

"Whatever you say," he said.

* * *

I needed to give this some serious consideration before I called Townsend, needed one last look at the files Hans had e-mailed me. Things were spinning too fast, too goddamned much going on, and I had been too far removed from the loop. I felt the weight of Hans's humiliation, of Lani's growing disillusionment with me, and the distance between where I was and where I wanted to be.

I allowed myself the cold comfort that I couldn't have played it any differently. If I'd gone to Townsend straight away, Kemp would have used my statement as a sideshow, my brother's mess would have come to light, and Hans would already have been fired. As it was, at least Hans could continue to claim ignorance about whatever I had been up to at that house, maybe accept a formal reprimand, even a transfer to another bureau, but still keep his job.

The timing was delicate. I had to walk a very thin line, needed to close the open issues raised at Townsend's murder scene before the case went to OCID and things spun thoroughly out of control. At the same time, I needed to do my best to protect Valden's little secret, or this whole cat rodeo would have all been for nothing.

The tipping point, it seemed, was how much Townsend knew about my personal activities. I needed to determine whether he knew anything about the gun Hans had provided me, or about our act with the manager at the Mandalay Plaza, or if they knew that I had been the one to hog-tie and aggressively encourage the soon-to-be murder victims to cooperate with my off-the-grid investigation.

I went below to my laptop and looked over the reports and photos one last time.

It was no surprise the case was going to Organized Crime. The whole thing had begun to feel like a professional job, right down to the severed fingers. I knew where the victims driver's licenses had gone, but that didn't mean it hadn't been a hit. Missing fingers were something else.

It was the motive that still eluded me, hanging out there in the mist. What made it worse was not only had it started to smack heavily of OC, but the victims had been my brother's blackmailers. That put the bent-nose crowd far too close to Van de Groot Capital, and coincidence didn't exist in the world I knew.

I closed the file, checked my e-mail one last time before logging off. A few minutes later I was back on deck, a soft wind coming in off the stern, the last hammering drums from the luau pounding the night air, and Townsend's number clenched tightly in my fist.

It was past ten P.M. in California, but the call couldn't wait until morning. And I didn't want to talk to Townsend at the office.

Truth was, I felt like those descriptions of old soldiers on the front lines. About war being interminable stretches of boredom interrupted by moments of blinding terror. This whole deal had been like that from the jump. Empty stretches of impotence, punctuated by unexpected eruptions of violence, betrayal, abrogation and reprisal.

I punched in the number I'd written on the crushed piece of paper I held, waited through three rings and got a recorded message. A pager. The voice asked me to enter the number I was calling from, followed by the pound sign. I did, and set the phone down beside me on the captain's chair while I waited. I knew the drill. A cop will routinely give his pager number to a confidential informant rather than a phone number, so the callback was likely to be quick, give nothing away.

Sure as hell, it came before five minutes had elapsed.

The voice was terse. "I was just paged."

"John Townsend," I said. "This is Mike Travis. I heard you were looking for me."

"Where are you?"

"On my boat. Where are you?"

The torches from the luau were still burning, casting flickering patterns against the high walls of the hotel. The audience had left, but the oily fumes blew across to me in the strengthening breeze.

"At home," he said. "Are we done screwing around?"

A dry laugh stuck in my throat. "Nobody's screwing around, John. You called me and I called you back. Are you recording this?"

"No, you asshole—" There was hesitation on his end, regret at the tone he'd taken. "Listen. I'm well aware of your reputation over here, Travis. You know I respect you. I've seen your work."

"Thanks."

"Yeah, well, I've got this gaping hole in my case, and it's got you smack in the center of it."

"Where's Kemp in all this?"

"Nowhere," he said. "I'm not a rat, Mike. We all feel bad about Hans, okay?"

"I heard your case was going to OCID."

"Who told you that?"

"The proverbial little bird."

Townsend grunted. "Yeah, it is. And I want to get yours and Hans's names cleared out of it before it goes. I'm trying to do you a solid, here."

"Then I'll help you out," I said. "You want to know what I was doing at that house?"

"Very much."

"One of the victims worked at the Mandalay Plaza Hotel. He

was in hotel security. My brother was staying at that hotel. In fact, he was there to meet with Bill Kelleher."

"The congressman."

"Yes. Some items my brother considered sensitive were stolen from him during his stay there, and he had reason to believe that the thief was one of the men you found in that house," I said.

"Stolen from your brother, or Kelleher?"

"My brother."

I heard the scratch of pen on paper, the ruffle as he flipped to another page. "And he called you to take care of it for him?"

"Yes."

"Why didn't he call us?"

"My brother is a very private man. As I said, he considered the items to be sensitive and wanted their recovery handled discreetly."

"Uh huh," he said. "And what's your brother's name?"

"Valden Van de Groot."

A short blast of static came over the line, then silence.

"You said Valden Van de Groot is your brother?"

"Yes."

"And he'll corroborate what you just told me?"

Lying was not something of which I was particularly proud, but it sometimes proved to be a useful skill. "He will if you ever get through to him," I said.

"What kinds of things were stolen?"

"Computer disks, documents, things like that."

"So it was you who trashed the electronic equipment in the bedroom at the victims' house?"

I smiled, and it hurt. "With the baseball bat you found. The one with my prints on the handle."

"And the victims were alive when you left."

"Cross my heart." I watched the torch fire dance across the hotel wall, the play of shadow and light. Just like this conversation.

"Any way you could prove that?"

"Any way you could prove they weren't?" I said.

I was getting a clear sense that they knew nothing about the Stoeger nine-mil Hans had lent me, or my having gone cowboy on the two dead guys. It was time to go on the offensive and get this shit wrapped up and done. I was sick of the whole idea of my having run, and I needed to get back to Kona.

"Listen, Travis, we don't—"

"You know me, Townsend. You think I'm going to shoot two guys in the back of the head, then cut off their goddamned pinkies? Are you fucking high? I got what I was looking for. I didn't need to kill anybody."

Townsend changed course. "And what *was* in the box you took from the house?"

"The things that had been stolen from my brother."

"Breaking and entering. Assault and battery."

"Entering," I said. "Take another look at Kemp's photos, Townsend. The guy let me in voluntarily. The only things I broke were his computers. Oh, and I might have hurt his feelings. Why don't you jot me down for a couple counts of vandalism and bad manners and call it a day."

Several beats of silence were followed by a long sigh.

"I'm going to need your brother's number," he said finally, and I gave it to him.

"Let me ask you something," I said. "What about the girl who found the bodies? What does she say?"

I waited as he decided whether to tell me. "She had a date with one of the victims."

"A date on a Monday morning?"

"They were planning on leaving town, Travis."

"For where?"

"We don't know. A long trip. She said he'd been talking about money. That he was about to come into a shitload of it."

From Valden's blackmail, I guessed. Or something else.

"She mention where the cash might be coming from?"

"Nope. Claims she didn't know."

"Then somebody pulled the guy's rip cord, hit-man style, and the case goes off to organized crime."

"That's about the size of it," he said.

I explored my lip with the tip of my fingers. The swelling was going down. "You never liked me for the murders."

"That was Dan Kemp fucking with Hans Yamaguchi. Kemp and his goddamned camera."

"And you allowed it to happen."

"I don't control that prick, Travis. Nobody does."

A small gust blew down from the mountain, felt like cold breath on my neck.

"Take it easy, Townsend."

"I'm sorry about Hans, Mike," he said. "I heard it went hard on him today."

"Yeah, I heard that, too," I said. I tilted my gaze to the sky and saw the stars wink out, one by one, as a cloud passed slowly overhead.

CHAPTER THIRTY-ONE

I sat in the Captain's chair on the *Kehau*'s afterdeck, a steaming mug of Mango Ceylon in my hands, and watched the arrival of a new day. I wanted to sit there for the whole program, watch the sun creep over the mountains and illuminate the moisture that hung in the air until it edged all the way into the morning sky.

But I had to reach my brother in New York before Townsend started his day in LA.

"Someone from LAPD is going to be calling you, Valden. Probably today. It'll likely be a detective named John Townsend. Take his call."

"Me? What for?"

"To back up a story I told them about why Hans and I were at the house where the security guard and his friend were murdered."

"I don't have time for this."

"Make time," I said. "You can't put these guys off, or it'll get worse. Much worse."

"What do you want me to say?"

"Stick close to the truth, don't get too detailed."

I told him the story I'd given Townsend.

When I'd finished, he said, "That's it?"

"And one other thing. Hans Yamaguchi."

"What about him?"

"It's looking like Hans could lose his job because of this."

"Because of me? Because of the Mandalay thing?"

"It didn't help. And if he does, you owe him, Valden. He would never have been involved if you hadn't called me."

"And now I owe him?"

"I'm family, Valden. It's one thing to put me at risk, but I would have never gotten to the guys in time if it hadn't been for Hans. And you'd be out $3 million."

"Three million dollars," he repeated.

"Versus the cost of a divorce. What's that? Half of everything you own? Maybe more? And lose your kids in the bargain. I'm thinking that might have been unpleasant for you."

"I'll think about it." His tone said he thought I was full of shit.

"While you do, remember this: Hans has a family, too. If he gets fired, he'll lose his pension, health benefits, the whole ball of wax, Valden. He's been in for more than twenty-two years."

"I said I'd think about it."

"Do that," I said. "And don't fuck up with Detective Townsend. You tell it exactly as I told it to you."

The conversation hadn't taken long, but it was enough to defile my enjoyment of the sunrise, so I went below to throw some breakfast together. I opened the sliding windows, invited some clean morning air into the galley, and began slicing some fresh papaya, mango and guava. I cracked a couple of eggs, whipped them in a bowl, and a few minutes later, the smell of sizzling bacon brought Snyder up from his bunk.

He took a seat and watched me cook, working the sleep out of his system.

"I was thinking we'd run the *Chingadera* up to Keehi Lagoon. Blow out the exhaust. What do you say?"

"I could use a change of scenery."

"Up for diving yet?"

I ran my fingers across the lump on my head. "I don't think so."

He looked past me to the stove. "Let's get this thing on the road, then, Travis. You've been indoors too long."

Chingadera was in the water, Snyder dragging her to stern, careful to keep her from banging the yacht's hull as I swung the davits back in place and stowed the canvas in the deck locker. The morning air had grown still and hot, with only a breath of the trades to cool it. The few clouds in the pale sky were diaphanous and frail, like pulled cotton.

The ice chest rattled as I hefted it over the rail to Snyder, who was standing at the bow of the skiff.

"I don't think I fully appreciated how thoroughly they kicked your ass," Snyder said. I was wearing a tank shirt, the lumps and bruises on my face, arms and chest showing green and black and angry red.

Down below, Snyder's cell phone rang. For a second, I debated not going down to get it, but this wasn't a morning for that. I was still waiting to hear back from Thel Mishow and Hans. But when I picked it up, it was about the last person I would have expected.

"Mike, this is J.R." He sounded agitated, distracted.

"J.R. Lennox?" I said.

"Yes, sorry, I should have . . ." There was a long pause as he composed himself. "You gave me your card when we met in California, told me to call. The number wasn't working, so I got this one from your brother."

"Sure, J.R.," I said, wondering what the hell he was getting at. "I saw the news about the fires. I'm sorry."

"This isn't about the fires."

"I'm not following you, J.R."

"Mike, they've taken my son."

CHAPTER THIRTY-TWO

It wasn't long before a white stretch limo pulled to a smooth stop at the curb where I'd been pacing ruts in the pavement at the entrance to the harbor. It had been long enough, however, for me to throw on some clean clothes, wash my face, run a comb over the lump I hoped was still hidden by my wind-tangled hair and throw my mind into overdrive. I didn't wait for the driver to open the door, just climbed in and settled into the soft leather seats and closed the door behind me.

The driver eyed me in the rearview. I sat alone in the backseat.

"Mike Travis?" he asked.

"Yes."

He rolled up the transparent screen between us without another word.

The car moved away from the curb and pushed through the late morning traffic on Ala Moana Boulevard toward Kalakaua and the seemingly endless stretch of high-rise hotels that lined Waikiki Beach. I shifted in my seat, adjusting the weight of the Beretta nine that was tucked into the back of my khakis and grating painfully against my newly acquired bruises. I looked out across the park where morning people biked and skated and jogged, taking special interest to identify the place where I'd received my beating.

When I turned back, I noticed the driver in the rearview again, clearly eyeing me. I located the button on the armrest beside me, raised the solid privacy screen between us and mentally revisited the brief conversation I'd had with J.R. Lennox half an hour before.

"You're certain it was an abduction," I had asked.

"There's a note, Mike."

"A ransom demand?"

"Of a sort," he said. "Listen, Mike, I need—"

"Have you called the cops, the FBI?"

There was a charged silence inside of which I sensed the depth of his fear.

"There aren't going to be any cops," J.R. said. "Dad and Hobart are both firm on that."

I started to ask who Hobart was, but he cut me off. "I know you used to be a detective," he said. "And I need your help. I want Randall back, and I want him back fast, unhurt."

"J.R., this really isn't my area. I don't know how much help I can be to you."

Outside the car, I could hear the rumbling of traffic along the service road that bled off the main boulevard and out toward the highway. The sun bounced hard against the side of a passing delivery truck and into my eyes.

"I understand you recently got your brother out of a sticky situation. That's the kind of person I need on my side. All I'm getting right now is advice from the company's security people."

I didn't like his reference to my visit to LA, and didn't know who his sources were, but they were damned well-informed about Valden and me. I didn't like it, not even a little.

"You twisting my balls, J.R.?"

He sighed heavily.

"No, Mike," he said. "I'm not. I'm against a wall here. My son's been kidnapped and I want him back."

"What's wrong with the help you've already got? The Lennox family must have access to the best security talent in the world."

"They work for my father," he said. "I'm sure you know how that is."

I did know how it was. And I kind of liked J.R., understood him, even felt a little sorry for him. Now his eight-year-old son was missing and he wanted whatever help I could give him to get his boy back.

He broke into my silence. "Listen, Mike," he said. "I've read enough about these things to know that they're sometimes inside jobs. The truth is I don't know whom to trust, except somebody from the outside. Somebody who understands the family dynamic. Somebody like you."

I hadn't been trying to make him grovel.

"Okay, J.R.," I said. "Enough."

"You'll help me?"

"I'll do everything I can."

"Tell me where you are," he said, afraid I might change my mind. "I'll send a car right away."

The limo came to a stop underneath the portico at the Ala Moana Surf, one of the finest luxury hotels in Waikiki, where a bellman in a starched white uniform had my door open for me before I could even reach for the handle. I stepped out of the car, walked across a plush carpet embroidered with the hotel's lion-and-shield logo, and into the hypercooled air of the lobby.

Inside, the decor was all exotic wood and potted palms, and looked more like my idea of the Bahamas than the South Pacific. Tanned country club types lounged in designer furniture, wearing aloha shirts and white cotton pants with creases you could shave with—card-carrying members of the touch-of-silver-at-the-temples set, who winked at one another and wore their Bally loafers with no socks. These were the people who snapped their fingers to get the attention of waiters, treated the housekeeping staff like furniture and stiffed valets and bellmen—people with no comprehension of the irony inherent in tropical-wear that bore the logos of fashion designers.

J.R. Lennox stood alone at the far end of the lobby, near the elevators.

"Mike," he said, and offered me a damp handshake. "Thank you for coming."

He took hold of my arm and pulled me farther into the recess of the lobby where he'd been awaiting me. His eyes seemed unfocused, but charged with the static electric energy of a man pushed too far too fast.

His expression changed once he saw me up close. "What happened to you?"

"An accident in the park. Forget it."

He seemed to consider something, then his attention slid from my face and appeared to fade into the distance.

"One thing before we go up there, Mike," he said. "My father doesn't know I've called you. He doesn't know you're here."

I looked out the window, squinted into the stark daylight of the courtyard. "What're you telling me, J.R.?"

He followed my gaze briefly then turned away, blinking against the brilliant sparkles of glare that reflected off the fountain, gathering his thoughts into words.

"I don't know exactly how to say this," he said. "I've been up in that room for the last several hours listening to all this . . . *strategy*." He turned his eyes back on me. "This is my *son* we're talking about here. This isn't some goddamned transaction. Everyone in there is a Lennox employee. I didn't know what else to do. So I called you."

"Who is involved so far?"

"Besides my father and me?" he said. "Ray Hobart, and one of Ray's lieutenants."

"Who is Hobart?"

J.R. rubbed his chin, closed his eyes for a moment. "Head of security for Lennox Biomedical."

"A bodyguard?"

"No," he said. "More like a private cop."

"Former military, I assume. What does he do for the company?"

"He's in charge of creating and implementing the security procedures for our offices and manufacturing plants. He sees to it that the senior executives are protected when they travel abroad."

"That includes you, obviously. And your son."

"Yes, it does."

"Sounds to me like a conflict of interest."

"I believe so, too," J.R. nodded. "That's why I need you here."

"Does your father trust Hobart?"

"Completely."

"I don't get the impression that you feel the same way."

"I used to," he said. "Had no reason not to."

"And now?"

"Now I don't know, Mike. I don't know much of anything at the moment."

A twinkle of laughter drifted across the lobby to us, a foursome of beautiful people waiting as the valet brought a rented Jaguar convertible up front; feral smiles, backslapping and air-kisses as one of the couples got into the car and pulled away.

"Let's go on up," I said, and J.R. seemed to pull his strength together, stood a little straighter.

We stepped into the empty elevator; heavy doors slid into place, closing us into a burlwood-and-polished-brass cocoon.

I caught J.R. furtively assessing my injuries in the reflection again.

It was a long, quiet ride to the twenty-fifth floor.

"Who the hell is this?" the shaven-headed man at the door asked of both of us. His skull was the shape of a mortar shell and his shoulders nearly as wide as the doorway.

He attempted to deny my entry with a stiff arm and a smile that looked like it belonged on someone else's face.

"Watch what happens if you lay hands on me," I smiled in return. "You'll be getting your nutrients through a straw."

"That's enough, Pollard," J.R. said. "Let him through. He's with me."

The suite felt cramped, close and dim, despite its size. Oversized bay windows that ordinarily looked out onto Diamond Head and the white beach below were sealed shut and concealed behind a set of blackout curtains and heavy drapes. The only light in the room emanated from a pair of floor lamps glowing yellow at either end of a seating area that separated two master bedrooms. Something stale and bitter hung in the air.

Pollard closed the door and took up a position inside.

Phillip Lennox fixed his son with a cold stare, then turned toward the man who had first spoken to me. "He's a friend of J.R.'s." His intonation suggested that we should be tolerated in the same way one tolerates children who are seated at the grown-ups' table.

To J.R.'s credit, he didn't let either man back him down.

"Mike Travis," I announced to the room in general. "Friend of the family."

If I blinked, I would have missed it, but something passed between the men like a cold chill. Phillip Lennox stood and crossed the room, greeted me with a firm, quick handshake.

This was a man who always moved fast, as if trying to stay in front of someone.

"Then you know that we're dealing with a crisis here," Lennox said, shooting another glance in J.R.'s direction.

"I'm here to do whatever I can to help get J.R.'s son back."

The man who had been lurking silently beside Lennox decided to assert himself.

"The first thing you can do is stay the hell out of—"

"Ray Hobart," Phillip Lennox interrupted him. "Shake hands with Mr. Travis."

Hobart was a tall man, about my height, but he'd allowed a build that had probably once been described as athletic to go soft around the middle. He had lifeless prosthetic eyes that looked as though they had been glued onto his face. His dark hair was cropped short in military fashion, and he had the appearance of a man who had once been comfortable in third-world countries with a sniper's scope pressed against the lenses of mirrored shades. He grunted something meant to pass as a greeting as he grasped my hand, and squeezed a little harder than necessary. I smiled and squeezed in return. Hobart's expression said he didn't much like my kind. I read that to include anyone without a military background, or who was not a part of the official Lennox inner circle.

"How long has Randall been missing?" I asked.

The room remained silent except for the hum of the air-conditioning. J.R. answered when no one else spoke.

"Since about seven o'clock this morning."

"That's five hours ago."

"That's correct," Phillip Lennox said, "we're aware of the time frame." His voice was flat, so empty it seemed piped in from somewhere else.

I looked at Lennox and Hobart, then turned to J.R. I was an

outsider, unwanted. That much was abundantly clear. The security man eyed me with the same expression as the senior Lennox had, and I knew I'd walked in at the middle of this movie. There was so much backstory buried here it would take the Jaws of Life to pry it all out.

"He was last seen at the beach," J.R. added. "Randall was enrolled in an early bird kids' program overseen by the hotel. The children are still on mainland time, so they tend to get up early in the morning."

Hobart turned his back to all of us, peeled open a curtain and fixed his eyes on something far below. A triangle of golden light strayed across the carpet.

"They're supposed to be supervised." J.R.'s voice faded into an elongated stretch of nothing.

"You mentioned receiving a note," I said.

J.R. looked to his father, and Hobart returned his attention to the conversation. He let the curtain fall back into place and restored the room to semidarkness.

"For Christ's sake," Hobart said. "Mr. Lennox, are you really going to—"

The older man cut him off again without turning his head. "Thank you, Ray."

Ray Hobart shot me a look embroidered with the threat of violence, but I'd seen it so many times before—on the faces of bikers, gangbangers, and other self-appointed badasses—that it didn't have the desired effect.

"We received an envelope, Mr. Travis," the elder Lennox said. "It was delivered to the room by one of the bellmen at about eight thirty this morning."

"Who brought it to the hotel?" I asked.

"One of those corporate document delivery outfits."

"Was there a purchase order attached?"

Lennox showed me a patronizing smile. "One of Mr. Hobart's people is looking into that as we speak." His speech pattern and content carried not so much a tone as a viscosity.

"And what is the demand?"

There was another stillness, a silence so thick you could curl up and sleep on it.

"A statement from my father," J.R. said, finally. "A general press release denouncing Congressman Bill Kelleher."

"More specifically," Lennox added, "denouncing my support of the congressman's foreign trade bill."

"What's the deadline?" I asked.

Lennox pulled back the cuff of a long-sleeved cotton shirt, exposing a thin gold Patek Philippe. "Noon."

I looked at my own watch, then to the faces of the three other men in the room. "That's right now," I said, alarmed that I was the only one who appeared to be alarmed. "I assume you've complied."

Lennox shook his head as he gazed at the floor and gave me a chuckle of condescension. "No, Mr. Travis, I have not."

"What are you not telling me?" I didn't understand his calm, and my ears began to ring. "There's something else?"

"You're out of your league, son," Hobart said. "We've got this." He seemed so proud of himself I could practically see the jazz hands.

Lennox took control again. "What Mr. Hobart is trying to say is that in situations like this—cases of extortion, that is—we've found it wisest not to relent, not to negotiate. It only encourages the perpetrators to try it again."

I shot a glance at J.R., coming to a full understanding as to why he'd called me in.

"This is your grandson, Mr. Lennox," I said. "This isn't that simple."

"It's a version of blackmail all the same," he said. "The fact that it's my grandson they're holding, rather than some dirty photographs, is not germane. We have to look past the details and deal with the root of the situation. And the root of *this* situation is political."

"I believe you're underestimating," I said. "You've already had two of your company's buildings burned to the ground. I can only assume, under the circumstances, that these matters are all related. Are you prepared to pay with Randall's life if you're wrong?"

Phillip Lennox waved the idea away. Wrong didn't seem like a concept he often considered in any context involving himself. "Don't be melodramatic. We've dealt with this kind of situation before, and I think we know what we're doing."

"So, what *are* you doing?" I asked.

"For now," Hobart said, "nothing."

His statement was firm, final. This was clearly coming out of his operational playbook.

"I assume this was your call, Hobart."

"It's our standard protocol."

"I had also assumed you had the intelligence of a colostomy bag," I said. "But I may have overestimated."

"When we do not respond or attempt to negotiate," Phillip Lennox interrupted, "they'll see that we're playing hardball, too. They won't want to take it any further. Not in the name of politics. It could easily backfire and defeat their purpose. They're not going to kill the child—Randall—over this. They'll either let him go, or demand money instead. If it comes to money, then we'll get Randall back when we make the trade."

The older man stood, looking like he was about to deliver a speech to his Board of Directors.

"But my political influence cannot, *cannot* be extorted,"

Lennox said. "Imagine if I allowed it just this once. Our lives would never be the same again. We'd be under the threat of kidnap, blackmail, every manner of shakedown you can think of, for the rest of our lives, Mr. Travis. And my executives operating worldwide would become targets, as well."

I had seen this dynamic before. When indignation turned to self-righteousness, you'd better batten down the fucking hatches. It was clear that this man had a moral code unique to himself. As if theft were not stealing if he admitted to it afterward.

"You are familiar with the adage about putting a frog in a pot of cold water and slowly heating the stove?" I said. "The water begins to boil before the frog is ever aware he's being cooked. You know the story, right?"

Hobart took a step toward me. "Is that some sort of code we're supposed to understand?"

"Dig the sand out of your ears," I said. "I'm suggesting that you hold the goddamned press conference that the kidnappers are demanding, and once you get Randall back, you go public with the fact that it had all been a sham. An extorted statement. End of story."

Lennox shook his head. "That's exactly what I *cannot* do. I'd be admitting my—our—vulnerability to this sort of thing happening again. At the very least, my word wouldn't be worth a thing, wouldn't ever be fully believed again. People would always be waiting for the other shoe to drop. Trust me. We've got this under control, Mr. Travis."

I looked at my wristwatch again, watching the seconds sweep by.

"Relax," Hobart said. "What we do now is wait. I'll have the boy back in time for dinner."

J.R. had seated himself on the couch, his head hanging low between hunched shoulders, elbows resting on his knees. He put a hand across his mouth and squeezed, pressing the flesh of his face until his cheeks gathered up under his eyes. The futility of arguing with his father and Ray Hobart had left him deflated. I took a seat on the couch beside him.

I leaned my head back and stared at the ceiling, willing myself to think of anything I could say that could alter the present course. We both knew that J.R. had brought me in to save this situation, but I still felt his disappointment as if he'd spray-painted me with it.

"Hobart," I said. "You know from experience that a battle never goes according to plan. Never."

I'd spent too much time on the streets not to hold the image of death clearly in my head. Real death, with real blood; real loss and real pain. Mine wasn't experience born in a boardroom, or strategy sessions with the corporate legal team. Mine came from staring violence right in the goddamned face, looking it straight in its red, crazy-assed, drug-addled eyes. It was out there. Plenty of it. More than you ever wanted to believe. There were people to whom it meant less than zero to take a life. They could blow someone's shit away with one hand and eat a double-cheese, extra tomato and onion, with the other.

Both Hobart and Phillip Lennox remained unmoved.

My mind went back to Randall, the only way I had ever seen him, a little eight-year-old boy in miniature Armani holding fast to his father's hand. An only child in a very rich man's world.

In the end, we did what Lennox and Hobart wanted. We waited.

As it turned out, we didn't have to wait long.

CHAPTER THIRTY-THREE

The cell phone in my pocket rang, and Hobart made a grab for his sidearm. Everyone's nerves had been strained to the limit.

"It's mine," I said to the room, flipped the phone open and stepped into one of the darkened corners.

Hobart and his cohort, Pollard, eyeballed me with contempt, tried to plaster expressions of competence onto their faces.

"Mike, it's Thel Mishow. I've got some more information on the Mandalay Plaza. Can you talk?"

I glanced at Phillip Lennox still seated in his overstuffed chair, fingers laced around a smoldering cigar, staring at me.

"Not so much," I said.

"I understand," Thel said, lowering his voice. "I'll be brief. What we've found is that a number of the subsidiary corporations and partnerships in the ownership structure are of Chinese extraction."

"Of which persuasion?" I asked, attempting to remain oblique to the roomful of ears now tuned-in to my side of the call.

There was a brief hesitation as Thel decoded what I meant.

"Ah, yes. Good question," he said. "The answer is: both. The old Hong Kong capitalists, *and* the new, post-British variety.

Odd though, if you ask me, having both the communists and the Hong Kong old guard in the same transaction together with Phillip Lennox."

I worked to remain expressionless.

"Anything else?"

Thel cleared his throat uncomfortably. "Are you sure you can talk right now?"

"Is there anything else?" I repeated.

"As for more detail, I'd have to say there's not much. Because of the Chinese incorporations, we haven't been able to determine who the actual *shareholders* are yet, but we're using every channel we have access to in an effort to find out for you."

Hobart, Pollard and Lennox had all begun giving me the hard-eyes. It was time to ring off.

"I appreciate it."

"I'll call you when I have more," he said. "By the way, Patricia Dunross told me you'd had some trouble. Is everything all right?"

"Fine," I said.

"We were discussing another matter and she happened to mention it."

Bullshit.

"No problem," I said casually, a non sequitur. I was tired of being stared at, and I couldn't tell how much of Thel's side of the conversation they could actually hear.

"Call me later, Mike."

"Soon," I said, and cut the connection.

Hobart took three long strides across the room and glared at me. "Who was *that*?"

I faced him, our noses now inches apart.

"A friend of mine, *Ray*. You want to screen my calls?"

He fixed me with a touch of that third-world spook stare,

thought better of it and broke it off before this went too far. I saw him file it away for later.

"Gentlemen, please try to relax," Phillip Lennox said. "We're all under pressure here."

The crackle of fired tobacco was the only sound in the room. I watched arabesques of smoke dance toward the ceiling.

And more seconds ticked by.

The finger arrived in a tiny box.

The third man on Ray Hobart's security team, Ted something, found it outside the door of Lennox's suite, packed in dry ice and wrapped up in garish holiday paper. Ted had returned from following up on the purchase order for the delivery of the original ransom note, traced it all the way back to a phony business address supposedly located in a vacant lot in Pearl City. It was barely after one o'clock, scarcely an hour past the original deadline.

Phillip Lennox unwrapped the package himself, tearing through the paper and throwing the pieces to the floor.

"Goddamned smart-ass bastards." His words caught in his throat when he lifted the top from the box.

J.R. took in his father's expression and crossed the room in a single stride, and peered into the box that his father had dropped on the table. I was two steps behind J.R., arriving in time to support him when his knees began to buckle.

It was a pale piece of meat and bone lying on a bed of dry ice. The bloody end was ragged, and looked as though it had been masticated. The tiny finger had been severed neither swiftly nor cleanly.

The air in the room grew thick in the stunned silence. J.R. turned and vomited into a waste can.

"This is likely a ruse, Mr. Lennox," Hobart said, and shot a glance at Ted. "Probably a fake. This is not Randall's finger. They want to throw us—"

Lennox's face was stone, his eyes luminous, manic.

"Shut up," I said.

Hobart took an involuntary step backward. "What I'm saying is that—"

"Shut the fuck up, Ray," I said again. Their strategy, such as it was, had gone to hell, and everybody in the room knew it. "Experience comes at a price. Randall just paid it."

CHAPTER THIRTY-FOUR

In the time it took me to utter those words to Ray Hobart, the pieces came together for me.

The murders in Los Angeles, fingers severed from the hands of the victims; the case being transferred to the Organized Crime Intelligence Division; the tangled ownership of the Mandalay Plaza Hotel and the maze of unidentifiable Chinese partners. Add to that the two arson fires at Lennox Biomedical plants and the kidnap and mutilation of J.R.'s son, Randall.

"Phillip, J.R.," I said, looking at both men in turn. "You can no longer assume that this is anything but very, very real. Your battle plan just changed."

J.R. nodded.

"Are you following me?" I asked, driving the point home to the senior Lennox, who hadn't seemed to hear me. "These people are not fucking around."

It would have taken a fool not to feel the power shift inside that room, and while Hobart might be an Olympic-class asshole, he was not an idiot. To save face, he knew he needed to reassert himself in the eyes of his employer.

"Sir," he said to Lennox, "I'm going to send Ted down to hotel security, see if they've got anything we can use. Video.

Anything at all. I'll talk to the manager myself. Somebody must have seen something."

"Fine, Ray," Lennox answered, his voice empty, vacant. "See what you can find out."

I waited until the door closed behind Lennox's security team before I spoke again. J.R. stood at the window, drew back the curtain and looked down at the beach where his son should have been. His face was a pallid mask of revulsion and fear.

I took a seat across from Phillip Lennox and waited until he gathered himself enough to meet my gaze.

"Tell me about the Chinese, Mr. Lennox."

A flash of something, then it was gone. "I don't know what you're talking about."

"Mr. Lennox," I said, "with all due respect, there's no more time for horseshit."

He took his seat in the big chair, gave me the corporate glare, the one that was supposed to stop me in my tracks. But I didn't work for Phillip Lennox, didn't give a rat's ass for his money or his power or his politics.

"You know who did this," I said. "You've known from the beginning."

Thick gray brows knit together in a frown, eyes screwed tightly shut. Lennox pulled in a deep, jagged breath. The dam of control he had fought so hard to maintain was beginning to burst.

It started with his hands, fingers quivering until full-scale tremors traveled all the way up his arms. He leaned forward, elbows on his knees, stared at his shoes and looked as though he were about to be sick. His mouth hung open, like a fish on a dry pier, attempting to catch his breath.

"Are you all right?" I said. It was beginning to look like he was having a heart attack.

He nodded, wrestling with something inside of himself.

I went to the bar for a glass of water, came back quickly and pressed it into his quaking hands. He drank it down in one long pull, wiped his lips with the back of his hand and placed the glass on the table beside him.

J.R. no longer could make eye contact with his father, just kept staring out the window onto the long ribbon of sand, at the tourists laid out on hotel towels watching outrigger canoes as they sliced through rounded turquoise waves.

"Tell me what's happening here," I said. "*Now.* Before this whole thing comes apart any worse than it already has."

Lennox raised his head finally, his expression glazed, the look of a man unacquainted with the loss of control.

"It started with the hotel," Lennox began.

"The Mandalay Plaza?"

He nodded, locked his eyes on mine again. "You know what OPM is?"

I didn't answer.

"Other People's Money," he said. "It's how rich people get richer. Hell, Travis, your father—his father before him—they knew about OPM. They built Van de Groot Capital with it."

"Go on," I said.

"It's the American way, son. You leverage other people's risk capital, you fight tooth and nail for the project's success, and the profits belong to all of you. Everybody wins. That's how it's supposed to work."

"What does that have to do with the Mandalay?"

He focused on a spot in the air behind me. "The Mandalay Plaza was going to be my Trump Tower, the very centerpiece of the business district in Los Angeles."

"But?"

"But the investment capital didn't all belong to me."

He came out of his thousand-yard stare, dropped his eyes and trapped my gaze.

"I'm a board member of IBC, the International Business Circle. It's where I first met your brother, Valden."

"Go on."

"He invited me to several meetings of his YPO group . . ." Lennox batted his hand in front of him, frustrated by his own digression. "Anyway, the IBC sponsored a trip to China, just a small group of us, twelve or fifteen is all. Ever since Tiananmen Square, everybody in the business world has known that China was on the verge of making some significant changes regarding its views on capitalism and international investment. So we went over to meet with some of the prime movers in Beijing and Shanghai, met some very interesting people, in fact, people who are very much in favor of opening up their country to free enterprise."

His face took on the familiar zealous light I'd seen before, most recently when he had given the speech at the fundraiser at his home; it was a look you might have seen in the eyes of Samuel Adams talking revolution, or Billy Graham speaking about Jesus. The fevered glow of the true believer.

"Do you have any idea how big a market that would be?" Lennox said. "There are billions of potential consumers who have never before figured into US business models. The potential impact on our economy is almost beyond imagining."

The room was diffused with light from the window where J.R. still stood. Dust motes drifted on the chilled air while I listened to Phillip Lennox describe his fever dream.

"We spent four days there," Lennox went on. "We met with some of the most important men in the country, men who want to create a new China. Among them was a man named Xiang Ho, the head of a conglomerate of manufacturing, mining and shipping interests based in Hong Kong. After one of our conferences, Ho took me aside and expressed an interest in investment opportunities that might exist for him in the US. He was particularly interested in doing business with a global enterprise like Lennox."

The sentence drifted into silence. I waited, but nothing came.

"Mr. Lennox?" I prompted.

It seemed as though I had lost him to another faraway thought.

"But that had not been my purpose in going to China," Lennox resumed abruptly. "I wasn't there looking for investments for Lennox Biomedical. I was there to identify partners for some of my outside, personal investments."

"Like real estate."

"Among other things, yes. Those nights in China ran late, and our hosts were always anxious to show off what passed as sophisticated nightlife in their cities.

"In the days that followed, I became friendly with Xiang Ho and his young lieutenant and translator, Mr. Soong. Since Soong was fluent in English, it was quite natural, really. By the fourth night, we ended up staying out very late, drinking and talking and developing what seemed to be a certain amount of trust, forming the basis of a business relationship. We each talked of things that interested us, and as it turned out, Xiang Ho and I shared an interest in collecting artifacts from around the world."

Lennox stood, thrust his hands deep in his pockets and began to pace the length of the room.

"The next night, Soong took me aside and told me, with a wink, that he knew a man who was willing to part with a very precious religious artifact—my true weakness where collecting is concerned. In fact, Soong told me, this gentleman would be most honored to know that the object would be part of a prestigious Western collection such as mine. When I finally persuaded him to tell me what it was, Soong revealed that the relic was one of the true Buddha's teeth."

My mind traveled back to the lighted displays in Lennox's study.

"At the time, I laughed at the very thought of it," he said. "Which I'm sure was very rude. Nevertheless, I really thought Soong was having me on about it. But he was quite serious, and assured me that the tooth was authentic, though the provenance was somewhat irregular, to say the least. The item, he told me, had been the subject of a complicated transaction between a rebellious Tibetan monk and some corrupt Chinese military conscripts. Regardless, I registered polite interest, and changed the subject back to more mundane matters."

Phillip Lennox plucked the remnants of his cigar from the ashtray and tucked it between his fingers, unlit.

"About three months later, I received a package from Mr. Soong, a gift from him and his boss, Xiang Ho."

Lennox licked his lips, looked back to the floor as if that was where his shame lay.

"I'm no virgin where gifts and business and politics are concerned, so I understood what the message was. It was an overture that they wished to do business with me.

"It was out of the question to return the tooth, not only would it have been the apex of impropriety and disrespect, but a clear message to them that I had no interest in doing any further business with them at all, and would likely kill any possibility of investments from the other Chinese I'd met on that trip. Well, that was hardly what I wanted. After all, finding new capital partners was the purpose of the IBC excursion in the first place."

"So you offered Xiang Ho and Soong the opportunity to invest in the Mandalay Plaza with you," I said.

He nodded, his humiliation coming to full bloom.

I glanced over at J.R. If he was listening at all to his father's conversation with me, he showed no sign of it.

"Out of gratitude for the gift, I offered them the chance to participate in the Mandalay Plaza investment, on terms that I considered to be very reasonable. A short time later, we formed a partnership to buy the land and fund the predevelopment costs of the project.

"At that time, I had borrowed a good deal of money—to carry the project—from a bank with which I do a bit of business. Mr. Ho's investment capital paid off those loans and created a pool of additional operating cash that we would use in order to move the hotel forward. From there, we formed some additional partnerships, some corporations, all for the purpose of completing separate and distinct aspects of the project's construction and for setting up the management company."

That began to explain the complicated pyramid of the hotel's ownership structure.

"Something obviously went wrong," I said. "What was it?"

"At first there was nothing wrong. Then, out of the blue, I was visited by a man who claimed to be an attaché of the Chinese embassy. The man represented himself to be a senior officer of what amounts to be the Chinese version of the CIA."

J.R. allowed the curtain to fall and the room dropped back into the gloom that had characterized it since we'd arrived. He drifted over to the sofa across from his father and took a seat beside me.

Lennox looked uneasily in his son's direction, but there was no eye contact. The atmosphere was leaden with loathing, but something inside Phillip Lennox had changed. I wasn't sure if I was watching a metamorphosis or a meltdown.

"I'm not a man who is easily intimidated," Phillip Lennox

went on. "Nor am I easily deceived. But suffice it to say that over the course of that meeting I was convinced by the man's story, and his none-too-subtle intimations that my new partners were deeply involved in Chinese organized crime. He showed me a document. He convinced me that it would be in my best interest if I were as sympathetic as humanly possible to my new Chinese partners."

"Xiang Ho and Soong," I said.

"Yes."

His voice had grown stronger, more impassioned, as if he were delivering a keynote address. Phillip Lennox was mercurial in the extreme, with a nearly pathological need to dominate. I have developed a sincere appreciation for the delineations between good and evil, truth and obfuscation. But it was the man's complete absence of a moral compass that disturbed me more than anything else he was saying. It was a common personality flaw among sociopaths and recidivists.

He paused to light his cigar before he went on, his head momentarily lost inside a silver cloud of smoke.

"I didn't hear another word from them for months," he said. "And the project continued as smoothly as one could reasonably expect. That is to say, there was a hitch here or there, but overall, it was proceeding quite nicely. So nicely, in fact, that I had begun to believe that the whole episode with the embassy man had been a misunderstanding of some kind, or even that he was an imposter, or some kind of agent provocateur acting for someone else's interests entirely."

J.R. shifted in his seat and rested an arm along the back of the sofa. He studied his father as though he had never seen him before.

It was then that I recognized what was happening with Phillip Lennox. I'd been here before, in interrogation rooms.

Once the floodgates came open, you did everything you could not to stanch the flow, and let it all come out. There was always need behind a confession; and this was proving to be nothing short of a confession.

"So I had one of my own security men check out the Chinese attaché. My man found nothing. Not a trace. After that, I thought it best to leave things alone. Months went by without any contact outside the normal course of the project, neither side asking, or even intimating, that anything out of the ordinary had transpired—"

The suite's phone rang loudly, interrupting Lennox, and causing J.R. to start so badly he lapsed into a coughing fit.

Logic dictated that now that Randall's finger had been delivered, this call would be from the kidnappers. As the phone rang a second time, I quickly moved to the bedroom extension and instructed Phillip to simultaneously pick up the living room extension as I counted backward from three. He began to protest, but I cut him off.

"We do not have time to fuck around. Do what I told you."

Lennox stood, suddenly uncertain, as the phone rang again.

"Goddamn it," I shouted. "Pick up when I get to 'one.' *Do it!*"

Time slowed to a crawl, and the phone rang again. He shook himself from whatever had gripped him, then moved to the phone beside the couch.

Both our hands hovered over the receivers as it rang a fifth time.

"Three . . . two . . . one," I said, and we both picked up.

CHAPTER THIRTY-FIVE

The silence on the line was so complete that I thought we had missed the call.

Lennox didn't utter a word, only pressed the phone mutely to his ear.

"Are you there?"

"I'm here," Lennox said.

"Did you receive our package?"

"You bastard, you goddamned—"

"Now, Mr. Lennox," the voice interrupted, "don't be rude. I'm calling you with good news."

Lennox said nothing.

"You don't want to know what it is?"

"What is it?"

"That's much better. I assume you have people listening, attempting to trace the call perhaps? Don't bother, it can't be done. Besides, I truly don't think you want outsiders to hear what I have to tell you."

"Where is my grandson?"

"I didn't hear any clicks, so I suspect that no one got off the line. I've given you fair warning. The choice is yours."

"*Where* is my *grandson*?"

"He's a fine boy, Mr. Lennox, very brave."

I caught Lennox's eye, mouthed to him, "Ask to talk to Randall." Proof of life.

Lennox nodded.

"I want to talk to him. I want to speak to my grandson."

"Ahh," the voice was mock-disappointed. "I'm so sorry. That can't be done. He's sleeping."

"You sonofabitch, Soong," he hissed. "If you've—"

J.R. looked up from the trance he'd been in and gazed at his father. He turned to me as though he didn't know how we'd all gotten here.

"Really, Mr. Lennox, please. Quite the contrary. I'm calling because I want to give him back."

"Why?" he said.

I winced.

"Because I no longer need him."

I knew it meant that the caller had something damaging on Lennox, but Lennox's mind had wandered somewhere else.

A moment's hesitation, then, "When?"

"Perhaps as early as tonight," he said. "But it's up to you."

"What do you want?"

"You know what I want," he replied evenly.

Lennox's hand was tight on the receiver, his knuckles white, his face mottled with anger. "You know I won't—"

"Mr. Lennox, your House of Representatives has delayed the vote on Kelleher's trade bill for one week." Joey Soong paused to let it sink in. "I want a draft copy of a speech that you will agree to make, denouncing that bill. *And* I want a letter, signed by you, that authenticates it."

"I've told you before—"

"I'm not finished yet. You will then schedule a press conference within the next forty-eight hours in order to deliver your statement. I expect you to bring every pressure to bear upon your friend the congressman to withdraw the bill from the floor completely."

"That's ridiculous, he'll never agree to that."

"I think that, for you, he might," Soong said. "In fact; I think the congressman would do anything you asked of him."

Lennox squeezed his lips tightly, and cast his eyes to the wall. He took a deep breath before he spoke again.

"And if I give you the statement you're asking for, you'll return Randall to me?"

"The statement, and all the rest of what I've asked for. Including your commitment to have Mr. Kelleher withdraw the bill from the House floor."

I watched Lennox's mind begin to work, plotting new moves, calculating new percentages. He twisted the phone cord between his fingers as he paced the floor.

"I can hear your puzzlement," Soong said. "You're wondering what's to keep you from going back on your word after I return your grandson."

Phillip Lennox didn't reply, but stopped pacing long enough to cast me a sideways glance. His eyes were ice.

"Hostages are a bother, Mr. Lennox," he said. "And I am now in possession of something even more potent."

"What are you saying?"

Soong laughed. "Do you remember the document that our friend from the embassy showed to you?"

"Yes." Lennox's voice was hoarse, his expression morphed to something that resembled panic.

"What I have is even better than that."

"No one would believe you."

"They won't have to believe me. They will be able to see it for themselves."

The color drained from Lennox's face.

"Haven't you been following the news, Mr. Lennox?"

"What?"

"Your coast guard rescued a cargo ship yesterday," Soong said. "It was discovered while foundering in the open ocean, and had been abandoned by its crew. The coast guard is keeping it afloat with temporary pumps. They are towing it to Pearl Harbor as we speak. I'm told it should arrive there within the next two days."

"What does that have to do with me?"

His voice told me he already knew.

"One of the pieces of cargo on the manifest was destined for your facility in Baja California. I think you know what I am speaking about."

Lennox looked as though he was going to pass out.

"If I don't see your speech on television, and hear of the trade bill's withdrawal before that ship arrives in Honolulu, I'll make sure the entire story becomes public. Every detail. So you see? I no longer need the boy."

Lennox's face had gone white, the collar of his dress shirt ringed with sweat. "You'll be implicated, too."

Soong laughed again. "I am a Chinese citizen. I'll be back home by the time your press airs the story."

"Bastard," he said.

"I'll call you again in an hour, and you can give me your decision. Either you agree to exchange your grandson for what I want, or I will send him back to you in small pieces like the one you already received. One piece every hour. And believe me, Mr. Lennox, I know how to keep a person alive for days this way. Please save me the trouble."

"How do I know you'll keep your word?"

"To disclose the cargo situation even after you've done what I've asked? Think about it, Mr. Lennox. Why would I do that?

Why would I kill the golden goose? You're far more valuable to me with your wealth and influence intact. But, remember, you are of no use to me at all if you are unwilling to use it."

"Where is my son?" J.R. said. He was coming back to reality.

Lennox stood motionless, the tone from a dead line buzzing dully from the receiver still gripped in his hand.

"Is he all right?" J.R.'s eyes were moist, expectant. "Is Randall okay?"

Lennox set the phone gently back in its cradle.

"He's okay," I said. "They want to give him back."

J.R. looked to his father, then turned back to me. He seemed to have come alive for the first time since I'd met him in the lobby. "That's wonderful!" he said. "That's great . . . isn't it great?" He wiped his eyes with the back of a hand, and I felt his enthusiasm die into the empty silence of the room.

"Your father has to do something first," I said. "He has to agree to make a public announcement, and persuade Kelleher to withdraw his trade bill."

J.R. looked confused. His face went dark, but different than before.

"Dad?" he said, looking back and forth between Lennox and me. "What's happening?"

Phillip Lennox looked ill as he faced his son. "The stakes have gone up."

I felt it before I saw it—an almost electric snap that brought J.R. to his feet, his expression one of incredulous rage. "The stakes have gone *up*?"

He took a step toward his father.

"Did you say the stakes have gone *up*? Are you out of your goddamned mind? They've got my *son*, your own *grandson* held hostage." He stopped and pointed behind him at the small box that still lay on the table. "They *cut off* his *finger* for Chrissakes! And you say the stakes have gone *up*?"

He cocked his fist and let fly before I could reach him. The elder Lennox raised his arms to defend himself, but too late.

The force of J.R.'s blow slammed his father into the corner. The older man slid halfway down the wall, even as he continued his struggle to ward off the blows being rained down on him.

"You sonofabitch!" J.R. rasped, as he pounded his father without mercy.

I wedged my way between them, finally able to gain a position to shove J.R. to one side. His knuckles were skinned and bloody, his breath coming hard, his face slick with sweat and snot and tears. His father had collapsed into a fetal ball, the front of his shirt stained with the blood that had begun to flow freely from his nose and mouth.

The room stank of loathing as I stood in the gap between them, their chests heaving for air, their eyes hard and red. Lennox looked up at his son as J.R. drilled an accusing finger toward his father's ravaged face.

"You *will* do what is necessary to get Randall back, you sorry fuck. No more negotiating. No more waiting."

Lennox locked eyes with his son for a long moment, and I saw something pass from them. He swiped the sleeve of his shirt across his mouth, smeared blood high across his cheek, and nodded so slightly I nearly missed it.

Phillip Lennox had sequestered himself behind the double doors of his room, scrawling out a draft of the speech that was meant to secure Randall's return, when Hobart and his man, Ted, returned.

"What the hell happened in here?" Hobart said. The stink of sweat and something primal still lingered in the air.

"The Lennoxes worked out some family issues while you were out," I said.

Ray Hobart made for the doors of Lennox's room, rattled them in frustration when he found them locked. "Mr. Lennox? You okay in there?"

"I'd leave him be, Ray," I said.

Hobart gave me a look that suggested I go fuck myself, and rattled the doors again. "Mr. Lennox?"

No answer.

"Any luck with the security tapes?" I asked Hobart.

Ted answered instead, shook his head. "Couldn't see a face."

"Where's J.R.?" Hobart said.

"Taking a walk."

Hobart knocked again, rattling the doors on their hinges. "Mr. Lennox?"

"Leave him alone, Ray."

He turned back toward me with an expression of confusion. "What's he doing in there?"

"There's been a change of plans," I said. "He's decided to ditch yours and get Randall back instead."

I stood outside on the suite's balcony, looked south past Diamond Head, far into the distance where Kona lay. I leaned against the railing and pulled in a lungful of clean air, laced with the fragrance of plumeria, sunscreen and sea salt. A patchwork of colored towels was spread out on the sand far below, and the carefree sounds of laughter and crashing surf drifted up to me. The scene was punctuated by the blasts of an air horn aboard the catamaran that was returning to the beach from a sightseeing trip up the coastline. Somewhere down there in that crowd I knew J.R. was walking the beach, wondering which patch of sand had been the last to touch the soles of his son's bare feet.

It took a special kind of strength to be the son of a man like Phillip Lennox, a kind of self-possession that shrugged off other people's desires to believe that nothing ever could be difficult for the son of a wealthy man. J.R. had it easy; J.R. had it made. I was sure he'd heard it all his life. I had heard it in my own life and taken a different road. But J.R. had stuck with the program. He'd worked his way through the corporate maze at Lennox Biomedical, having to work twice as hard as the next guy just to be considered an equal. A lesser man would have coasted, but J.R. had not, and even so, I knew he'd likely never be accorded the respect that had been given to his father.

Another burst of laughter carried up from the hotel swimming pool, and I turned my attention to a clutch of lotion-slathered children, standing in a line that snaked beneath a roiling manmade waterfall, waiting a turn on the waterslide. Their parents lay on nearby lounge chairs, sucked cool drinks through long straws, squeezed fresh wedges of lime into colorful blended cocktails, and waved down passing waitresses for more, more, more. These were people who brought their *au pairs* along to look after the youngsters, and snapped twenties off designer money clips if the kid asked for an ice cream—the kind of people who'd never give a guy like J.R. an inch, never an ounce of respect. And he was down there somewhere, alone, listening to the same sounds that I was listening to, knowing he'd give every last dime he had to hear his son laugh that way again.

CHAPTER THIRTY-SIX

It was after three o'clock when the phone rang again.

J.R. still hadn't returned from his walk along the beach.

I came in from the balcony as Lennox was coming out of his room. Hobart was moving for the phone.

"No," I said. "Don't pick up."

Hobart looked at Lennox, and Lennox shook his head. "Don't pick it up, Ray."

"We'll do it like before," I said, and Lennox moved to the extension. I counted back from three.

"Mr. Lennox?" Soong said.

"Yes."

"You've made your decision?"

Lennox shot me a glance, remembering what I'd told him to do. "Not before I talk to Randall. I want to hear his voice."

Soong considered it.

"Fine," he said at last. A moment later, we heard the sound of scuffling feet, then the quick, shallow breathing of a frightened child.

"Daddy?" Randall's voice was shaking.

Lennox clenched his jaw.

"Randall," he said. "It's your grandfather. Are you all right?"

The boy started to cry, deep keening sounds. "Grampa."

"Randall?"

"That's all," Soong said.

In the background, the boy's desperate noises grew faint as he was taken away from the phone. "Now, what have you decided?"

Lennox's voice was a whisper. "Yes."

"Very good," he said. "Now, please get a paper and pen."

There was one on the desk beside me. I picked them up and nodded to Lennox. "Ready," he said.

Soong rattled off an address on a street I wasn't familiar with, told Lennox to be there at ten o'clock. Because I knew the tides, I knew the moon would rise late that night. So did Joey Soong. He wanted the handoff to take place in a location that was as dark as possible.

"Mr. Lennox," he said, "I won't bother to tell you to come alone. I know you won't. I just want you to know that I will not be alone, either. And I want to discourage you from doing anything that might cause further harm to the boy."

"You've caused him enough harm already."

"The timing was unfortunate," Soong said. "Had I known of the ship's arrival even an hour earlier . . ." His voice trailed off like a shrug.

We all knew that was a lie.

Phillip Lennox hadn't taken Soong seriously, and Randall had paid for his grandfather's mistake in judgment. Regardless, whatever was on that cargo ship had Lennox more terrified than the thought of losing his grandson. But the old man's moral and emotional integrity wasn't my immediate concern.

I wanted to get Randall back to his father, and walk away clean.

It was time for us all to go home.

CHAPTER THIRTY-SEVEN

It could have been simple.

But I should have known better. I've known men like Phillip Lennox all my life.

We'd talked it to death, sitting there in that spacious, expensive prison of a hotel suite: J.R. insisting I be there for the pickup, Hobart protesting for all he was worth. I tried to explain that this was not a military action, that the best way to handle it was slow and easy. Give Joey Soong what he wanted and walk away with Randall alive and relatively well.

Hobart argued fiercely for a show of strength, but Lennox finally settled it, took the security man aside and had a quiet, private discussion that ended the matter. Though I couldn't hear what they said, it did not require an abundance of imagination to guess what the contents of that conversation might have been.

I obtained a city map from the hotel concierge and brought it up to the room. Once we located the approximate area where Soong demanded to meet, we all got in Lennox's limo and did a little recon.

"I don't understand why he'd do it this way," J.R. said. "Why not just bring Randall to us, bring him here."

"To the hotel?" I asked.

"They took him from here," he said. "They obviously know where we are."

"Soong's a freak," Hobart said. "He wants to show control."

Hobart was feeling his oats again, back in his element. He reminded me of a boil that needed to be lanced again and again.

"He wants to keep things as they are," I said. "As low-key as possible. The way it is now, nobody outside of the people in this car knows about any of this. How do you get a scared and injured eight-year-old boy into a public space like a hotel without making a scene? Why take the risk?"

"They delivered the finger," Hobart said, like that explained it all.

"Fingers don't cry or scream."

Hobart turned away, looking out through the darkly tinted window. The rest of the ride across town was long and mercifully quiet.

The address Joey Soong had mandated for the trade turned out to be a large vacant lot in a run-down industrial area on the north side of Chinatown, on the opposite side of the canal. Traffic was nearly nonexistent, and what buildings there were didn't look like they saw much business anymore. Corrugated steel wept rust, cracked wire glass hung from broken frames. A cluster of shower trees, heavy with crimson flowers, dropped petals that blew in deep, wind-driven piles along the roadway. Scattered tufts of wild kiawe grew unchecked in the soil of the undeveloped lots.

Lennox's driver pulled to a curb and stopped. We all got out.

"No streetlights," I said, taking a long look up and down the streets and sight lines. "Gonna be dark as hell."

Hobart nodded. "Why wouldn't he wait 'til the last minute to tell us where to meet?"

"Because it doesn't matter," I said.

He gave me an expression that told me he thought I was an asshole. "Of course it matters," he said. "We could have people here waiting."

"Here?" I said. "Chinatown's two hundred yards away. Soong is Triad. Who do you think has more juice in this part of town? Phillip Lennox? You?"

Lennox flinched, and Ray Hobart tried to appear as though he hadn't heard me.

"These buildings are no good," Hobart said. He was looking for places Soong could stake people out. But the roofs not only were pitched too steeply, they didn't look like they could support a man's weight.

J.R. and Phillip returned to the air-conditioned cool inside the limo. Their opinions were of little tactical use, and they knew it. Hobart and I left them to their tense and stony silence while we walked in separate directions, scanning rooflines, tree lines and the view from the street. By the time I returned to the car, Hobart was already there, smoking a cigarette, leaning on the limo's trunk.

"J.R. trusts you," Hobart said. His words rolled out on a blanket of blue smoke.

"It appears he does."

He gave me a derisive huff that came out through his nose, then took another drag off the butt. "You ever in the military?"

I looked across the open field, across the canal to the roofs that sheltered Chinatown.

"Is this the part where we measure our pee pees, Ray?"

Hobart took a last deep hit and flicked the cigarette onto the street. It landed on the pavement in a shower of sparks and rolled to the gutter.

"I was humping my second tour in 'Nam while you were still beating off to *National Geographic*."

"Listen, Ray," I said. "You wanna be bad? Okay, be bad. But do it somewhere else, some other time. All I want to do is get J.R.'s son back to him, then I'm history. You'll never see me again. But don't make a mistake and push a button when you don't know what it does."

He wiggled his fingers. "Spooky."

"I'm finished here, Ray," I smiled. "You go on back to biting the heads off chickens, or sniping at the neighbor's cats, or whatever the hell you do for fun. Just don't fuck me up tonight. We clear?"

Half an hour later we were parked at the entrance to the Ala Moana Surf.

Phillip Lennox was out the door before the valet knew we were there. Ray Hobart followed close behind. I was sliding across the seat as J.R. grabbed my arm, motioned me to stay. He signaled the valet to close the door and leave us to our conversation.

He started to say something, but I silenced him with the time-honored finger to my lips. I punched a button on the limo's control panel and raised the partition.

"Go ahead," I said.

"What do you think, Mike?"

"There are a lot of moving parts here, J.R. What are you asking me?"

"What do you think about Ray Hobart?"

My eyes strayed out the tinted window, watched Lennox and Hobart shoulder their way through the crowd surrounding the bell stand and disappear into the lobby. "I believe he considers being an asshole a major part of his job description. And I think he takes it very seriously."

He showed me a tight smile. "I mean professionally."

"My grandfather used to tell me that if the only tool in your toolbox is a hammer, you'll try to fix everything with a hammer."

When we returned to the hotel suite, the room was nearly dark. Phillip Lennox sat alone in the overstuffed club chair he had adopted as his command center. His face was deep in shadow, his hands clenched into fists that rested on his neatly pressed slacks.

J.R. stared at his father in silence as long seconds ticked by. "Where is everyone?" he asked finally.

The elder Lennox shook his head slowly.

"Where are Ray and Ted?" J.R. asked again. "Where's Pollard?"

"I let them go."

"Let them go where?"

Lennox shook his head dismissively.

"There is only one way this can end, J.R.," he said. "This might be the most humiliating night of my life. I don't need an audience for that."

CHAPTER THIRTY-EIGHT

It was about a quarter to ten when we pulled to a stop along an abandoned side street in the old warehouse district. It was dark and moonless, nothing but a scattering of stars to pierce the black blanket of sky. Lennox's driver left the car running, but killed the headlights. The parking lights remained illuminated, as we had been instructed. Flying insects eddied blindly inside their glow, hungry for the light.

Phillip Lennox, J.R. and I waited in unsettling silence for long moments before I slid the release and dropped the clip out of the Beretta, checked it one last time before I rammed it back home.

J.R.'s eyes went wide. "You're not going to need that," he said, the tone more question than anything else.

"An old habit," I said.

"I thought we said no guns," he said again. "I thought we decided."

"I know, J.R.," I said. "But that was for Hobart. He wanted to storm in like the goddamned infantry."

"But—"

"It'll be fine," I said. "Nobody's gonna shoot anybody."

J.R. was wild-eyed with anxiety, had been all afternoon.

Lennox looked at his son with a chilling calm, idly fingering a file folder he held on his lap. "Fifteen minutes it will all be over," Lennox said. "All of it."

It turned out to be less than that.

Off to our right, in the distance, a pair of headlights bounced across a dirt access road that ran beside the canal, and turned onto the empty lot beside us. A minute later, the Toyota Land Cruiser pulled up to a spot about twenty yards away, turned broadside to us and stopped. A cloud of dust overtook it, trapped it in its own headlights and enveloped the vehicle inside a luminescent halo.

An offshore breeze swiftly cleared the air as three men got out. One of them carried Randall under his arm, like a football. The Toyota's lights pierced the darkness, lit the space between the three men and Lennox's limousine. Their shadows lengthened as they reached a spot about midway between our two vehicles and they came to a halt. The one carrying Randall placed him on his feet and the other two men stood their ground. The boy's hand was wrapped in a bandage of white gauze, darkly discolored where blood had seeped from the stump of his severed finger. I nodded to Phillip and J.R. and we all got out of the limousine.

Joey Soong spoke first.

"You brought what I asked for?" His voice seemed loud in the expanse of empty darkness.

Soong stood between his two foot soldiers, one hand maintaining a solid grip on Randall's neck. The other two were larger, meatier than Soong, and I noted an unmistakable shape inside the fist of the man to his left. I didn't have a good angle on the other one, couldn't see if he was carrying, though I assumed that he was, too.

"I have it," Lennox said. He held up the manila folder for Soong to see.

Soong took a step forward, the reflection from the Land Cruiser's headlights catching his smile. Randall squirmed, then winced in pain at the rough squeeze Soong inflicted on him.

"Give me my son," J.R. said. I felt his apprehension turn to anger.

"You must be Phillip Jr.," Soong said. "A pleasure. You should be proud of your boy's bravery."

The night air turned electric.

"Mr. Lennox," Soong said. "I remind you that you have two days—perhaps less—to make good on the rest of your promises. When the coast guard arrives with the cargo ship, it will be too late. We understand each other, yes?"

"I understand," he said, his voice barely audible over the background hum of the idling cars.

"Fine. Then please put the folder on the ground in front of you, and return to your vehicle."

"Give me my son," J.R. repeated.

"In a moment. First, your father will put the folder on the ground, then you will return to your vehicle. I will take the boy back with me. When I am safely inside my car, I will read what you have given me. If I find it acceptable, I will allow him to walk across to you. Alone."

I held my focus on Joey Soong, but kept Phillip Lennox in my peripheral vision. He stooped to place the file at his feet, and in the same moment, a hiss split the air between us.

Soong's body jerked and spun backward, his grip beginning to take Randall down with him. But the boy maintained his balance, took a lunging step toward us. I knew in an instant what had happened.

Then everything turned to shit.

I snatched the Beretta from my waistband, but not before one of Soong's men turned loose with his pistol. I saw the flashes of fire spit from its barrel before I heard the blasts, the man's face briefly illuminated by the combustion of his ammunition, concentrated on his target.

The Land Cruiser kicked up a storm of rocks and dust as the rear tires bit into the dirt of the empty lot and coiled into a tight turn, trying to take up a protective position between us and them.

Soong's second man fired, and Randall fell forward, collapsing into a heap at Soong's feet. J.R. screamed as he folded onto his hands and knees. A half second later I two-tapped my trigger and dropped the one who'd shot the boy. J.R. was crawling across the dirt toward his son, and I trained the Beretta on the second of Soong's soldiers just as another hiss came from somewhere behind me, and a slug took him squarely in the forehead.

The Land Cruiser braked hard, the driver leaping out the door the moment it skidded to a stop. Three more snaps creased the air, and I watched as large-caliber bullets punched holes in the passenger side door, pitching a cascade of safety glass into the air.

I lay on my stomach, sighting down the Beretta and waiting for my shot, intending to go for feet and ankles. But I could barely make out the Toyota through the dust. In the movies, the hero goes for the tires. That's bullshit, a myth; all you get is ricochet, and things were bad enough as it was. I squeezed off three more rounds, but only kicked up puffs of dirt as the driver dragged Soong through the door. A second later, it was nothing but taillights and dust clouds and tears.

CHAPTER THIRTY-NINE

"You lying sonofabitch!" I shouted.

"You fucking killed him!"

I was insane with rage. Phillip Lennox was prostrate on the ground, panting, eyes wide, wild and darting in every direction. A dirty wind riffled the papers in the file folder that had fallen open beside him.

My ears rang and my nostrils stung from the chemical odor of cordite. Approaching sirens pierced the edges of my consciousness, but my eyes were locked on Phillip Lennox.

"You planned this, you lying bastard!"

He showed me a blank and uncomprehending stare, the look of a stunned, scared and stupid man.

I stood and looked across at J.R. His young son, Randall, lay limp, cradled in his arms. My feet crunched across loose rocks and gravel as I crossed that empty distance and knelt down beside them. It felt like a long walk.

A bullet had taken the boy in the back, above the hip, and had exited high on his left side. Bright blood oozed from the pulsing wound, and leaked from the corner of his mouth, soaking both the boy and his father. Randall's eyes were open, half-lidded, glassy and unfocused. I pressed my fingers gently to his neck and felt a weak pulse growing weaker, no way for me to be certain that the bullet hadn't grazed a lung, or worse.

"Put your hand over the wound, like this," I told J.R. "Hold it tight until the paramedics get here. Don't let go."

He did as I instructed, without question, with nothing more than a nod of his head. His face was wet, smeared with dirt and tears as he whispered softly to his son.

Two of Joey Soong's men lay dead. One had a tight cluster of holes in the center of his chest that I'd put there, the other had been left with only the front half of his head. From behind me, somewhere off inside the maze of disused buildings, I heard a car door slam, an engine turn over, and the squeal of rubber on asphalt. The sound rolled across the empty streets, echoed through vacant metal structures before it died away, blending into the sounds of traffic along the boulevard. I knew they'd ditch the guns and disappear within the hour. Ray Hobart and men I knew only as Ted and Pollard. A show of strength. Fuck.

Hospitals.

They smell, they're noisy, and with the possible exception of the maternity ward, are brimming with nothing but grief and suffering.

J.R. sat at the edge of his son's bed, surrounded by the hum and buzz of machines and pumps and monitors whose sole function was to try to keep Randall Lennox alive. Outside, the sun had come up over the *pali*, throwing the sheer vertical slopes into pale light and shadow, but neither of them were aware of it.

I had spent the past nine or so hours answering questions and giving my statement to the police. They had retained possession of my Beretta, but had finally cut me loose.

Phillip Lennox had waited for his lawyer before uttering a

word to the cops. The attorney finally arrived a few hours later, on a Lennox corporate jet. Both the lawyer and Lennox were already gone by the time I had been released.

"They don't know if he's going to make it," J.R. told me. His words felt like he had taken a lead pipe to the side of my head. "The bullet got a piece of his lung, did some damage to other internal organs . . ."

I looked at the boy lying unconscious, tubes snaking up into his nose, down his throat, and his little arms speared with heavy-gauge needles. Bags of fluids hung from metal poles and dripped slowly into his veins. A computer monitor beside him scrolled uneven lines across the screen, flashing numbers that meant nothing to me. All I saw was another young child that had been caught in the crossfire.

"He has a hell of a grip, Randall does," I said. "Got a hell of a handshake."

J.R. smiled, unsuccessfully pressing back the tears that welled again inside his eyes.

"I brought you some coffee," I said.

J.R. had moved to the cot that the nurses had brought in for him. He had refused to leave the room, not even for food.

"How's Randall doing?" I asked.

"The same."

I'd spent that night aboard the *Kehau*, brought some coffee and a bag of fresh *malasadas* back for J.R. the next morning. They were still warm by the time I arrived at the hospital.

We ate them in silence as nurses came in and out, checked IVs, monitors, fluids, and did the other things they do. I pulled a deck of cards from my pocket, talked him into a round or two of gin rummy that neither of us had our hearts in, doing everything I could to keep this from feeling like a deathwatch.

"What's going on out there?" he asked me, tossing the cards on the cot.

"In the world?" I said. "No idea."

He looked at Randall, then back to me. "You don't have to stay."

"I know."

That afternoon, a man entered the room unexpectedly, uninvited.

He had an erect manner of walking, a nearly military posture, and was dressed in a dark, chalk-stripe suit and expensive Hermès tie. His hair was gray, swept back off his forehead, revealing a prominent widow's peak. His gaze swept past me, locked on Randall for a long moment before landing on his father. He carried an envelope in his hands.

"J.R. Lennox?" he asked.

J.R. stood. "Yes."

"May I speak to you in private?"

J.R. threw a glance my way.

"No," he said. "This man saved my life, and that of my son. Anything you have to say, you can say it in front of him."

"My name is Jeffry Brusseau, I work for Timberlake, Psaltis, Matteson & DeYoung. You're familiar with the firm?"

"Yes."

"Then you know we've done a great deal of work for your company, as well as represent many of your father's individual concerns."

"I'm aware," J.R. said again. Suspicion trumped fatigue.

Brusseau held out the envelope. "Your father personally instructed me to deliver this to you."

J.R. snapped the packet from the man's hand, and the room seemed smaller, claustrophobic and suffocating.

"I'm sorry about your son," he said.

"Is there something else?"

"No."

"You may leave now, Mr. Brusseau."

The clack of the lawyer's heels faded away down the corridor before J.R. opened the envelope, withdrew a handwritten note and a small sheaf of papers. I watched his face as he read it, saw his hands begin to tremble.

"Turn on the TV," he said.

The story was everywhere.

Most of them had intros like, "A bizarre story of greed, slavery, and medical science has ended with the apparent suicide of billionaire Phillip Lennox . . ."

Philip Lennox had attempted to salvage what he could from a situation that had spiraled out of control, his last-ditch effort being a failed undertaking to bring an end to his problems by assassinating Joey Soong.

While his own grandson lay unconscious in a hospital bed, Phillip had spent the final day of his life working with his lawyers to ensure the orderly transfer of everything he owned to J.R., including the chairmanship of Lennox Biomedical. Phillip Lennox had then prepared a lengthy and detailed statement in which he took responsibility for everything that had gone before. He publicly and categorically denied any wrongdoing on the part of his only son, J.R. He sealed it, together with the opportunity for any further cross-examination, with a 38-caliber bullet to his brain.

The upshot was that Lennox Biomedical had spent decades researching solutions to the spread of the worst of the world's known communicable and sexually transmitted diseases. But documents had been leaked from a Lennox laboratory facility in Mexico that provided evidence of research of an entirely unsanctioned variety. Ugly Fact: the aftermath of September 11, 2001, was Big Business for Big Pharma. The threat of global pandemic as a weapon of mass destruction had suddenly become very real. A company that could stay ahead of the curve through the discovery and dissemination of preventive vaccines or curative medicines would win, and win big. Lennox Biomedical's research on the AIDS virus had opened a significant number of doors, scientifically speaking, and now, given the escalation of fears regarding the intentional spread of diseases like Ebola, avian flu, SARS, smallpox and all the rest, it was about to pay off in spades.

J.R. watched the whole thing unfold on television, nearly catatonic.

The story got uglier when the coast guard towed an abandoned Malaysian-registered vessel into Honolulu harbor. It had been seized by pirates several years earlier in the South China Sea. Its name had been changed, its silhouette altered to deter identification, and it since had been used to ply the smuggling routes from Shanghai, Indonesia and Mexico. The ship had taken on water in heavy weather, been abandoned by her crew and gone adrift for some time before being spotted by a commercial fisherman.

Once aboard, the coast guard discovered, among other things, two steel cargo containers that had been used to confine a number of Chinese nationals, the vast majority of whom had already perished by the time help had arrived.

Among the living was a young woman who, according to Phillip Lennox's own last confession, had been sold to a Lennox research lab located near a small town in northern Baja. She had been one of an extremely rare group of people who had been repeatedly exposed to a variety of STDs and other diseases, yet had never contracted a single one of them. Over the years, Lennox Biomedical had undertaken to gain access to such people, and their DNA, by any number of unsavory methods.

On the TV screen, a transcript of a passage from Lennox's final personal message scrolled out beneath a publicity shot that had been taken of him years earlier. In it, he explained that the young woman had been sold outright, as nothing short of human chattel, to Lennox by Joey Soong through a complex underground network of Chinese organized crime organizations. She had been in the process of being smuggled, together with all the other unfortunates aboard that foundering ship, along a well-tested route that landed streams of illegal aliens onto a remote stretch of beach in Mexico. She was not the first, nor would she have been the last.

But it was all being done for what Phillip Lennox called the "greater good." That "the suffering of a few might serve to eliminate the suffering of future generations."

"They're going to find you," I said to J.R. "It's not going to take them long."

"The press."

I nodded. "You need to stay in front of this for both your sakes."

He glanced at Randall, then back to the TV screen. "I need to meet that woman first."

I was with him when he met her.

She and the nine other remaining survivors had been brought to Honolulu General, housed within a secure ward and treated for severe dehydration, malnutrition, dysentery, and a number of disorders I'd never even heard of.

Single beds lined the walls, separated by diaphanous white curtains, and looking like a scene from a World War Two field hospital. Representatives of the US Citizenship and Immigration Services—formerly the INS—were present, too. Through interpreters, they had been interviewing those who were strong enough to speak, gathering statements and evidence regarding their ordeal.

The young woman's name was May Ling, the only surviving female victim, and she told us her story even as she clung to a little boy from whom she refused to be separated, a little boy she claimed to be her son.

As she unraveled the account of her life, I found myself humbled to the point of nausea, and deeply moved by her inner strength. In my life as a cop, I had witnessed countless indescribable acts of violence and cruelty; nothing had prepared me for May Ling's story. The notion of trafficking in human beings for profit—primarily women and children—sickened me to my core and filled me with shame for the human race.

"I am lucky to be alive at all," she told us. "The People's Republic of China allows only one child per family. Because male children are more desirable, it is not uncommon for the father of a baby girl to drop her down a well."

It was something I had heard before, but somehow couldn't allow myself to believe. Apparently it was true. These unauthorized babies were often allowed to come to term, only to have their lives extinguished at the moment of birth using a syringe filled with formaldehyde stabbed into the crowns of their newborn heads. This was not something the PRC advertised to the outside world. Nevertheless, some girls managed to survive, in no small part owing to the love and courage of people like May Ling's long-deceased parents.

When she finished her story, J.R. kissed her softly on the forehead and whispered something to May Ling. He told the interpreter to translate.

"I can't tell her that," the interpreter said.

"Tell her," he demanded.

The interpreter hesitated for so long, I thought she'd refused, when finally she turned and spoke to May Ling in rapid Cantonese.

May Ling listened intently, something soft coming into her eyes. She reached for J.R.'s hand, pressed it tightly to her cheek, repeating something that required no translation. She looked so young in that brief moment. Even through the hardship and abuse she had endured, it was plain to see not only her beauty, but her strength. I thought of Kwan Yin, the goddess of mercy, and the silver strands of incense that swirled about her feet.

A few minutes later, I followed J.R. as we left the secure ward.

He pushed through the doors to the men's restroom, moved hastily to a stall, sank to his knees and vomited. It was a quarter of an hour before he had purged himself. I looked on as he washed his face, unable to meet his own reflection, his eyes distant and red-rimmed.

We were in the elevator when I asked him what he'd said to May Ling.

"I told her that she and her son were safe now," he said. "That I will personally see to it that they remain in America if that's their desire. I told her she can live anywhere she chooses, and I will help her to begin a new life."

Early the next morning, my cell phone rang.

It was a little after three.

"They took him off the machines, Mike," J.R. told me. "I thought you'd want to know."

And the line went dead.

CHAPTER FORTY

I climbed into a bottle and stayed there for the better part of three days.

I wasn't useless drunk, just drunk enough to pace myself so that it required less than forty-eight hours to find the bottom of a half gallon of Absolut that still had the seal on it when I'd started. It's the nights I don't remember much. But Snyder had the helm, and the *Kehau* was sailing a fine reach before the trades. It would be another four days before we would be back in Kona.

Even in the depths of my intoxication, though, my awareness of the costs and consequences of the events of the past two weeks in my life threatened to eat through the lining of my soul. The sun wouldn't burn it away, and the alcohol wouldn't purify it; I couldn't sweat it out, and there was nowhere for me to run.

I'd seen J.R. make good on his promise to May Ling. I had been in the room when his lawyer called to say that he had found a statute in the immigration law that had been established to protect people who had been smuggled into the country against their will. The Trafficking Victims Protection Reauthorization Act. It not only made May Ling and her son eligible to remain in the US, it allowed her to sue her captors.

J.R. was footing the bills in an effort to locate Joey Soong and anyone else he could find who had been involved in May Ling's abduction. I knew J.R. would never let go until Soong was roasting on a spit in some remote corner of hell.

I had shaken the hand of J.R. Lennox, accepted a shuddering *embrazo* as he stepped from his limousine and into the executive aircraft terminal. I had seen him climb the stairway to his Gulfstream IV.

"Make it right, J.R.," I said.

I silently wished him a better kind of life as I watched the jet disappear behind a long reef of low clouds.

After that, I had gone back to the harbor, readied the *Kehau* to make for home, turned the helm over to Snyder, and slid into that bottle. On the morning of the third day, I climbed back out.

The afternoon had gone gray, but the sun poured through intermittent holes in the cloud cover and formed bright circles of light, like stepping-stones that had been laid out across the hammered steel surface of the sea.

"I'll take the helm," I said, a steaming mug of Mango Ceylon in my hand for a change.

"All yours, bud," Snyder said, and went below to get himself a beer.

It wasn't long before he nodded off, leaving me to my thoughts as I scanned the horizon. My mind picked at loose strands, like the bitter end of a rope that couldn't be properly spliced. The beginning seemed so long ago, that first message from my brother, his first panicked call for help. I tried to fit it together with everything that came after.

I kept coming back to Congressman Kelleher, his aggressively anti-Chinese political agenda, and his meeting with Valden at the Mandalay Plaza. And it began to come together.

The simplest way to have torpedoed Kelleher's trade legislation would have been to dig up dirt on Kelleher himself. Joey Soong—either by applying pressure to Phillip Lennox, or by some means of his own—likely bribed hotel security in order to find something that could be used to compromise the congressman. Unfortunately for Valden, Kelleher played by the rules when he was on the road, and there was no dirt to be gathered. But the security man and his computer buddy went entrepreneurial. They saw my brother, found out who he was, and went after him when the Kelleher well ran dry.

I was Lennox and Joey Soong's bad surprise when I showed up in LA and came far too close to exposing the Chinese connection. So Soong had the blackmailers murdered, had their fingers carved off in that time-honored tradition as proof of the kill.

When Kemp attempted to turn the investigation toward Hans and me, Soong was probably laughing his ass off. But when Thel Mishow began looking into the ownership structure of the Mandalay Plaza on my behalf, things heated-up back in Hong Kong. I had been ambushed and beaten in the park as a warning. A warning I hadn't understood until now.

It had all been about Kelleher, and Valden had been in the wrong place at exactly the wrong time. I couldn't help but imagine whether everything might have been different if my brother hadn't stepped out on his wife that night, or whether Phillip Lennox had already set an unalterable course.

I engaged the autopilot and made my way forward.

I checked the rigging, the lines and the set of the sheets. I leaned over the rail, watched the quicksilver sea slip beneath the hull and caught the taste of salt spray on my tongue. I thought back to the spinner dolphins Snyder and I had seen on the uphill run, recalling how Lani loved to swim with them in the early mornings at Kealakekua Bay.

I went back to the cockpit, took my place in the chair and breathed deeply into the empty place I felt in my chest.

Snyder had awakened from his nap and was resting his arms along the aft rail and watching the wake trail away.

"You all right, Travis?"

I had quit being an LA detective to find peace, to come home to Kona to build a life. Lani had seen me through all of it, all the chaos and loss and collateral damage. Her voice was still an echo from the last time we'd spoken. I thought about who I really was, what we both seemed to want, and didn't know how much more I could expect her to take.

"I had a friend once," Snyder said. "He was a pilot. He used to say that God is God, but the devil is us."

Snyder stood there quietly after that, as lost in his own thoughts as I was in mine. As the sun slipped below the horizon, I sat at the wheel, glanced up at the sails that pushed the *Kehau* through the swells toward Kona, and watched rain bleed from a distant cloud.

CHAPTER FORTY-ONE

We tied off to my mooring in Kona Bay the same day Congressman Bill Kelleher's trade legislation hit the House floor. It failed by a narrow margin, but he vowed to keep up the fight.

Two hours later, I accompanied Snyder to his bar to collect my mail and run the errands I had been planning for the past two days.

"Hey, guys," Lolly said. "You're back. How about a beverage? My treat."

"Just my mail," I said. "But I appreciate the offer."

Snyder went behind the bar and tapped a beer for himself as she pushed through the swinging doors that led to the office. A minute later, she returned with a box stuffed with mail.

"I had to sign for this one," she said, handing me an overnight letter.

I looked at the return address. Dunross, Frankel & Wood.

Inside was a copy of an article clipped from the Honolulu newspaper. A yellow Post-it with a handwritten note from Patricia Dunross had been stuck to it. *Thought you'd want to know about this* was all it said.

I unfolded the paper and saw that May Ling's tragic story

had become front-page news in the city, prompting a spontaneous outpouring of donations that already reached well into
six figures.

At my recommendation, J.R. had retained Patricia to represent May Ling in finalizing the details of her immigration and
ongoing litigation against Joey Soong and the White Orchid.
Apparently, Patricia Dunross had taken it upon herself to set up
a charitable foundation in May Ling's name, as well.

Patricia was quoted widely throughout the article, stating that
it was May Ling's wish to use the contributed funds to establish
a home where people such as she and her son could find shelter
while they sorted out new lives in America. It ended with May
Ling's own words: "Someday, I want to repay."

"You okay?" Lolly asked me.

I had to clear my throat. "I believe I'll take that beer," I said.

She came to the door wearing a pair of board shorts and a
bathing suit top. Her hair hung loose across the smooth brown
skin of her shoulders, and her eyes took me in an inch at a time.

"Hello, Lani."

"Been home long?"

"Long enough to shower."

Her smile was weary and thin, but she stepped aside to let me
in. I slipped the sandals off my feet, left them on the stoop and
came inside.

"There are some things I need to say and I don't want you to
interrupt me," she said.

"Okay."

"I dreamed of you again last night," she said.

"You sound angry."

"I am, and you're interrupting. You're like a goddamned
song I can't get out of my head."

I waited through the silence she left floating there, listened to the mynahs and mourning doves in the palms outside her apartment.

"Do you have any idea how much I care about you?" she said finally.

"I—"

"*No, you* don't," she finished for me.

I saw her face flush beneath the tan. She shook her head.

"You don't even care about *yourself*, Mike. You're last on your own list."

She moved into the kitchen and I took a seat at the breakfast bar.

"First, your brother calls and you fly off to LA. The next thing I know, your ex-partner calls and you disappear again. You don't even tell me where you're going, or when you're coming back. When you do come home, you look like . . ."

Her hands swept the air in front of me.

"Like *that* for Chrissakes. Beaten up, bruised and God knows what all. What am I supposed to do with that, Mike? I mean, what is that?"

I fingered the shrinking lump on my forehead, glad she hadn't seen it when it was fresh. But I knew she was right. The part of my life I hadn't spent completely focused on being a cop, I'd spent trying to lock it away. I lived behind an invisible line and I didn't know exactly how I had arrived there.

"Lani," I said. "I was trying to protect you. I didn't want you involved."

"That's what I'm talking about," she said. "You never want me involved. But I want to be. I *want* to be involved. I'm thirty-freaking-three years old, Mike. I think I can handle being *involved*."

"I meant to say I didn't want you *hurt*."

"Oh, that's even better." She turned away from me, laughed without humor, then her voice went soft and low. "Mike, all I want is a little stability in my life. But you've got a choice you need to make."

It was the truth, and I knew it. I had thought of little else for the past two weeks.

"I love you, Mike," she breathed. So quiet, I almost missed it.

I kissed her softly, and felt her hands on my shoulders, my neck, the back of my head. She kissed me in return.

"I have something I need to show you," I told her.

"Where?"

"Do you trust me?"

She gave a look that went straight through me.

"You'll need to put something on," I said.

Pale orange light glowed from a place well beyond the entry gates of the Kamahale plantation. I saw the puzzlement in Lani's eyes as we drew closer to the source, driving slowly through the dense rows of coffee that grew along the edge of the road.

My business partner, Tino, had done everything I had asked of him on the phone a few days earlier. He had been busy. With the help of a contractor friend of ours, he had carved an acre—a perfect square—from the lush green fields. The light from at least three dozen tiki torches flickered along the perimeter of the land where I now hoped to build a home with Lani.

I held her as Lani stepped down from the Jeep, and stood beside her in a silence broken only by the night music of tree frogs and crickets deep inside the jungle. A warm breeze pulled at her hair as she gazed down the gentle slope to the lights of Kona and the vessels that lay at anchor in the bay.

When she turned to me, the torchlight played across the most beautiful smile I think I have ever seen.

"Mike?"

I was kneeling on the red soil, a tiny velvet box in my outstretched hand.

I slid the ring onto her finger and kissed her.

"What about the *Kehau*?"

"I can still do my charters," I said. "But kids need a place to run and play. They need swing sets and bikes and tree-houses."

She moved beside me and wrapped her arms around my waist.

There were no more words. There was no need. Everything I needed to know was reflected in her eyes. I held her close, felt the warmth of her breath against my chest as the sky faded to purple and the first fine dusting of stars appeared from behind the clouds.

Echoes II

(Eleven Years Later)

I have developed a fondness for rain, even though it sometimes brings with it visitations from the specters of the dead.

Other times, when the light is exactly right, and there is precisely the proper concentration of moisture in the air, a nearly alchemical reaction takes place when the atmosphere begins to glow with other-earthly hues of amber, gold and ochre. I have never witnessed this phenomenon anywhere other than here, in the tropics, and in all the years that I have called these islands my home, I have experienced it only twice. It never lasts long. Mere minutes.

This morning marks the third.

I believe in the portent contained in certain moments.

"What happened to the girl?"

"What girl?" I asked.

"The young girl at the bar. The one who started that whole thing with your brother."

"You focus on unusual details, Randall."

"You promised you would tell me everything."

"That's one I don't have an answer for. I was never able to find her. Never even knew her name."

He looked off toward the ocean, through the gently falling rain. His eyes were glassy with fatigue, yet indefinably alive with something else. We had talked all night.

"Maybe she quit that life," he said. "Maybe she finally found someone."

I was happy to know that this young man possessed that kind of hope. I both admired and envied it.

"He would never talk about it," Randall said. "My father."

"I know."

"He wanted you to tell me."

"I know that, too. But you needed to wait until you were old enough to hear it. You understand that now."

Randall Lennox pinched the bridge of his nose with his thumb and forefinger, pressed his eyes shut and leaned back in his chair.

"He always said you saved my life," he breathed.

"He was wrong."

He opened his eyes, rested his elbows on his knees and studied my face.

"In what way?"

"Your father saved your life, not me. He could have gone along with whatever plan *his* father had in mind, but your father refused. He loved you very much, Randall. So he called me. I was a virtual stranger at the time. But he knew he had to do something to help you, and he did."

"The whole thing changed him. My dad. Broke him in a way, I think."

"It changed a lot of people."

A gust of wind disturbed the leaves overhead and scattered droplets across the planks beneath our feet.

"I miss him," Randall said.

"You should. He was a good man."

I heard the kitchen door slide open. She moved softly toward us, as though she might disturb the gilded rainfall.

"Look out there," Lani whispered, her eyes reflecting the sunrise.

She carried a tray in her hands, three cups of hot tea trailing diaphanous ribbons of steam. She offered one to Randall, one to me, then took the last one for herself, then sat cross-legged on the lanai and tipped her face skyward.

"You've been up all night," she said finally.

"Eavesdropping?" I asked.

"A little. I hope you don't mind."

"It's Randall's story," I said. "Ask him."

Lani turned toward him and inquired with her eyes.

Randall smiled. "I don't mind."

The golden light had begun to turn to amber morning and was already beginning to fade away.

"You're welcome to stay another day with us, Randall," I said.

"I've imposed enough as it is. Besides, I have to get back to school."

"Northwestern, isn't it?"

He nodded his head.

"You like it there?"

"Cold in the winter."

"Stay for breakfast, at least," Lani said.

She stood and so did Randall. She wrapped an arm around his shoulder, pulled him close and led him back into the kitchen.

"Don't be long," Lani called to me as they stepped inside the house.

"I'll just be a minute." I needed the silence.

The sunrise came softly then, like the skin of a ripened peach; the day did not so much break as awaken. The last remnant of the golden glow was disappearing, like a watermark, before my eyes.

I stared eastward, through the pale light and mist, breathing deeply the scents of loam and wet soil and stone, of leaves that had fallen to the ground and begun to rust. I leaned on the koa railing of Lani's and my lanai and sent up a prayer that had no words.

Then I prayed I might somehow capture the image of this morning in my mind, to preserve it, uncertain as to when, if ever, I might witness it again—perhaps in the work of Renaissance painters and their representations of archangels descending from clouds. In the meantime I would continue to remind myself that this was no illusion, and to learn to be content inside the light of a lesser heaven.

ACKNOWLEDGMENTS

As usual, this book wouldn't have been written of not for my wife, Christina, and her endless supply of patience, love, enthusiasm and support during the process. The same goes for my daughters and their families, too—you always make it fun when the whole thing's said and done; thank you Allegra, Christan, Britton, Nick, Ashton, Kheler, Liam and Declynn. And thank you, Mom & Dad. Aloha pau ole.

Big-kine mahalos to everybody at Quinn's (Almost By The Sea) in Kona, Hawaii. Thanks for always saving a seat for me. And to all the wonderful and interesting readers whom I have had the pleasure of meeting at conventions, book signings, and all those other gatherings of literary-minded folk: Thank you for trusting me with your valuable time (and money). The bottom line is, these books are for *you*. As the rock band, Supertramp, says in their song, "Sister Moonshine," *If no one wants to listen, what's the story?*

Finally, my most sincere thanks to my agent, Peter Riva; and to Mara Anastas and all the great professionals at Open Road Media for being in my corner. I couldn't be more fortunate nor more grateful that you're all on my team.

Until next time . . ."

ABOUT THE AUTHOR

Baron Birtcher spent a number of years as a professional musician, and founded an independent record label and management company. His first two novels, *Roadhouse Blues* and *Ruby Tuesday*, are *Los Angeles Times* and Independent Mystery Booksellers Association bestsellers. Birtcher has been nominated for a number of literary awards, including the Nero Award for his novel *Hard Latitudes*, the Claymore Award for his novel *Rain Dogs*. He currently divides his time between Portland, Oregon, and Kona, Hawaii.

BARON BIRTCHER

FROM OPEN ROAD MEDIA

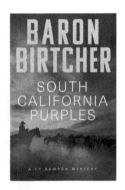

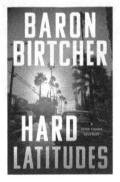
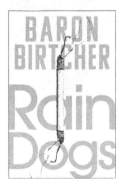

OPEN ROAD
INTEGRATED MEDIA

CPSIA information can be obtained
at www.ICGtesting.com
Printed in the USA
JSHW020843210523
41985JS00001B/19